THE GALLANTS

From an Engraving by J. Raphael Smith after Gainsborough

His Majesty King George IV
as Prince of Wales

THE GALLANTS

FOLLOWING
ACCORDING TO THEIR WONT
THE LADIES!

BY

E. BARRINGTON

Where none admire, 't is useless to excel;
Where none are beaux, 't is vain to be a belle

Illustrated with Portraits

THE ATLANTIC MONTHLY PRESS
BOSTON

PRINTED IN THE UNITED STATES OF AMERICA

TABLE OF CONTENTS

ILLUSTRATIONS

THE KING AND THE LADY

HENRY II

KING OF ENGLAND

1133–1189

> When as King Henrie ruled this land,
>   The Second of that Name,
> Beside the Queene he dearly loved
>   A faire and princely dame.

WHETHER Fair Rosamond was really the daughter of Walter de Clifford of the family of Fitz-Ponce, whether she dwelt in the maze at Woodstock, whether she was the mother of William Longsword, Earl of Salisbury, and whether she was poisoned by Queen Eleanor, each reader may decide to suit his own romantic fancy. But Henry II did love her — "with what love he had" — and took sorrowful leave of her, —

> . . . twenty times, with waterie eyes,
>   He kissed her tender cheeke, —

when he set off for France to put down the rebellion of Queen Eleanor's sons in 1173–1174. History has it, too, that when Eleanor was imprisoned for her encouragement of the rebellion, Henry acknowledged Rosamond.

His Rose of the World died about 1176, and as the ballad and the chroniclers relate:—

> Her body then they did intombe,
>   When life was fled away,
> At Godstow, neere to Oxford towne,
>   As may be seene this day.

Granger Sculp.

Henry II

I

THE KING AND THE LADY

In her little low house at Rouen the holy Canon of the Chapel of St. Nicholas noted down these words of Dame Petronille, woman formerly to Eleanor, Queen of Henry Fitz-Empress, the Second Henry of England. Even then, at the end of her life, she trembled very exceedingly in revealing these secrets of the great. Yet, for admonition, they should be known. And what is here writ is true.

Of the Lady Queen Eleanor I would fain say little; yet must I, since all was of her shaping, and as she sowed so she reaped, and by the justice of God will so do for all eternity.

No greater Lady of birth and right dwelt ever in this world; for she was herself Duchess of Aquitaine, that land of the trouvères and of song, and to the holy French King Louis was she wife, and after, wife to Henry of England, great lords both. Wherefore of this world's glories was she full fain and of them she fed full, and for this her immortal part mourneth in great torment.

I saw this lady first when she sat Queen of a Court of Love in Bordeaux, her chief city. By the river she sat, under a bower of roses — roses about her in myriads; and so strong was the scent of them that the Lady Alix de Coutances, seated at her feet, swooned from the heat and perfume. But the young

Duchess drew it in smiling, and it flushed her face like strong wine. A rose herself, all color and bright flame she seemed among those other roses.

The Duchess Eleanor had plenteous hair, dark as night and braided about her head with jewels, for she would not follow the custom that a maid's tresses should fall about her shoulders or braided to her knee. On her head she had a garland of red roses and about her neck sparkling jewels set in fretted gold in the design of a peacock with spread tail, very precious, of Saracen's work, that her suzerain and lord to be, the holy King of France, had sent her. This lay on her bosom, splendid in the sun. She had a kirtle of cloth of silver that fitted her shape and full breast, and over all she wore a long white pelisson of great brocade from Byzantium, edged with fur of ermine because she was a sovereign Duchess. Very haut and proud was her face, and her long golden eyes that, seeming to see nothing, yet saw all. She had a trick of looking sidelong and smiling at a man beneath her lashes; and if on this he dared a return, she would flash a look at him that made him shrink. Yet a very magnificent lady, tall as a young poplar, and showed beneath her robe her silver brodequins that men said were the smallest in Christendom. But I have seen smaller.

Before her stood Bertrand d'Arles, the trouvère, and all round her sat the ladies and nobles to hear him sing, and the song he sang to his lute was a chanson of her own making. Wherefore she listened with a flush of pride and a musing on her that for once softened her into a girl.

And thus he sang:—

> In the orchard the dawn is breaking,
>   Look forth, ma douce amie!
> See o'er the dewy hills the sun is waking —
>   Monseigneur Dieu! what hath he done to me?
> Lo, how the sweet night dies before his shining,
>   Slain of this cruel baron the high sun,
> And I, that for my lady's arms am pining,
>   Must weep and weep to see my joys foredone!
> Monseigneur Dieu, sitting enthroned on high,
> Remember me, how for my love I die,
> And grant the pity of her soothfast kiss,
> A little bounty dropped from thine own bliss!

She smiled a little when he ceased, and even I could see in the glance she cast from her long amber eyes that there was a secret thought between her and Bertrand; and he was such a man as a lady might well favour, — lean in the body, eagle-faced, — and sang indeed like one of God's choristers.

A Court of Love followed, where was tried the piteous case of the young Comtesse de Saintonges against her old husband; but all this I have forgot. Only I see the Duchess Eleanor seated above the rest, dark and glorious — a great lady.

Very soon came the news that the French King, Louis the Saint, had asked her in marriage, most deeply desiring the marriage between her rich lands of Aquitaine and his kingdom of France. My brother, the Seigneur de Vermandois, laughed aloud when this news came to his Seigneurie; and when his wife asked him why, he said:—

"From a marriage of the dove and eagle what should follow? No peace, but rending!"

And on her replying, 'But our Eleanor is no dove,' he laughed again and said no more. After, I knew that the French King was the dove, and he had need to be, to bear with our haughty Duchess.

For she would have none of Paris. Sunless and cold she held it after her warm and languid Provence. Cold and cloistered also the court of the saint; and ever and again she would come riding down at speed of horse and man to Bordeaux, and laying aside her dolorous royalty, be once more our Duchess, and sit by the clear waters, crowned and throned amid roses.

It was on one of these days that she chose me to be a woman about her, knowing my mother had served her mother with loyal heart. For her sake she loved me a little, but she could love none greatly — no, not even Bertrand d'Arles! So I entered upon the service with great fear, for blows and hard words were plenty in our lady's chamber, though in public all was summer sunshine, for this lady would be loved and feared.

All the joys of this world she tasted, and would have sweetened her lips on the next; for when St. Bernard preached the Crusade at Vezelai, the Queen-Duchess must needs make a plaything of that also. A fair penitent, she knelt before the high altar, and, receiving the Cross from his hand, wore it upon her shoulder like a knight Crusader, and she and her ladies sent their cast-off distaffs to the knights and nobles who shunned the Crusades, to shame them. So that on the Pentecost, when the King of France marched for the Holy Land, the Queen-Duchess and her ladies went with him as fellow soldiers.

No need to tell that journey and the shame she brought on the King! as well may witness Raymond de Poitou, and even the infidel — the Emir Sal-u-din. And from this Crusade of bitterness and defeat she returned, loathing the monkish King, crying aloud for freedom from him and his cloistered ways, weary of her very life because of him, black-browed and sullen with anger.

Behind her chair I stood, when he who should be King of England, Henry Plantagenet, surnamed Henry Fitz-Empress, was presented to her, the shaven King leading him by the hand, and saying:—

"Madame my Queen, show favour to this damoiseau, Duke of Normandy, who shall rise higher."

I saw the red glow in her face as he knelt to kiss her hand, for though younger by ten years than she, he was a great gentleman already. Short of hair, gray-eyed, clean-lipped like a boy, strong of arm, light of foot, he moved like a woodman — a hunter and a soldier rather than a man of palaces and councils. The courtiers called him Courtmantle, for he went in jerkin and hose, but yet very splendid with fur and jewels; and for me, I compared him with Monseigneur Saint Michael, so much a warrior he seemed with his fighting face and gold head above his furs.

He was a goodly sight for such eyes as hers, and when he was gone she sat staring into the wood fire — for it was Christmas and cold — until the monk King returned; then she flouted him until the blood stood on his lip as he bit it striving for patience.

Three years later she demanded her divorce of him

as in the fourth degree of kinship, and well I knew
the cause, knowing also that she would gain it, as
what did not our Eleanor gain when she would! But
it was ill to gain, for the King held that Aquitaine
and France were one, be he and she what they might,
and it was wrenching a cantle from his heart to break
that bond. But she had the ear of His Holiness, and
what she would she had.

So she departed, taking her great inheritance with
her; and when Henry Fitz-Empress heard what was
done, he knew her mind, and counted her lands and
gold and weighed them against herself, for he loved
her not. Piers the Norman that was with him at
Courtelai hath told me that, when the letters came,
he frowned all day a black Plantagenet frown, sitting
in his chamber of dais; and the next day he sent
letters, asking her in marriage, and for answer, he
had the one word, "Come."

With great pomp they were wedded, and with
pomp they sailed for England; and I, who was ever
near the Queen-Duchess, wondered in my soul how
she should live in that gray land of rain and mist.
She shivered when we landed and drew her pelisson
of vair about her, and King Henry said: —

"Fair Lady, lose no heart, for the sun shines merry
here also when the leaves wax long and green in the
shaws. And my English love a laughing Queen;
therefore greet your new kingdom with smiles."

But if she smiled then, she smiled little when we
came to London, to the Tower, for among her ladies

was Rosemonde de Clifford. Of her I knew nothing, but it seemed the Queen knew more, for I saw her black brows draw together as the noble demoiselle came up to kneel and kiss her hands, averting her glance from Henry, who sat beside Eleanor on a chair of state. And henceforth I watched.

Very tall was this lady and slender, with great gold hair braided above each ear like a cup, so that her face was set in gold as the faces of saints in a Book of Hours — pure ivory it seemed against a glory, having little color in cheeks or lips. Her eyes were a green blue like the beryls in the clasp of the Queen's missal, and the lashes so long that she could look through them unseen, as birds do in the reeds; and so she looked upon Eleanor and dropped them. Her gown of blue sendal fitted her body closely and was set with goldsmiths' work about her long throat, and on her head she had a network of gold chains set with blue jewels. She held herself with a stiff grace, not gliding and languishing like the ladies of France and Provence, but straight like a young saint on a Church banner. No saint was Rosemonde, but most gentle, patient, and sweet-voiced — with long cool hands, ready to plead or pray, swift in almsgiving, pitiful to man and beast. But this I knew not then.

"Iseult of the White Hands!" whispered our Eleanor bitterly to me, as the fair de Clifford drew back among the other ladies. Very learned was Eleanor in all the loves of bygone days and had herself made a lai on Sir Tristan and the two Iseults — the dark and the fair. But Henry was no Tristan:

a swearing, fighting Plantagenet, a lover of the tall deer, no lover of the harp; and had our Eleanor been wise, she had shut her eyes and gone her way. For all kings are not as the monk King of France, to whom a woman was a painted picture; and when she had him, she loved him none the better for the milk that ran in his veins, for a man must be all fire for her and steel for others. But this she did not find — no, not with Bertrand d'Arles, who sang of her as a thing divine, and when he laid his harp aside found solace in Marguerite Spagnolles. This we knew right well, but she did not know.

In the Tower was her son born — a lionceau indeed; and the King laid him in his shield and held him up to the barons that crowded the Queen's chamber. His face was hard and flushed as if with pride, and he cried:—

"Lords, let us receive with joy what God and Madame give us! Here is a boy shall carry the leopards into France and further. Welcome him, barons all!"

And they clashed their swords, and the Queen turned as she lay and looked on the King. The child she never heeded.

But Rosemonde was not long a Queen's woman. She grew paler and paler, and her eyes feared like a bird's when the hawk hangs on steady wings above him. This I knew, for I watched and pitied.

Later, when the Queen sat by the window that looks out upon the muddy river of the English, the Lady Rosemonde sat before her upon a low tabouret,

her hands folded in her lap, an image of patience.
Thinner she had grown, so that the small bones
showed in her face, and her shape was like a willow
wand under her close cymarre. Her hands were so
white and frail that in my heart I also called her
Iseult Blanchmains as did the Queen. She sat among
the ladies as if she were not of them and had no
friend at all. And the thing grieved me inwardly, for
to me she was ever courteous and sweet of speech.

And the Queen said, "See — the King passes!"

And we looked out and saw the Royal barge, with
Thomas of Ipswich, Lord Mayor that year, sitting
at the King's feet, and at his elbow a Bishop, and
they rowed down to see the ships at Queenhithe. So
the King looked up to the window and saluted with
his hand, Eleanor waving her kerchief; and I saw
the blood rise slow in Rosemonde's white cheek until
it burnt red and brought the water into her eyes
under the hard stare of the Queen. A blow had been
less cruel than that stare! And when it was past,
she rose and knelt before Eleanor, and, in a voice
that trembled, she said:—

"Lady, a boon! I ask of the Queen's Grace that I
may go down to Hever, to my father's house, for I
have a wasting upon me and weakness."

The Queen's eyes pricked her like steel from head
to foot as she knelt with her eyes on the ground.
They searched out every secret of body and soul.
Indeed, I pitied the damsel, for Henry was a very
splendid lord.

"There is none to take your place, fair lady," said

Eleanor. "She whom King and Queen delight to honour is well beside them. And in this grim Tower I have need of your skill with lute and voice."

"Madame, my sister Aloyse is a sweet singer. And, moreover, she is skilled in broidery. I pray you accept her service for mine, for I am ill at ease."

"I also!" said the Queen, and all the ladies looked upon each other. "But I must needs endure, and why not Rosemonde de Clifford? Dismiss it, damsel, and content yourself. What! have we not pleasures and merry-makings at court to gladden a maiden's heart? And for the wasting and fever, my own leech shall heal it."

As she said this, Rosemonde stretched out her hands like one blind and fell forward, swooning at the Queen's feet; and all the ladies looked again upon each other and none gave any help. None but I — and I feared not Eleanor, for I was not high enough for her wrath, or so I thought; and with me the storms came and went. So I raised this Rosemonde in my arms, and summoning the gentleman of the antechamber, we bore her to her bed; and there she lay so long with her lashes sealed upon her cheek, that, thinking her a dying woman, I sent for Maitre Pierre, the Queen's leech that she had brought with her from Provence — a learned man, small and gray.

He, doing all his knowledge bade him with strong essences and cordials, at length made the fair dead image tremble, and it was then I said very earnestly to him, "Sir, is it death?"

And he replied, looking pitifully upon her, "No —
alas! ma bonne dame — but life. Guard well your
lips, for this is a King's secret."

"But the Queen's Grace?" I asked, trembling.

He shrugged his shoulders French-fashion and
went his way, a small bowed figure in his gray robe;
and turning, I saw her eyes were fixed upon me and
staring like a lost soul.

"I have heard," she said. "Oh, if it be thus, let
me die. Have pity! I would die and be at peace. It
is still and quiet in Winchester where the tombs
stand in the dimness and the incense floats about
them. There a woman may lie and none disquiet her
— no passion in the night, no hard eyes in the day;
but day and night in a silence of great peace."

The pity brought the water to my eyes. None
ever knew this Rosemonde but loved her, so child-
sweet she was, so piteous in gentleness; and nothing
witting, I kissed her brow that was cold as marble
and the sweat in drops upon it.

"What should I say? Trust me for silence. Speak
with the King this night that he may bid her let you
go. Talk not of death, sweet lady. She that bears a
King's son need not despair. His arm is strong."

"But how to see him, I know not," said Rosemonde, lying stark before me, and her voice like a
whisper. "I am beset with spies. With the King I
have not spoken in three months; yet must I see him,
for this is a greater matter than a woman's sorrow
and shame. Write I cannot, nor he read. Mother of
Mercy, what should I do? There is no way."

Then in my folly and pity I said: — "There is this way. To-night I will guard you, and to this the Queen's Grace will agree, that I may spy. And I will speak with the King. What token is between him and you?"

She thrust her hand in her thin bosom and pulled out a ring set with a small gold lion and a balas ruby in his claws.

"He will speak with whoever wears this. But I am watched, and since Jehane my woman went I have had none to trust. For God's pity, help me now, and I will pray like a soul in Purgatory that though I lie in flame you may sit in Paradise."

And so, by the choosing of Fate, was I made privy to the King's love of Rosemonde. I did not choose it, Saint Catherine knows, but I pitied her as a mother her child, and also I feared for very great harm to all these noble persons. So I left her lying, her long limbs folded beneath her gown like a lady on a tomb, and returned to the Queen.

She had none with her but a page, and him she dismissed to the other end of the hall, where he stood, looking upon the steps. And then she caught my hand.

"Eh bien, Petronille, what has she said? How I loathed her as she knelt before me, her eyes on the ground, pure as a saint to see and with her heart of hell! She would go, would she! But I will keep her here, and her shame shall be her gibbet."

"Madame," said I kneeling, "I know not if you are right or wrong. This is a matter that needs watching and discretion, for the de Cliffords are great barons. Certain it is that she is ill at ease. One should be with her this night. I desire not to inter-meddle in great matters, yet if it be your will, I will watch this night, and mayhap she will speak — "

The Queen's face shone with fierce joy; I sickened, seeing.

"Excellently said, my good Petronille. Stay not only this night with her, but many. You she will trust. Your face is like the picture of Saint Anne in the church of Saint Ouen, and she has no friends. That has been my care. Though spies could watch her, they could not win her heart. But you will do this and tell me all. Is it not so, my Petronille?"

I bowed my head meekly, but I would not speak. Surely it should be devils that serve the great, for it is devils' work they do! And before I could rise from my knees, the King entered, bright-coloured of blood with the sharp wind on the river.

I stood behind her chair, as he kissed her cheek lightly, telling her the doings of the voyage down the river and the shouting of the people, and how they should dine with the City of London come summer; and she smiled as if well pleased, and presently, I laid my hand over the Queen's chair, and looked at him.

He was yawning as if wearied, but I saw his eye catch on the ring and stay. He looked straight and hardily at me with a question, and behind the Queen's back I laid my finger on my lips. He continued his tale, and she saw nothing.

Two hours later, when Eleanor sat with my Lord
Prince, the King called me into the small bower
chamber, and looking behind the doors to see we
were private, he faced me.

"What says my lady?"

"Sire, that she would see you. She has that to
say that brooks no delay."

"So!" he said, and looked upon the ground. Then
again: "But you, Dame Petronille, what do you in
this matter? You are the Queen's woman. Is it
spying or honesty?"

"It is pity. Let Madame Rosemonde herself tell
you of it."

"Madame?" he said, and up went his eyebrows,
as if he laughed. He read my meaning.

"La pauvrette! she has no friends," he said, half
sighing. "If indeed you are one, Dame Petronille, it
shall be for your good. Take an earnest!"

And he lifted a long gold chain from his neck, and
would have flung it over me, but I stepped aside.

"Not so, beausire. I have done nothing. But this
night I watch with the Lady Rosemonde, and there
will be no spies. Come, therefore."

"I will come," he said, and strode away with
his dog.

I alone was present when he came to the chamber
where she lay, white as death, but a beautiful girl
certainly, with the eyes that take men captive and a
body like a swaying reed in her slacked gold loin-belt.

He came, wrapped in a long gown of silk, a noble
crimson with the French lilies on it in silver. Great

comely men were the Plantagenets, all ruddy and gold, and used this like a weapon with the hearts of women. Even now Eleanor loved him after her fashion — a love so shot with hate and jealousy that she would as lief have killed as kissed him. I stood by the vaulted door on guard, and because I dared not move I heard their speech, and the first word caused me to totter where I stood.

"Wife," he said, softening his lion's voice to her ear, "what is this? Come, smile on me and have good cheer. A King is your man, and who shall harm the Rose of the World?"

She said only, "Husband," and was silent. Then again, "Shame!" I could hear the sob in her throat.

And he, caressing her:—

"What shame? Ma mie — ma belle amie, were we not wedded of God and Holy Church, and that before ever I took the Queen? Is this not known to Wilfrid of Hampton, the Mass priest of Hever, and is it not known to you and me? Then what shame? Doth that not suffice?"

And Rosemonde, sighing bitterly: —

"For me, beausire, it hath sufficed, and I have endured the looks of women and the smiles of men. But for the child — the heir of England — this I cannot endure. Speak out, or slay me."

"Ma mie, would I not set you by me on the throne if that might be? Would I not wear my rose on my helm for all to see? But I cannot. See with me that this cannot be! If it could not then, how now, that the Queen is beside me and her son born?"

"And my son?" Her voice was like a cry.

"What shame? The sons of Kings are royal and their mothers go proud and tall because of them! This shall be — What name shall he bear? William, from the Conqueror his ancestor, and Longsword because of the great sword I will gird on his thigh. And he shall be a haut Duke and ride with the leopards on his shield and our broom-bough on his crest."

"And the bâton sinister?" she said faintly.

"We will make it a charge of honor. Sweet, fear not! Smile as you smiled at Rouen the day I saw you first in your long gold gown, when you leaned from the balcony to see the knights ride in two by two."

"How can I smile? I die with grief and shame. Who will believe, for none can know, that with Mass and ring was I made your wife and true Queen of England. For that last little I care, as well you know, but for the child —"

There was silence, and I knew the man was seeking in his heart how he might bend her will. Alas! he knew her well. Not Bertrand d'Arles played more skilfully on his lute than this man on the souls of women, and most of all on the soul of this sweet lady. So, after a while, he spoke.

"Rosemonde, your mother is with the saints." (I could hear her weep.) "But there is a mother of more than your earthly body — there is this land of England. How often hath not my Rose entreated me to toil for England, to fight, to pray for England. Remember you not that day at Shene when the thrushes sang in the coverts and all the world was

white with May, and you spoke proud and high?
'For this dear land I would die. What is there I
would not give for England?' Now, therefore, give!
For if I put away the Queen, I put away Aquitaine
from England. I challenge France, and you will see
this land a province of the French King, and men of
England will curse the name of Rosemonde de
Clifford. My lady, I am in your obedience in this
thing, for I am your husband and the father of this
child to be. Choose therefore for me, and from your
dear hand will I take dishonor if it be your will.
But you shall know first what must be."

Now I, listening, knew well that Henry would
take his own way in face of God or Devil; but this
she did not know. Love is blindness and a great
weeping. Never have I seen aught else in this world,
nor ever shall!

Again there was no word. But alas! I knew and he
knew also what would be her mind; for this Rosemonde was a very great lady, true and high and
gentle — the dove and the eagle in one sweet flesh.
But I caught my breath to hear, and he doubtless did
likewise.

And she said, "England," and paused. And again,
"England!" like one musing.

And he said not a word.

Then, very softly, she spoke. "Lord, I am English
born and bred. Neither my child nor I would hurt
this land that is our mother. True words have you
said. It is expedient that one woman perish for the
people. I did think — I believed that this our secret

was but for a while; but since it is not so, since it is for England, I will endure. Had you but told me —"

And then again she was silent. She would not chide where she loved. The Plantagenet was safe in the shelter of the England that as yet the Plantagenets loved not, for they were but Normans at heart.

He clasped and kissed her.

"O Sweet, most sweet, what a lady have I loved! O worthy to be Queen of the world and not only of this little land! God do so unto me and more also if some day — some glad day — you sit not on my right hand, the Queen of the King and of all he hath."

His voice died away in a murmur of love and worship. So it is with men who triumph.

"The Queen?" she said, and I heard the shudder in her voice. "She knows! Her eyes pierce me like daggers."

"But I will hide my Rose in a thicket so full of thorns that she shall find no way through. I have mused long, and I remembered fair Woodstock by the river, where the meadows are cloth of gold with buttercups, cloth of silver with daisies, and the thrushes sing all day. There is a little house in the heart of the Maze — a house like a bird's nest all hid in leaves, and there shall my Sweet sit, and Dame Petronille, who is the wise and kind, shall be about her, and I will come through the Maze like a knight errant to la belle au bois dormant, and wake her with a kiss."

I had not thought he could be so gentle. Certain it is he loved this Rosemonde with what love he had:

but I think it was little enough, though she, poor soul,
fed on it, believed it, worshipped him for the scant
measure, as is the way of women. So in all things he
triumphed.

At the last he strode out, and his brow darkened,
as he beckoned to me.

"If the Queen knows this, Dame, as well I believe,
that poor sweetheart's life is not worth the purchase
of an old pantoufle! and Woodstock Maze is the only
hope for her and me. The Queen is cunning, but
my love and I will outwit her. Who is on my side
— who?"

So he said, like the King in the Holy Book; and I
answered, "I, beausire!" — for indeed I loved that
Rosemonde, as did all who came near her, excepting
only the King that thought he loved her well.

It needs not to tell of the plotting: of how I asked
good leave from the Queen-Duchess to return to
Aquitaine, because I could not endure the damps of
England — and indeed I endured them ill. She gave
unwilling leave, but, as I think, suspected nothing,
and gave me a jewel at parting, a gold asp with eyes
of diamond sparks, but I never wore it, for I loathed
the coiled murderer.

So I rode to Woodstock, with Simon of Winchester
for my guard; but my heart was heavy, for I knew
the mind of Eleanor, and had seen her downcast eyes
when she asked delicately and smoothly of de Clifford
how fared his daughter the Lady Rosemonde.

But when Simon threaded through the Maze,
guiding me, I banished fear, for I thought no creature

not a sleuthhound could nose without the clue through those intricate ways. I scarce could see the sun, and we turned and twisted and doubled in the close walls of green; and there I might have wandered until God's Angel trumpeted, but that Simon held the clue; and what it was, he would not say. So at the long last we entered the little garden close in the heart of it, and there stood the little low house, brown and quiet like a wren's nest in a hedge, and at the door was Rosemonde clothed in apple green, and her great hair in two mighty gold plaits that fell to her knee, twisted with pearls — the very Queen of the wild woods.

The time drifted away in that quiet place like flowers falling — it made no sound nor stir. The days grew to months and the great day came, and we had not seen the King. Simon of Winchester — a good, simple man, but not, as I think, understanding all that hung on his tongue — told us how the Court was at Windsor or Shene, and where not, and how the King had taken ship for Normandy, but would soon return.

So the day came and passed, and we were now one more in the House of the Wood, for the little William Longsword lay in his mother's arms; and praying for forgiveness, I could but liken the poor soul to the Queen of Heaven, so fair she was, so mother-pure and sweet.

And then was her poor heart torn again, for erelong came Simon with the King's sign-manual to convey the child into safe keeping at York, and his mother must see him go.

But two days later the King came, winding through the Maze by the clue known only to him and to Simon. Great joy was there in the meeting of him and Rosemonde. No longer pale and thin, she bloomed forth like a rose-royal, the Empress of all the garden. I, who have seen the courts of Aquitaine, France, and England, do say that never was such a lady as she, with a beauty of light and laughter about her, beyond all naming or painting, so that where she came the hearts of all naturally waited upon her, and she had been a Queen of hearts had she been a peasant.

So he made great joy of her, she sitting at his feet, and I saw her sigh when he told her that next day he rode to the sea and so to Harfleur.

"Sad life to be a King's wife!" she said; "lonely days and weary nights — and a heart that knows not rest."

"Yet would you forget the King, if you might, Rosemonde?"

"That would I not! Better a heart that aches with love than a dead heart. But better still, a cot here in the woods, with my King for a simple archer and my little son on my knee, and me to bake and brew for them, and the weary crown forgotten."

So she sighed; but for Kings is no refuge from the crown but in the high tombs where they lay down sceptre and state.

He stayed but a few hours, and as he went I, looking, saw tangled about his spur a little ball of broidering silk, and I thought, Can it be the clue? But she was at her prie-dieu, and I said nought.

Days went by and Simon had brought confections and sewing silks and gold threads, and a message from the King that in three months he would return, and that with the child all was well.

Now on a certain afternoon the air was hot and still, with a leaden sunshine such as comes before thunder. The birds were still in the trees, and on the little garden-plot the rose leaves fell as if dropping from the heat, and fluttered to the ground.

I sat at the broidery frame, stitching the gold borders on the robe of the Queen Dido forsaken and weeping, in a design that Rosemonde's ghostly father, Wilfrid of Hampton, had made for her, when I heard a step on the grass, and before me came a woman, bending, as if she traced her way by something on the ground. She wore a close coif and a veil that hid her face, but I knew the Queen-Duchess.

Now at such times it is not thought that moves hand or foot — it is the passion that makes the mother deer face the lion if no better may be; and when I saw her put by her veil and gaze at the house that sheltered us, with those fell, fierce eyes, yellow as a lion's, I thought not at all. I fled like a lapwing to Rosemonde where she lay upon her bed faint with the heat, and cried in her ear, "Fly, while I hold her in talk! Fly! Take sanctuary in the nunnery at Godstow." No more; and seeing the white terror of her face as she sat up stark and still, I walked forth of the door quiet as a gossip at a christening and did obeisance to Eleanor that stood and steadily regarded me.

"Greeting, Dame Petronille!" she said, in her hard voice that with her yellow eyes had brought her the name of the Shrew of Aquitaine. "Greeting! Is this the France you sailed for so many months agone? Well indeed for you that you are out of England, where the English Queen has still a word to say concerning her subjects."

So she mocked, but at that hour I knew no fear.

"Madame la Reine, I have obeyed the King's command. And there is none in this house but me."

She smiled a smile I knew — a cruel smile if ever the great Devil set one on the mouth of a woman.

"The King is in France, the Queen in England. Give way, Dame Petronille! I would see the Rose of the World that a King hath plucked and flung by!"

And still I knelt before her and clung to the skirts of her great velvet robe.

"Madame, there is none but me."

And this I thought was truth. But as I held her, she, like the she-wolf that she was, drew a dagger of jewels from her girdle. I knew it well — had I not seen Bertrand d'Arles give it her with kisses? She struck at me — and whether she meant it for my throat, God knoweth; but it glanced and took me in the shoulder, and I have the mark now. And even then Rosemonde came forth, white and tall, and stood before the Queen.

"Spare this poor faithful heart, Madame," she said. "What is her crime? It is I only that have sinned against you. I give myself to your mercy. But for her I ask grace."

"My mercy!" The smile of the Queen was dreadful. It crooked her lips like an old woman's, and indeed I saw her for the first time old, with the deep lines about her mouth and her throat bagged like a vulture's.

"What do you standing, wanton?" she cried. "Kneel — kneel before your liege lady!"

And, folding her hands very sweetly, Rosemonde knelt and spoke.

"Great wrong have you had, Madame, though not as you have thought. I kneel to beseech your pardon for more than myself. I have sinned against you — though I knew it not."

The leaden sun struck us with blows like a strong man armed. So hot and still that the earth, like the Mouth of the Pit, knew not coolth nor refreshing. I huddled against the sundial and the blood soaked slowly in the woolen of my gown; but still I watched and prayed.

"Bold to sin and craven to ask mercy! Crawl lower, Rosemonde de Clifford! Swear that never in life will you see the face of my Henry again."

And Rosemonde, meekly: —

"Would I had never seen it, for it was to his great losing. Madame, I swear this if it lie with me; but for him I cannot swear, and you know it."

How could she but know that the poor lamb spoke the truth? Who should let the King from his heart's desire? I saw her eyes darken and gloom. Very terrible the woman was, in her coif and gorget stiff as a knight's armor, and the haggard vulture's face above it.

"That is true, and being true there is but one way. So dainty a lady should choose her death. See, Rosemonde, when first I set foot on English shore I knew I was mocked of the King and you."

"Never that, Madame," she replied patiently — the sweet soul was ever patient! "The King's Grace honoured the Queen. But true it is he loved me before ever you set foot in England."

So she held the King's secret!

"Loved!" God's pity for Rosemonde! That word had slain her.

"What are words between us two?" said the Queen. And I feared with deadly fear, for I saw her mood was like iron upon her, and stilled her voice and dulled her eyes. She looked like one drunk with wine.

"See here, woman — I have brought this cup and this dagger. Choose."

She took from her bosom a small closed cup of gold, set with green stones, and I knew it for that Sal-u-din the Emir gave her when there was that between them that Christian Queen should scorn. And in her other hand was the dagger still wet with my blood. And a faint giddiness took me so that, though I could hear and see, no word could I say.

"Choose!" she whispered: "the swift stroke or the sleep that lies in this cup. And because I am crowned Queen and Christian woman, I say the cup is the easier way. It is sleep, and sleep without pain or dream. Choose, for with either choice the waking is in hell."

She held out the cup with a hand that did not

tremble and in the other hand the dagger, and Rosemonde, white to the lips and kneeling, said: —

"Madame, I have a little son. Have then pity on a mother. The nunnery at Godstow is close and sure. Neither King nor baron may enter. Give me leave to hide my head therein."

And she: "Could I breathe the air you breathe? Could I live if you have life? Talk no more, but choose, for the thunder comes quickly."

And even as she spoke fell some slow drops of rain like blood upon the grass.

Then Rosemonde, still kneeling, put her hands together like a young maid at the Mass, and she prayed: —

"Crowned Queen of Heaven, Mother and Maid, have pity on my extremity, and on my child. For love's sake and my King's." And again, "Merciful, have pity, for I have wept and suffered. Receive my spirit."

Having said this, with one hand clasping the gold reliquary that the King had given her to wear in her bosom, she stretched forth her hand and said in all simplicity: "Madame, for this small mercy of the cup I thank you. You have had wrong. I ask your forgiveness."

But never a word said Eleanor as she unclasped the cup. Sure, if hate could walk the world as a woman, it were thus and thus. So Rosemonde, kneeling, received the cup and drank, and it fell and tinkled as it fell. And the thunder broke upon us like a leaping lion.

No sleep — no sleep for Rosemonde! for the Queen lied in her throat. Sharp pains, rending agonies, dread anguish of soul and body tore her. She fell writhing, with the pains of hell upon her, and Eleanor smiled.

"Madame, the dagger, the dagger! O mercy of God, slay me!" she shrieked; and her shrieks pierced the air, and sure they pleaded like angels at the throne. Was it for eternity she shrieked? — God He knoweth, and not I: but it pierced my ears — my soul; and still she shrieked, and I swooned at long last, and even in my darkness heard the cries of soul and body rent apart in torment.

Now when I waked, the thunder was rolling fearfully away in the distance, and in the wet fresh air a bird sang, and there was a clear shining. I dragged myself to my knees, and looked about me, and beside me lay Rosemonde, gray and still in death, like one wearied and at peace at the end, and her hair like wet seaweed in the grass; but the reliquary was in her hand. So Simon of Winchester, coming later, found us. He knoweth.

Later, Rosemonde was coffined, and in Godstow stands her tomb covered with a pall of gold that the King gave with many Masses for her soul, and upon it these words graved: —

HIC JACET IN TUMBA ROSA MUNDI
NON ROSAMUNDA

(In this tomb there lieth not Rosemonde, but the World's Rose.)

But who shall know the hearts of the great? For I looked that he should see the Queen no more, nor touch her hand in this world nor that to come; and this was not so, for she bore him children, and he and she ruled as King and Queen to his life's end. Also, very speedily he found him a new love, the Lady Aloyse of France; and God He knows that should not have been, for reasons many and heavy. But these matters are above a simple woman like me.

Only this I know — his sons were his scourges, and in and by them no peace had he, and he loathed the face of the Queen. And it is told that as he rode against them in battle he said this to the son of my Rosemonde: —

"True son of mine are you — true son of a true mother, and England is yours as mine. For these are but misbegotten whelps."

So sin and shame fulfill their day.

Blessings also. For strange it is and true that in the arms of the son of Rosemonde this King died at Chinon, deserted of all else, and laying his head on her son's bosom as one content.

And, O King that sits above the thunder, Judge of the world, deliver us from evil Kings and Queens and all their deeds!

And let all of their charity pray for the soul of this Rosemonde, who with much sorrowing passed through pain to God's mercy.

HER MAJESTY'S GODSON

SIR JOHN HARINGTON

1561–1612

"For thanks to the swete God of silence, thy lips do not wanton out of discretion's path like the many gossipping dames we could name, who lose their husbands' fast hold in good friends, rather than hold fast their own tongues," wrote Sir John to his wife. Evidently her discretion merited his frankness.

Elizabeth did not forget the loyalty of her godson's parents, who had been imprisoned with her in the Tower during Mary's reign. But even so, it was well for Saucy Jack that he was born a wit and a poet, and knew how to trim his sails to the capricious winds of her Grace's fancy. For the divine right was exercised right royally in private as well as in public affairs, and it may be that her courtiers had need of more tolerance toward their "great Prince" than she had toward her subjects.

Sir John and his merry fellows, adept and shameless flatterers as they were, — endorsing fully the saying that "Poets may lye by authoritie," — knew how to win her fickle pleasure, and thus was it fortunate for young Harry Compton and his poor Lettice that these gallants were determined to see young love in the ascendant.

And at the end, who can say where the fullest measure of satisfaction fell? To the lovers, forgiven and saved from poverty; to the father, his child happily restored; to the Queen, her hasty action vindicated, her personal power reasserted; or to the aweless youths — who, after all, were responsible both for the problem and for its solution?

Sir John Harington
From a Miniature by J. Hoskins, Senr.
in the possession of the Duke of Buccleuch

II

HER MAJESTY'S GODSON

Being certain letters from Sir John Harington, Queen Elizabeth's "Saucy Godson," to his wife Mary, Lady Harington.

What follows is founded on contemporary sources, in many cases in Harington's words, and the story of the lovers is a true one.

HERE write I on our royal progress, Moll, and we are come to Chartells for two nights or it may be three, Her Grace lying here with all her attendance ere we pass to Elvetham where are prepared many pleasures. And a great welcome have we here of old Sir John Spencer and his fair daughter Mistress Lettice. And since it be your will to hear, sweetheart, here sit I your humble scrivener.

And first, we have had fair weather. The gracious countenance of my Godmother hath not been once overcast, though if a storm leap not from the blue ere long it is much, I discerning last night a cloudy sunset. But Chartells is a noble park. It lieth quiet in the woods where the windy rooks do caw all day with a voice that, though not angelical like lark or nightingale, hath that in it of England that, if a man do but remember oversea, bringeth before his heart this little island that is the home of so many high and heroical virtues.

Now at Chartells this sound falleth all day from

leafy towers of beech and elm. And the great old house standeth in the midst of green lawns like a man knee-deep in grasses, and these lawns be trimly set with flowers, some of village seeming, yet sweet, such as coronations, pansies, sops-in-wine, gillyflowers, and the like. And, trust me, Moll, sooner would I see these rustic gentry than the new French and Italian garden monsieurs that Philip Sidney and other Italianate gentlemen have brought from the outlands. And there be alleys of roses white and red, gloriously blended, and lilies like kings' sceptres, and beyond all this, bowered in stiff-clipt yew, Mistress Lettice's herb garden with agrimony, lavender, vervain, balsam, and other such fragrance, where the maids do gather for the still-room. And be it my good hap to make clear my title to Harington Park, we will make of it a Chartells, and you shall be a country madam and I a rustic knight, writing only verses to my Godmother's eyebrow, and journeying twice a year to Court to junket lest I be clean forgot — for this is the way of the world.

And I tell you herewith that I have hopes, Moll — hopes! For before we left Greenwich did I send Her Grace your paste of apricocks and conserves of cherries by Philip Sidney, I being sick of a rheum, and he saith: "The Queen hath tasted your dainties and saith that your lady hath marvelous skill in cooking of good fruits. And as for your law suit touching Harington Park, please the Queen all you can, for all the great lawyers do fear her displeasure."

So said, so done, sweetheart — for I weary of

court. I have spent my time and almost my honesty
to buy false hope, false friends, and shallow praise,
and fain would I purge and live cleanly ere it be late.
Could I boast with chanter David, *In te speravi,
Domine* — but 't will not be yet.

Therefore I have presented a jewel, Moll, of rare
device, being a heart of gold garnished with sparks
of rubies, and three small pearls, and a little round
pearl pendant, out of which goeth a branch of roses
red and white, wherein are small rubies, pearls, and
two little emeralds; and this I took from Kit Blount
in part payment of a gaming debt, but breathe not
this to the moon! So I put it behind her cushion,
with this verse writ out of mine own fruitful brain: —

> For ever dear, for ever dreaded Prince,
> You read a verse of mine a little since,
> And so pronounced each word and every letter
> Your gracious reading graced my verse the better.
>
> Sith then your Highness doth by grace exceeding
> Make what you read the better for your reading,
> Let my poor Muse your pains thus far importune,
> Like as you read my verse, so read my fortune!
> *From your Highness's saucy Godson*

'T was neat, methinks, and she was well pleased,
though she gave me a tweak after her wont, saying
to Greville: —

"'T is a pretty fancy, and in the perfumed case
do I scent the roses of Harington Park! But that
merry poet, my godson, must not come again to
Greenwich till he is well rid of his rheum — and
leaveth the ladies' sports and frolics, wherein he
is too forward."

So standeth it now. But to my tale.

(Interrupt by Her Grace's summons. Resumed)

We made a great entry to Chart Town two mile from Chartells, Her Grace a-horse-back, habited in a gown of black velvet pinked, and a caul upon her head exceeding glorious with pearls and jewels, and a hat spangled with gold and a bush of feathers, and the Mayor and Corporation offered on the knee a loving cup having a purse therein of twenty marks' value containing a hundred pound in gold angels. So Her Highness, receiving it graciously, did weigh it in her hand, saying to Mr Secretary Cecil: —

"It is a good gift. I have but few such, for 't is an hundred pound in gold."

Whereupon the little Mayor plucked up heart and says he: —

"If it like your Grace, it is a great deal more."

"As how, Mr Mayor?" demanded my Godmother. And he: —

"It is the faithful hearts of all your loving subjects."

"We thank you, Mr Mayor," saith her Grace. "That is indeed a great deal more."

But I saw her eye follow the cup as Mr Secretary bore it off. Say what you will, sweet Moll, I love my Godmother well. She is full of gnarls as an oak tree and of whimsies and quidgets as a breeding woman, and of subtleties and turns as a very Machiavel, but a royal Prince withal, of such stately stomach and carriage as no other Prince in Europe can match, and when she smiles 't is sunshine.

Now this day after noon-meat I walked in the garden, bethinking me of Harington Park and dreaming of dreams after my wont, and so I came at last to a fair pleached alley beyond the bowling green, and then a little lawn where sat retired fair Mistress Lettice Spencer, our young hostess, with Sir Fulke Greville, he very splendid in bombasted breeches of purple flowers damasked on cloth of silver and a cloak likewise (and I know not, Moll, that my last doublet is of sufficient fancy for Her Highness's eye, she having commended Greville, but not me, and all the men now going in magnificence), and Mistress Lettice in white satin, very beauteous. And it is the old knight her father that gave me my first caudle cup, he being a good friend to my father and her Grace's trusty servant when she was but the Lady Elizabeth in the old Queen's days.

So, seeing them earnest in talk, I doffed my cap and adventured to sit on the seat of rustic bark beside them; and I said: —

"Fair Mistress, have you and this gentleman quitted the court for a hermitage among the roses, or do you await any happy wight in these sweet shades before you return to the revels?"

And she, dropping her eyes like a maid: —

"Sir, we await Master Harry Compton, and he is good company for that he hath always the last tale and jest." And I: —

"Fairest lady, he is good company and a very wit and addle-pate. Surely her Grace herself liketh well of his songs, so also the court ladies. But you,

Madam, are not of the court, yet he is no stranger to Chartells."

I touched her shrewdly there and she blushed, not like the common sort, but pale like the young dawn. 'T is a pretty lass, Moll — I know but one fairer, and you have smiled on her oft in the glass. Her eyes are exceeding long and narrow and of a languishing darkness, with long lashes. Not full-lipped, but the lips delicately cut and like a thread of scarlet, as says the Holy Book, and because her face is pale, this is a noticeable thing, as though an image of marble were tinted with rose. And her chin is percht upon a pillared throat that daintily sets off her falling ruff, and she moves as it were to music, but shy as a deer glimpsed through the trees. I liked well to see her pretty shame. And says she: —

"Sir, Master Compton hath been little here of late years. Time there was — "

And so ceased, with the tear in her eye. And I, jesting: —

"He is no great miss, Mistress. Sure all men are alike — and all are unworthy a regret." But she, reddening: —

"Not so, Sir. 'T is not Master Compton's will to be a stranger to Chartells, but my father objects to him that he hath made the Italian tour and is now infect with foreign customs and manners. And — and other reasons hath he — "

She touched my heart, Moll, with her innocency, for he who ran might read where lay her heart. And Fulke Greville, who loves young Compton, said:

"Very certainly is Italy in this age a land of monstrous crime and sinners, but some there be that, like the bees, suck only pure honey from poison flowers, and such is Sir Philip Sidney, my good friend, and Compton also, being in all things a most worthy gentleman."

"Sir Philip is the very mirror of knighthood," says Mistress Lettice, "and though so delicately featured and complexioned, his carriage is awful to all base persons, and if my father did but consider what this young gentleman himself saith he hath learned from his tour, poor Harry should not be despised." And the word "Harry" having 'scaped her lips, she was like to weep for blushing, poor sweet soul. And even as she said this word, Sir Philip approached, fanning himself with his gloves, for the day was warm.

Thou hast not seen Philip since a boy, my Moll — and I would thou didst, for he is of no common stamp, but one in whom all the perfections meet. Though I say it of a man, he is exceeding beautiful, favoring the Dudleys and the maternal line rather than the Sidneys, his hair a dark amber, his stature high, his face long and most nobly shaped and featured. Also there goeth with him an air as of the higher countries, so that he seems ever above his company, be it what it will, and this by no assumption of his own but a thing universally admitted. If it could be thought, Moll, that greater spirits visit this sublunary sphere disguised like princes who would not be known, so would I think of him. And he cried: —

"I give you greeting, fairest lady, and you, Greville, and you, Master Harington; and give me in return a seat, for I have been standing in the presence of my gracious Mistress till I am like to drop; and there is some anger toward, and as yet we know not what, but she is now closeted with that tale-bearing lady, Mrs Bess Russell."

So he was seated and there beneath the trees did Mistress Lettice ask him of the latest court news, inclining her pretty ear with diligence, for to her 't was all new and a romance, being a country lass.

"Why, as for that," said he, laughing, "my lady Katharine Howard hath but now told me of poor Mistress Mary Arundel's misadventure — how Her Grace telling her she would be suitor with her father that she might marry the man she would, did gain his consent, and so told the young lady. So then the sweet simpleton, blushing at so much condescension, did give her Grace goodly thanks and with wet eyes said: 'Then now I shall be happy, so please your good Grace!' 'So thou shalt, but not to be a fool,' saith Gloriana, 'for his consent is given to me, and in your possession never shalt thou get it! Go to your business. A bold one i'faith, to own your folly so readily!' It groweth on her Grace that she will hear of no marriage but her own."

I laughed as Sir Philip ended, but the lady sighed.

"Go not to court, fair lady," said I, "until he, whoever he be, be tied to thee with that golden ring that even the Queen herself must acknowledge. 'T is a hard life at court."

"Hard indeed," answered Sir Philip, "yet for the love I bear my Sovereign I would not leave it. 'T is a royal lioness indeed. Her gracious temper is easy ruffled, and it may be she loves too well the mud-honey of flattery, and politic is she as her grandfather the Seventh Henry of blessed memory. Yet what a woman, what a Queen have we in Her Grace! Well might Kit Hatton say that 'the Queen did fish for the souls of men and had so sweet a bait that none could escape her network.' Not once nor twice have I so found it."

"True is it," said Greville, "and whereas to the high she is high, to the lowly she is a very mother. The earth hath not such a Prince for affability. I should know this that am ever by her. Come ploughman, come beggar, the hour is yet to be that she scorneth them, or they have worse words than 'God ha' mercy, fellow!' or 'Give him a reward!' A great Queen."

"For my poor part," saith Mistress Lettice, "seeing I am in the company of honorable gentlemen, will I say that Her Grace, however fair as a young Princess, is now over old for these lightnesses of dress and speech that sit not well upon the majesty of a great Prince. Forty-four years! As well be Methusalem!"

"So it seems to your fresh youth, sweet Mistress," said Greville. "But I take leave to defend Her Grace's beauty against all comers, even those fair foes that be armed with tongue and bodkin."

So Sidney smiled upon her: —

"I do not know if Her Grace be old. So great things

hang upon her for this realm, so great loves and fears surround her, that the hope of all the earth attends her steps, and for me and many her face shineth as the sun in its strength, where beauty is but a rushlight and I neither miss nor seek it."

He paused, yet more he would have said, but up comes Laneham, sent to summon Mistress Lettice to her Majesty's presence. She waxed white as an Easter lily, and looked fearfully at him.

"What can it be — what can it be? I fear very greatly. She is not merciful to maids!"

"Fear not, sweet lady. Her mien to-day is gracious," says Sidney; and so squired her along the pleached alley, we following.

Now this rose walk at Chartells leadeth to a fair great lawn with a fountain and a great spreading beech tree beside it, very pleasant, and flowers about it in trim parterres after the French fashion, and the air full of bees and sweet scents. And here was a rustical throne set forth with rich tapestries, and the Queen with her ladies at her feet and the gentlemen about her. And says Sir Philip: —

"Even in Italy, that land of antique magnificence, is there no such scene as this, for here is splendor tempered with a sweet homeliness that giveth content to all beholders, and never do I think Her Grace so well beseen as when she sitteth thus in English gardens."

"And such English roses about her royal person as these ladies," says Greville; and indeed they made a brave show.

Sir Walter Raleigh, standing by, shrugged his shoulders after his fashion, laughing: "Witches! Witches!" But Sir Philip took him up.

"Every fair lady is a witch and mistress of the potent spell, and these more than most, being more lovely."

"I meant not so," said Sir Walter, "but the truth is these do nought but make mischief with Her Grace. They cannot speed a suit nor save a head, but for gossip, tattle, and mischief have they the very Devil's power: therefore call I them witches, for they have no will for good, but only ill. Look now on Bess Russell — that Puss Velvet-paw! If I am not much mistook, she is mischief-ripe."

If so, thinks I, Moll, let Harry Compton beware, for she hath long pursued him!

Says Greville: "I have a grudge that way myself, for I am like Robin Goodfellow that the dairy wenches blame when they upset the milk-pails. So whatever gossip these ladies tell her Grace, they blame it all on me."

"'T is true." says Sir Walter. "Look on old Francis Knollys, frowning on them. 'T is a perpetual war between him and these damsels. 'T was but last week that he sleeping close to their dormitory, they made such a noise as wholly hindered his sleep. For when retired for the night they would so frisk and hey about that it was vain for him to attempt sleep or study. So what does he do, when they were at their pranks, but break into their dortoir in his great nightcap, and so, horn spectacles on 's nose and book in hand, he marches up and down steadfastly, reading sonorously in Latin."

"And what did the ladies?"

"Why, Sir, they fled screaming; but two presently returned, earnestly entreating of him to depart. 'Why so I would and will,' saith Sir Francis, 'if an armistice be drawn and delivered, it being declared that I shall have peace in mine apartment and that all these rushings, friskings, and heyings shall cease.' And so departed victorious."

Thus pleasantly discoursing, we approached Her Highness; and since my Moll would hear it, I say she was most richly beseen. For she wore the garland of diamonds sent her Grace by the Sultana Valide, mother to Amurath the Sultan, and very nobly it sparkled in the red hair that graced her Majesty. Her bosom was uncovered, maiden-fashion, and she had a rich partlet, and a white silk gown bordered with great pearls, and a kirtle sheened with silver. And at her right hand our host, Sir John Spencer, looking no sweeter than soured milk. So she beckoned to Mistress Lettice, and the young lady approached and made her reverence, almost sinking for shame to be so public. And says her Grace, frowning upon her: —

"What is this, damsel, — I hear of love passages between thee and Harry Compton? For I am credibly told and informed that you purpose marriage — nothing regarding the consent of your Sovereign and natural parent. I will have no such ungracious flouting wenches."

And so all eyes fixed on Mistress Lettice where she stood, courteously supported by Sir Philip Sidney's arm, and pretty it was to see that young Harry instantly stepped forward from the gentlemen and stood beside her, pale and resolved, like to a man that advanceth to the gun's mouth. And says he, kneeling: —

"For ever dear and dread Sovereign, true it is there have been love passages between me and this young lady, tending to honourable marriage, but, be it said, not without sounding of her father, for to him I declared my passion and he would none of it, alleging me Spaniolate and Italianate, for that I have visited that country with Sir Philip Sidney and with your Grace's own royal permission, adding with great contempt that he would advance her fortune by marrying her with a rich old lord in your Majesty's service, for that I was but a younger brother and a penniless man."

"God's death! So said he? And who was this lord?" demanded her Grace. And Bess Russell white as death. So Harry: —

"That, Madam, know I not, and knowing scarce would tell, for I meddle not in other men's matters howsoever they meddle in mine. But hearing this, Mistress Lettice told me with weeping tears that she could never disobey her father yet would never wed another, and so purposes to follow your Grace's chaste ensample, remaining a virginal Diana to her life's end."

And certainly, Moll, I could but admire at this

lad's cunning in thus baiting a hook for Her Grace.
For turning to Dr. Whitehead, the old learned divine
that stood behind her, she smiled, saying: —

"What think you? Was not this obedience and
modesty in so young a damsel? 'T is only you and I
in all this court, as I well believe, Whitehead, who
keep the faith of single blessedness, and I like you
the better for it."

"Madam, for that same cause, I like you the less!"
says Whitehead very grave; and Her Grace could not
forbear laughing, but turned from him to Sir John
Spencer.

"Well, mine ancient friend, for so I must term
you, declare now to your Queen what is the fault of
this young man. For, though marriage be a purpose-
less folly and condoned by Holy Writ only for our
feebleness, yet there must be exceptions if the race
be not to decay altogether; and why not these two?"

So Sir John, sturdy as a pollarded oak with his
black velvet doublet and long staff, kneeled before
Her Highness despite the rheum in his knee, and
says: —

"Madam, I neither despise nor love Master Harry
Compton. But I will not have him marry with my
daughter, because his late father Lord Compton did
me a grievous displeasure in the matter of Heathden
Hollow and the rights thereto pertaining; since when
the name of Compton stinks in my nostrils. And
the young man is Italianate, and Sir Philip Sidney
himself hath well rendered the proverb:

An Englishman that is Italianate
Doth lightly prove a devil incarnate.

and he is moreover idle, glittering, a mere courtier.
And furthermore — "

"Hold there!" says Her Grace. "'A mere courtier'!
And what, ungracious man, can be better service
than the service of your liege lady? Learn manners,
disgracious knight, and know that there is no greater
honour than to stand before kings. I do perceive
in thee a very froward and naughty subject, and were
it not for former services — " but here she broke off
and becked to me.

"Come hither, Godson Jack. What know you and
the other gallants against this springald? Is he light
in conversation and living — a drinker, a roisterer,
a follower of wenches?"

"None of all these things, most dear and liege
Lady," says I, "but sober and discreet as a bishop,
and, though merry, eschewing all idle quips and frivol-
ity. Such is Harry Compton, and sure he never cast
his eye upon a lady until this, and then he commended
her to deponent for some dim and far-off likeness
that he conceited in her to one too fair to be evened
to the like, even though she be a personable young
lady and of a sad and shame-faced carriage."

And sure, if Her Grace had seen the look I cast on
Compton, we had been all dead men; for never was a
merrier gallant.

"H'm — 't is well," said Her Highness, "and a
discreet carriage to be highly praised, though 't is
a sort I grudge not to others, for youth should still be
youth. Has any other gentleman aught to advance
for this errant pair, since it seemeth we hold a Court
of Love to judge their case?"

"Why, Madam, if I may be heard," saith Sir Fulke, kneeling, "I can bear witness for Master Compton that never was more loyal subject. For ever in his lodging he hath your Grace's tablet picture, and I have seen him peruse it and invoke it as an angel manifest, and upon it hath he writ: *The Sum of all perfection. The Desire of all Eyes. The crowned Nymph of England.* Sure such an one deserves his Sovereign's favor, and this, not for loving what all love, but for his constant heart and orisons rendered before a worthy shrine."

"And wherefore, thus loving, hath he condescended upon a lower love?"

Here was Her Grace more than a little tart, Moll.

"Alas, Madam," cried Compton, casting himself before her, "shall a man — and not one man alone, but all — be condemned to love for ever where there is no hope, thus laying aside all worldly comfort and assuagement to fit his heart to bear its daily torment? For if it be so, surely treason itself could merit no harsher punishment than is thus accorded to hopeless love and fidelity."

This young man should go far, Moll, or I mistake much! Her frown softened.

"Sir John," says she, "I am minded to let these fools act according to their folly. If they have deserved punishment here is means, for marriage is the one cure for love. Be gracious lord to them, and let them shipwreck to their hearts' desire."

"So shall they not, your Grace," cried he, bellowing like an angry bull at baiting. "If it were my life

ELIZABETH

Hall sculp.

demanded, that is my Queen's, but my daughter
God gave me, and though your Majesty ask who
might command, yet shall no consent be won of me.
And here do I declare that if this contumacious wench
wed with this lip-cheating knave, she is no child of
mine. And I bid him and her to remember that my
cousin of Whichcote is as likely an heir as a rebel
daughter. And better!"

Now all stood astonied, hearing this defiance,
and instantly rising, lion-like, she daunted the mala-
pert orator with her princely checks, bidding him out
of her sight. "And fortunate are you," said she, "in
that you are our host, and that the memory of service
received is in the heart of your Prince, else had you
slept in the Tower."

And so, standing above him with her stately port
and majestical demeanour, she drove him, as it were,
from her presence, while Mistress Lettice, the fair
Helen of this war, did weep disconsolate.

"And for thee, damsel," says Her Grace, turning
upon her, "though I much mislike thy conditions,
yet will I not be bearded in mine own court, and so,
like it or leave it, to-morrow shalt thou be wed in the
chapel here to this young eyas, and your ruin be on
your own heads."

And the lady Katharine Howard led the fair
Spencer away, she hiding her face. And so broke up
the Court of Love; and some salvage men, quaintly
apparelled, appeared to dance before our liege lady
on the green, and the bridegroom, scarce able to believe his good fortune, was rallied by Greville and
your unworthy husband, but Sidney sighing.

And so happed it, Moll, and well thou wert not in presence, for the mere sight of a wedded wife is disgracious in the sight of my Godmother — God help us all!

And presently she calling me, cried: —

"Godson Jack, what hast thou known of this sorry business, for sure I saw knowledge in thine eye?" And my knees were like water under me, for she was walking fastly up and down like a chafed lion and catcht my girdle when I did kneel, swearing by God's Son. It was long before more gracious discourse did fall to me, for she had taken some suspicion, but at long last was I put out of my trouble and bid go off. I did not stay to be twice bid, Moll; if all the Irish rebels had been at my heels I had not sped faster, for I did now fly from one I both love and fear. For love her I do, being so quaint and witty a Princess and gracious withal to her poor Godson. And moreover, if I could forget my own benefits received yet can I never forget how, when my parents were in the Tower, and she but Princess, with sweet words and yet sweeter deeds she encouraged and supported them. And never can a man come before a statelier judge nor one that can temper wisdom, learning, choler, and favour better than herself. But when the storm breaks, God help all shelterless! For there is then no doubting whose daughter she is.

And so, Moll, wishing me heartily in thy sweet bosom, I end. Yet in parting — have an eye, good Moll, to the smock that is a-working to present to her Grace, come her birthday. For I have told Philip

Sidney thou hast set in hand, on his behalf, a smock
of fine cambric wrought with black silk work and
edged with a bone lace of gold and silver, the ruffs
cut-work, set with spangles, and with this he is well
content. And 't were well, sweetheart, if thou prepare
a gift for me also, if 't were but a sheet of cambric
worked all over with sundry fowls, beasts, and worms
in murrey-color silk. But rather let it be a pair, since
Mrs Carre prepares some such thing and 't were
needful to out-top her gift.

(A year later)

O LORD, Moll, what doings have we here at Greenwich! Her Grace driven devil-mad with tooth-ache,
and all about her no better. The Lords of the Council
sat upon the matter with me unworthy in attendance,
and so, gravely consulting, resolved that I be dis-
patched incontinent to Master Antony Fenatus, said
to be of great worth in this disorder. So I went off
handsomely, and when all was said and done, his
counsel might a mere mumper have given, being but
to rub the tooth with fenugreek to loose it; and if this
fail, to have it out. And this Her Grace swore by
Peter and Paul should not be — her lion heart that
never daunted before Pope nor Spaniard quailing
utterly to think on this little nip. This she declared
before the Council, they on their knees beseeching
her for the whole realm's good to perpend and submit,
and she swearing the man was not born that should
thus handle her. Lord pity us, what a pother!

So then, we all kneeling amazed, up comes the
Bishop of London, and reverently besought Her

Grace to hear him, for that the pain was less than she could well believe, and says he: "I though an aged man and but few grinders spared me by the hand of Time, will joyfully submit to have one drawn if so be that 't will give your Highness's royal heart courage to endure this little tweak." And right lovingly he said this, and sorry indeed was I, sweetheart, that I had not myself imagined this offer, for Harington Park is worth every grinder in my head if that might help.

So she accepted this cheerfully, and he sitting down, the man was summoned, and the Bishop without moan or murmur submitted his jaw to the robber with a right grim and valiant countenance. And 't is the truth, believe me who will, that Her Highness, being thus emboldened, submitted also, with Leicester holding one princely hand and Cecil the other, and the peccant tooth appearing, the Bishop begged it in memento that he might set it in a gold box for ever. And 't was accorded. Sure a man might write and laugh for ever at the humours of the Court.

Since thou dost ask of Compton and his wife, here is the truth. Her Grace hath done nothing for them nor her father forgiven, and I have seen him very lean and woe-begone in the purlieus of Chepe, and have, with Sidney, done what I could to his aid, declaring it a debt to be repaid when the rich man her father shall relent, though indeed my mind misgives me if that be soon or ever. But I could not withhold my purse, for my own heart bade me give, and Moll, thou knowest well Sidney's talk that none can resist, so heart-winning is it, and when he can he roundeth in Her Grace's ear, as doth also her saucy godson, that the poor child his wife is shortly to give Harry a child scarce more innocent than herself; but still Her Highness moveth not. And 't is sooth that as she advanceth in life this not-giving mood groweth on her. And methinks this is known to herself, for the prisoner Queen of Scots lately sending her a piece of her own handiwork — *videlicet* three nightcaps wrought very delicately — and humbly offered as beseems her, my Godmother thus replied: —

"Tell the Queen of Scots that I am older than she, and when people come to my age they take all they can get with both hands and give but with their little finger" — a true word spoken in jest. So what hope, Moll, of Harington Park, or our poor turtle doves? So here I end as at present, with my heart's love that out-runneth my slow feet.

PENSHURST.

Two weeks hath my Godmother spent at Penshurst, with Sidney, my Moll.

No palace is Penshurst, but I who have seen the palaces of France do declare that where they win the envy and awe of men, this shall win their love, for it bears state, and yet a place where a man may sit at rest with his children about his knees, and looking over the woods and fat acres, praise God for his home and the kindly folk about him and this dear land of England.

And here Philip grew, and if a tree set take on the nature of the earth that bears it, how much more a man? and he does oft compare himself in this to the tree set at his birth, whereof Master Ben Jonson hath writ: —

> That taller tree whereof a nut was set
> At his great birth where all the Muses met.

'T is best in his own home is seen his lovely and familiar gravity conjoined with such sparks of heavenly wisdom as persuaded his own father to name him, *Lumen familiæ suæ*, and such indeed he is.

But Her Majesty honoured Penshurst with this visit not only because of his graces, but also he is nephew to Leicester who is ever more in her familiarity.

So she came with a great Court, and Lord! Moll, how the people pressed upon her, riding through Tonbridge! 'T was indeed a kind of rapture, an ecstasy as beholding one more than mortal. She rode the last stage with Leicester at one bridle rein and Sidney at t'other, and you had laughed, Moll, had you dared, as did not I, to hear the tender compassion wherewith when Leicester used his riding whip smartly to get the press back, she would cry aloud:

"Prithee, my Lord, take heed that you hurt not my loving people. Prithee, my Lord, hurt none of them."

And then aside, in a low voice: "Cut them again, my Lord! Cut them again!"

Never do I weary of observing her humours, and methinks of all the books ever writ is she worthy to be heroine.

It is known to you, my Moll, that her years are a

subject to be dealt with tenderly, for the majesty of a sceptre borne for so many years cannot alter the nature of a woman in her, and on this must I now whisper a rare jest.

Dr. Antony Rudde being appointed to preach before her at Penshurst, in a evil hour declined on the text, "Lord, teach us to number our days," which text he handled so suitably and discreetly that he thought it would in no wise offend her. And while he dwelt on the sacred and mystical numbers as seven and three, all went well; but when he tended further I observed she began to be troubled, he interlarding it with some passages of the infirmities of age, such as, "When the grinders shall be few in number," and with more quotations to the same effect, whereupon the Queen looked out of her closet, and so far from giving him thanks upon it, told him in plain terms "he might keep his arithmetic for himself"; and later observed she thanked God that neither her stomach, nor strength, nor voice for singing, nor her sight, was at all decayed; and so produced a little jewel that had an inscription in very small letters and offered it first to my Lord of Worcester and then to Sir James Crofts to read, and both protesting they could not, the Queen herself read it, making very merry. And so it blew off, but Rudde hugely abashed and discomfited.

Now that evening, she sitting awhile with her lute and discoursing sweet music, came Sidney to me with Sir Fulke Greville and said: —

"How now, Harington, how think you to adventure

a word with Her Majesty of poor Compton and his sad case; for I have word that things go from bad to worse with them, and no relenting in the old father, but stiff as a stubbed oak, even though he have lost his cousin of Whichcote which was his sole heir."

"Why, Sir," said I, "it depends, not to speak disrespectfully, on who shall take the bull by the horns. I own myself that I would choose rather to be audience than principal where any matter is in dispute with Her Grace, though I do avouch that to observe her in her humours is to me beyond any play that man hath writ or players played. Still, I believe that to-day the sun doth shine!"

"So then," says Sidney laughing, "you would push another into the imminent deadly breach and stand back yourself, Master Harington! Well, even so be it. Come now with me when the music is ended and we will meet our fate like gentlemen adventurers; sink or swim together."

So we advanced to where she sat with but two ladies in attendance, very magnificent in a cut-down gown of black velvet and white kirtle ornamented with animals, monsters, and flowers. Moreover, she wore the great pearls of the Queen of Scots, which she hath secretly purchased for very small monies from the Regent of Scotland. And since thou hast a woman's stomach for jewels, my Moll, I will tell thee that these are like no pearls thy fair eyes have ever seen, but as large as cherries, very rare and precious. They are six strings, strung as paternosters and falling far down her princely bosom, and four-and-twenty that

thou wouldst give the said eyes to own, being like
black muscadel grapes, very noble in their strange-
ness. And so, though I must not and do not compassionate that false Duessa, the Queen of Scots, yet
also she being a fair princess, I well think it must
have been a goodly sight (though not so goodly as our
Mistress) to behold her decked with them. O Moll,
't is well she lieth in duresse: certainly Her Majesty
sleeps the sweeter for not seeing this Helen (who
catcheth all men's hearts) with her own eyes.

So we approaching, Philip Sidney took the word,
first commending Her Majesty's playing as the very
music of the spheres, whether upon the lute or vir-
ginals, but more especially accompanied with the
ravishment of her princely voice. And this received
in merry sort, we passed to more general discourse,
and Philip letting as it were drop that he had word of
old Sir John Spencer having lately inherited more
monies from his cousin Mr. Spencer of Illington, her
Majesty said with a jest that the Crown might well
be the heir of Sir John's estate, he having now no
other, and so would she do thriftily in this world's
gear to invite him to Court and make much of the
old gentleman. Whereat all we laughing as in duty
bound, said Sir Philip: —

"Why, Madam, an heir he should have, for we
hear credibly that Mistress Compton, his daughter,
is to lie in and that so strait is their poverty, Harry
Compton being also in your royal disfavor, that
they have scarce wherewithal to provide the wise
woman for the occasion."

But here Her Majesty interrupted him with "Pish!" and began twangling on the strings of her lute as though she would not hear, whereupon any other than Philip had desisted, but he not so.

"Madam," says he, smiling upon her, "sure the match was of your own making, for when the grudging father dismissed them you commanded their marriage, and by this act these turtle-doves became your birds to be nourished at your hands. Where then shall they look if not to your Grace?"

"Let fools suffer according to their folly," says Her Majesty, "and I take it the more ill to be thus harassed because I have heard this day that Godwin, Bishop of London, an aged man who should know better, hath taken to himself a spouse, and it is bruited abroad that the jilt is but twenty! If it be so, before God I'll unfrock him!"

"Nay, Madam," says Sir Fulke slyly, "I cannot tell how far above twenty she may be, but this I know — she hath a son of forty."

Her Grace could not here forbear a smile, so this past over without breaking of heads, though she continued muttering angrily about "fools" and "knaves" and such-like, and so would have slipped off Harry Compton's griefs; but Philip would not have it.

"God's death, Madam, shall it be told that man or woman in England obeyed their Sovereign's command and suffered for the doing so? I know well that Mistress Lettice Spencer was so abashed by her father's ill will that she had obeyed him there and

then, but for your Grace's angrily commanding her
marriage in his despite; and now the poor young lady
is in desperate need because of her following that
same. Your princely heart will never suffer such a
check to its bounty."

Here, Her Grace giving a smart push to her lute in
her anger, it fell, all the strings jangling; and looking
despitefully upon us —

"God's wounds!" cries she, "When will you cease
to be a beggar, Philip?"

"When your Grace ceases to be a benefactress —
and that will be in the Greek Kalends!" replies he
with a smile that might tame the Hyrcanian bear.
Indeed, it a little softened her wrath, for looking upon
him more mildly, she said: —

"I had needs be made of money, for not a creature
comes in my presence but begs if not for themselves
for another; and as to the Lords of the Council, they
resemble the daughters of the horse-leech in Scripture
whose cry is ever to give. And for you, Godson Jack,
and you, Greville, well do I perceive that though you
have not the courage to beg yet have you all the
stomach, so I like you the worse for your cowardice!"

Whereby you perceive, dearest Moll, that modera-
tion took nothing! And she proceeded: —

"Well, for all you think me a niggard and a fool,
yet shall my slender management find a way out of
this business without the aid of your mighty coun-
selling. And now say no more, lest worse happen."

And so called to her ladies, and before God I declare
I know not what she would be at and whether harm

is done or good to the poor turtle-doves, or to my suit touching Harington Park. But she is in high displeasure with Philip, that darling of chivalry, and purposeth to leave Penshurst to-morrow, to his great discomfiture. Lord save us all, and send us an easy deliverance! And now commending me to thy love, as ever I end, thy true husband.

GREENWICH

(*A month later*)

THIS day attending Her Grace, she was pleased to say: "Hie thee away to the Chepe and tell Harry Compton that we will have the christening of his child here in the chapel, and myself will be gossip and determine the others. And I will not have this delayed for the mother, for it shall be in two days, and for this I have reason. Therefore let all be prepared."

And this I did and returned, leaving Compton amazed.

So on the appointed day I was called to the Closet, and lo, there Her Grace with Mrs. Fitton and Bess Russell at her feet, and who before her sitting on his knees but Sir John Spencer, that she hath not seen since Chartells. And she was pleased to say, hand on his shoulder: —

"How goes it with my trusty servant? And are you well recovered of the rheum that hath vexed you? We are ourselves ill at ease when so good a servant doth languish."

And he: "I am hearty enough to serve your Majesty this day or another day. Yet am I no cour-

tier, Madam, and if I may have leave, will gladly
retire now mine eyes have been blessed with a sight
of my prince."

And she, spreading her net very sweetly: —

"Not so, Sir John. True hearts are not so plenty
that a word sufficeth, and when the French Ambassa-
dor cometh I would have you with me, that he may
see the old fashion of stout hearts and good swords
is not changed."

Lord, Moll! how his face smiled! So potent are
the words of princes!

And she continued: "And how have the times used
you, my friend, since last we met?"

"Poorly, Madam, poorly. For I have lost mine
heir in a drunken brawl, and so end the Spencers.
But talk not of me, but of your gracious self."

"What do we this day, Godson Jack?" says her
Majesty to me, winking with her eye, — and 't is
God's blessing, Moll, I partly guessed her drift.

"Why, your Grace," says I, "there is a christening
to hand where your Grace stands gossip. 'T is in the
chapel at twelve, but I know not your latest pleasure
herein."

"Why so! I had forgot. 'T is a fair boy of one
Somers that I hold in favour. But who are my
gossips?"

"Philip Sidney, your Highness, and Sir Fulke
Greville should be the other, but he is called to
Tilbury on affairs."

"God's death!" says she, frowning. "Shall not
his affairs tarry? But this being so, will you stand

gossip with me, Sir John, and take the vows for a young Christian?"

"'T is too great an honour, Madam, and I have no gift prepared."

"That can be mended later. And now, Godson, go see all in readiness and that the father be present." And again she winked her royal eye upon me. And off I went, Moll, pondering who should play the father, for well I saw her pretty plot, and swore it should not fail through me. So meeting on the way with Compton, he pale and troubled, I bid him stand behind the arras, and gave him to know who should be gossip, and he and I together sought for Kit Blount that he should play the father, making all known to him, and he consenting with jests the which I spare my Moll's dainty ears.

But Lord! my heart beat hammer strokes when the bell gave twelve, and I being in the chapel did see enter the nurse with the babe, and Blount beside them, in damasked velvet of the best, casting a paternal eye on the suckling. Then came various of the ladies, who fully understanding the game, kept counsel, but with whisperings of "Pretty flower!" "Poor lamb!" as women use. And after them her Grace's self in her noble gown of purple velvet with gold aglets and a rich hat, and on the left Philip Sidney, and on the right Sir John Spencer. And so, very stately, she advanced to the font, being thereto received by the Bishop of London and the singing children. And clear and loud did my Godmother make her responses, good Moll, the others following, and she giving the name "John Spencer" with a gracious nod to the knight, and herself presenting the babe in her royal and maternal arms (for sure her subjects are her children)

So, all ended, we passed into the great hall, and here Her Grace made her gift to Blount for the child, being a fair standing cup of gold, garnished with small pearls. And Sidney followed ('t is like him) with a sword of Ferrara, the hilt damascened silver, praying the boy might one day wield it to Her Grace's honour and defence. And now all waited to see Sir John's motion. And he, looking heavenward, spoke in a low voice: —

"Since it hath pleased God to deprive me of a disobedient daughter and then of a disgracious heir, and since this child is fair and strong and innocent of all ills, and is moreover given my name of Her Grace, I hereby in this assembly take him for mine heir and do pledge him my sustentation and good will throughout life, and to this I humbly bid your Grace and all present bear witness." And so took the babe and kissed him.

And in a great silence Her Highness spoke like a Queen: —

"Sir John, that as a good Christian man ye have willed this charity to the young John Spencer, we thank you. And the more, for by the provenance of God, your godson is likewise your grandson of your natural blood. And if it be that God be reconciled to us sinners (as none may reasonably doubt), so be sure it beseemeth us not to digest a grudge for ever.

Take therefore joy in your children and in the affection of your prince, for both shall gladden your declining years. Harry Compton, come forth! 'T is not his doing, mine old friend, for I alone am guilty.''

So Harry ran and kissed the old man's hand, and he raised and embraced him. 'T was a scene so pretty, Moll, as never adorned a stage, and methought as they kissed her gracious hand all white and sparking with jewels, *O Dea certe!* So might a goddess walk on earth dispensing good. Yet, when they were gone to bring joy to the young languishing mother, says my Godmother to me very shrewd: —

"Godson Jack, now have I made four hearts happy, and none the less have saved my purse, to the which otherwise these turtles must have been chargeable, had I followed Philip's mad counsel with yours and Fulke Greville's. And so is good done, and a purpose accomplished and no money spent. And thus is wisdom justified of her children."

So strangely in this lady are the elements blended; but yet do I say, Moll, that there is no prince like her, for ever her errors do seem marks of surprising endowments, and when she is sweet she winneth all affections, and when she is contraried she can so alter her fashion as leaves no doubting that she is Tudor and old King Harry's child. Yet sure in the sun himself are spots, and let none marvel, for she is Boleyn also. Never have I seen greater understanding than she is blest with, and whoever liveth longer than I may well look back and become *laudator temporis acti*, wishing there were always a Queen in this realm, for to women bow also the knees of the heart. But, as for Harington Park, say thy prayers for patience, good Moll, for little hope have I. What think you? She desiring Ely House of the Bishop for Kit Hatton, and he refusing (it being the See's property), she hath thus writ: —

Proud Prelate: You know what you were before I made you what you are. If you do not immediately comply with my request, I will unfrock you, by God!

Moll, he hath complied. And Mr. Secretary hath his eye on Harington Park. No more do I say, but commit me to the blind Goddess that hath not hitherto utterly betrayed me. And so I bid thee heartily farewell, as thy loving husband to command.

THE PRINCE'S PAWNS

JAMES SCOTT

Duke of Monmouth

1649–1685

"The Princess of Orange walked in the Mall every day with Monmouth," writes an old biographer, "and, during the great frosts at this time, the Prince induced the Princess to learn with the Duke to skate, who was desirous of acquiring the art. Monmouth had taught the Princess some new country dances."

Yet it was of Henrietta Wentworth that the Duke was thinking when he wrote from Holland: "I am now so much in love with a retir'd life that I am never like to be fond of *making a bustle in the world again*," and it was Henrietta with whom he hoped to find peace and safety in Sweden.

But others had a different fate in mind for Mary's Cousin James, nor was it long in overtaking him. On the fifteenth of July, 1685, he stood on the scaffold and replied to his tormentors: "I dy very Penitent, and dy with great Cheerfulness, for I know I shall go to God." Then, pressing six guineas into the executioner's hand, with a promise of six more to come if the task was well done, he bade him see that his axe was sharp. Report has it that the axe was not sharp, and that "if there had been no guard before the soldiers, to conduct the executioner away, the people would have torn him to pieces, so great was their indignation at the barbarous usage of the late Duke of Monmouth at his hands."

Thus died the man whose beauty and courage, more than Charles's acknowledgment or his alleged power to cure the king's evil, seemed to proclaim him Stuart. And Mary, left alone, submitted to her rôle of pawn with a nobility no less true, if not so striking.

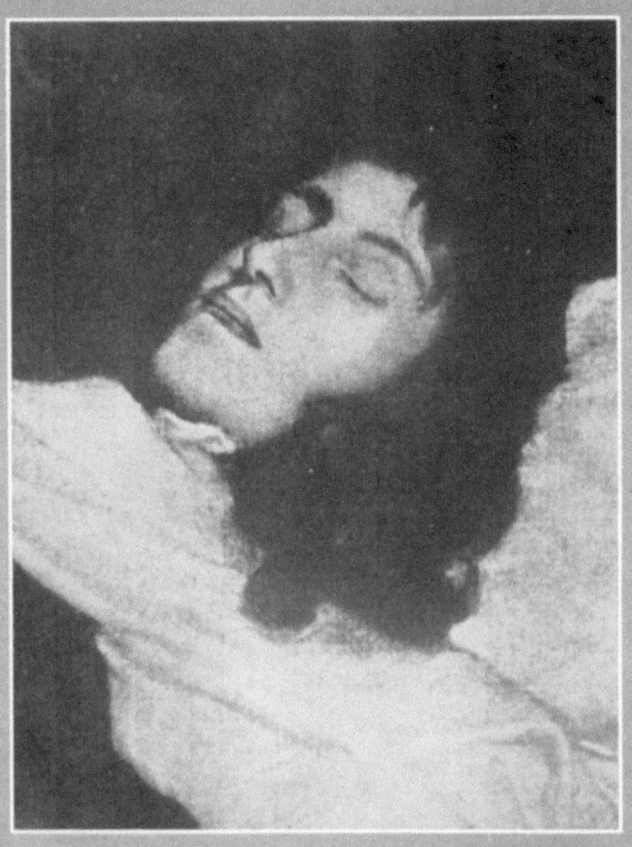

Head of the Duke of Monmouth,
after decapitation

III

THE PRINCE'S PAWNS

There is in the National Portrait Gallery of London a portrait of the dead Monmouth, of the most extraordinary beauty. The cruel mutilation is hidden by a drapery across the throat, and he lies as he lay in sleep, one lock of the dark hair fallen light as a feather on his brow. True Stuart, beautiful and fated, somehow escaping the tyranny of death to find a place in hearts that worshipped him, and not only so but in the world's memory, he lies in peace unbreakable. Over such beauty Death has no more dominion. The lips are closed, but the ghost of a smile — rather its sweetness than its motion — hovers about them — the eyes are softly shut under the dark brows; surely they would lift at a kiss and reveal the glance that no heart could resist. The white face floats in its cloud of heavy hair, as if on dark waters.

So — most beautiful, most unfortunate of men, he lies, and takes the inmost of his brief story with him.

"Sir, I have been your obedient wife for seven years and — "

"Madam, I purpose you shall so continue to my life's end, and were you Queen of England, as an accident may to-morrow make you, you shall know that I will still bear the rule."

"Sir, you have borne it, and I have borne much else. I may never be Queen of England. What is your quarrel with me now?"

William of Orange gazed at his Princess as one amazed. In seven years 't was the first complaint, if so it could be named, that past her lips. For seven years she had seen her maid of honour, Elizabeth Villiers, preferred before her — and not the only one. For seven years she had lived the life of all but a prisoner, pitied by all the courts of Europe among her damp ditches in Holland, at the Hague, Loo, and Hounslardyke, and she had endured all in a grave silence, unweeping. It is possible the Princess had wept out all her tears on leaving England, a most unwilling bride in her sixteenth year. 'T is known how she clung to her sister Anne, afterwards Queen; and with what a passion of affection her arms encircled her father, James, Duke of York. Her bridegroom, the Prince of Orange, viewed this excessive family love with anger, and biding his time silently after his Dutch phlegmatic fashion, meanwhile wended his own way, and fomented all the angers in England that ensued upon his wife's father being Catholic with an Italian Catholic wife.

A very silent man was his Highness of Orange, save when he unbent with Bentinck and Van Keppel and other Dutch nobles who, with him, fixed hungry eyes on the fat lands and exchequer of England.

The news of her hard treatment filtered out to those dear shores through her chaplain and almoner Dr Ken and others, and returned from England in a pity that might have warmed her frozen heart, had it reached it.

"This ugly Dutch little monster is horrible unkind

to his wife," writ one Englishman. "Dr Ken will speak with him about it, even if he kick him out of doors."

And another: "Sir Gabriel and Dr Ken both complain bitterly of the Prince, and especially his usage of his wife. They think she is sensible of it and that it doth greatly contribute to her illness."

So it went on, and her seclusion in her palace was all but such as the Grand Turk doth exact of his women, and she a budding beauty and a free princess of England. Yet not a word. She held her tongue with a wary discretion and in all things humoured her master. If she loved her kinsfolk across the sea, she kept silence on it now. If she shrunk to hear them abused and ill-spoke of, not a word. If Elizabeth Villiers flouted her openly, she met it with a serious calm, and William of Orange, who knew himself none too easy for a wife to live with, declared to Van Keppel and Bentinck that he could scarce have hoped one as pliable who carried so heavy a weight as a Crown in her pocket, and that Crown — England.

So now, walking in the Garden of Fauns, when she, looking at the ground, not at her husband, declared for the first time she had borne much, 't was in the nature of a blow to his self-esteem and he turned darkling eyes on her.

They walked at Loo beyond the Vivier, the great four-sided pond that fed all the fountains, jets, and cascades of the formal gardens; and because it was a bitter cold day in March, Mary of England was velveted and furred and her eyes and cheeks frost-brightened.

That day the princess looked more than common handsome. She was tall, her complexion a clear white, with dark eyes almond-shaped, clouds of dark hair, and such features, high born and bred, as Van Dyck loved to paint in the princes and princesses of the House of Stuart. She was indeed a true Stuart, and was said to resemble her grandfather, that most infelicitous King who laid his royal head on the block at Whitehall. She resembled also her own father, James of York, in his pensive and beautiful youth.

The black furs made her paler, like a star in the night. She had the mien and gait of a royal lady and looked down upon the little Dutchman beside her by at least two inches.

"Sir," she said, continuing the conversation, "if you declare your will, it shall be obeyed so far as is in my power."

He swore a Dutch oath, and kicked the hard gravel before his feet. It was not the dutiful words but the manner that angered him, and he scarce could tell why.

"My will, Madam, is this. The Duke of Monmouth is your illicit cousin. As such, and as the favourite illegitimate son of your uncle and mine, King Charles the Second of England, I receive him here. I entreat him with courtesy, with more, — with friendliness, — for reasons."

"Your reasons, Sir? I may suspect, but do not know."

Your uncle, King Charles, nears the end of his life. 'T is very possible, having no legitimate children,

though in a wide sense the father of his people" (this
with a sneer), "he may declare the young man legitimate and his heir. If so, I would have him under my
hand here. I am not the man to see my wife's rights
stolen by a by-blow. If, on the other hand, your
Catholic father, James, succeeds without opposition,
I am not the man, as a Protestant prince, to see the
people of England oppressed by the Pope and his
priests. In that case I shall loose Monmouth upon
him — Monmouth being the right pawn for my game.
And when the people of England's temper is thus
tested, if it is favourable, I strike."

"You strike at my father, Sir!"

"For his daughter's sake and the people's."

Still not a tremble nor a flutter. This young
woman's calm was excellent. She drew her furs closer
about her, for the wind was keen, and walked a little
more swiftly toward the grove called the Queen's
Grove, a deep wood, though now mostly leafless.

"And my orders, Sir, were to entertain the Duke
my cousin to the utmost of my power?"

"True, and even to win his heart — if he has one
— from his last love, Henriette Wentworth. But it
is not in the bargain that you shall turn red and pale
when he comes, that you shall soften in the eyes
when you watch him sing and play, that your hand
shall tremble when he takes it. Your heart is mine,
if you have one."

She looked him courageously between the eyes and
said: "This comes from Elizabeth Villiers. It is a
woman's work, not a man's."

He raised his light cane as if to strike her — and dropped it again.

"That word and your new-gained courage shows me more than you suppose, Madam. Well, I end as I began. The Duke of Monmouth is here as you are here, to play my game. You are valuable to me only in so far as you are Heiress of England and permit yourself to be pushed from one square of the board to another uncomplaining. Were your father's young wife to bear a son, and that son grow and displace you, you would be worth *this* to me and no more."

He snapped his fingers in the air as he walked, then turned and looked at her. She was still extraordinary quiet. Though he considered women worth but little study, he had preferred her weeping; but her eyes were bright and dry.

"Your will still is, then, that I see my cousin Monmouth alone, that I dance, skate, sing with him? You recall that none of these things have hitherto been permitted to me, and the news will spread?"

"I desire that the news shall spread. Continue as you have your instructions, but exceed them by not so much as a hair's breadth. A bird of the air shall carry the matter if you do. I suspect you on your way to meet him in the grove. That is well. Meet him — "

"And cheat him," she interrupted.

"But no more than I have laid down," said William of Orange, continuing as though she had not spoken. "You are a pawn in the game, but you may one day be a Queen in high earnest if you do your duty."

He made such a bow that the feathers in the hat
he flourished swept the ground, and walked slowly
back into the Queen's garden with its frozen lakes
and jets. She stood a moment observing him, then
following, overtook him.

"Sir, you recall that D'Avaux, the French Ambas-
sador, hath writ to his court, in the letter you inter-
cepted, that you, 'hitherto the most jealous of men,'—
his own words,—'who scarce permitted his wife to
speak with a woman, much less a man,' now press the
Duke to be perpetually with me and even alone?
That I, who never danced, are now bid by you to
dance with him? That — "

"There's no need to continue," he threw over his
shoulder, keeping on his way. "These things I know,
and you know your limits. Stay within them. For
the rest, I will watch."

She heard in silence, then walked back from him
to the Queen's Grove.

'T was a black frost — no snow lying, and the
trees stark as iron against the grey sky. Snow to be,
up above, but not yet fallen. Her foot fell rustling on
dead leaves, but otherwise it was an extraordinary
quiet unbroken by a breath or so much as the flutter
of a bird. She held her head high and had a queenly
air, as if she thought on somewhat that displeased
Her Highness; then she quickened her steps, and so
walked deep into the wood paths.

Suddenly across the frozen air came a low soft
whistle, and as she heard this, the answering blood
rushed up into her cheek and transformed her from a

frostbitten white rose of York to a Lancaster rose,
all colour and glow. His Dutch Highness had never
seen her thus, and could scarce have known the cold
silent princess in her stiff bodice and high cornette of
lace, had he seen this glowing, breathless young
woman.

"My cousin!" she said in French, and turned on
her foot to wait.

"My cousin," a man's voice answered, also in
French; and parting the boughs by a rock grotto, he
leaped out into the path and stood before her, topping
her by a head and more of his six feet.

Sure never was seen anything so beautiful as this
young Stuart, with his dark eyes and dark curls and
the light in his face and the smile on his lips that made
him king of all hearts. In the Court of his father,
Charles II, though there were many Knaves of
Hearts, was none such as he. Buckingham, Roches-
ter, Etherege, Sedley, de Grammont, Anthony
Hamilton, and many more, men worthy of their
bonnes fortunes and the lovely ladies who granted
or withheld — of them all was none who did not
own himself vanquished if this James Stuart looked
into the lady's eyes. Married at fourteen to the
heiress of Buccleuch for a name and a fortune,
he owned no bonds, but like the very god of Love
himself, shot his arrows here and there, and more
often than otherwise was not at the trouble to
gather up the victim. Do but see his picture at
Dalkeith House, armed and splendid, the dark
eyes under level brows, the mouth all strength

and wooing sweetness with the half smile hidden in
the upward corners of the lips. Or as a magnificent
young Duke in laced coat and knotted sash fringed
splendidly with gold, one gloved hand thrust against
his side, and say if any woman could resist the boyish
sweetness of him, the slim young body, the dark-
lashed and shadowed eyes? Sure of all Love's lords
this was chief. And no sugar-cate either, no duke of
dreams, and milk-curd sweeting of a court, but a man
for fighting and hard knocks and a gallant impudence,
and a something beyond all this in him — the wider
dream, the truth that poets know, the mystery that
touches the height. Indeed, this most beautiful young
man was compound of many essences, uniting to
create the strange perfume that was his spell and
accompanied him whithersoever he went.

So he leaped out and caught her furred hand.

"Mary, my beloved, are you glad to see me?"
says he in a voice golden as the distilled honey of a
perfect wooing.

"Shall you ask?" she answered, the tears standing
in her eyes for joy of his beauty and gladness. Could
any of her ladies have known the Galatea whom this
Pygmalion translated from marble into warm smiling
flesh and blood? Is not this why lovers love? Each
is as surely the creation of the other as of God's own
hand. "I never lived until you came to me!" cries
one. "I was dead, — the world was dead to me until
the light of your eyes awoke me!" answers the other;
and so each gives the gift of life, adoring the giver,
and looks on their work and beholds it good.

"No, what need!" says he fondly. "When I led you down the contre-danse last night, your warm hand in mine said, 'I love you.' Your sweet breath touched my lips as I stooped over you, and said, 'I kiss you.' Your eyes — O God, what word can I find for them — looked up and glowed: 'I love you.' Did any other see? How do I know? It seemed that all the world paused to listen and envy. But here are you now, kind and cold-cheeked and mine own. See, this grey sky is Paradise. O heart of my heart, are you content?"

"Content. James, did you but know — you talk of my beauty, but have you never seen your own? Look in the glass of my eyes. My beloved is one among ten thousand. Love, we Stuarts have beauty. Your great-great-grandmother and mine was Mary Stuart, whom the world will remember, and of all the Stuarts you are most beautiful. What is a woman's beauty to yours — lithe, slender, and strong like a drawn sword, steel sheathed in velvet and jewels? All day could I stand and look on you, and long and look on you, dear heart of mine!"

Words broke on his lips and hers. "Kiss me, my heart," he said.

It was when they drew apart that she told him the truth, now with no hesitancy.

"Beloved, I am sent here to cheat you, to spy upon your free-heartedness," she said, clinging against his arm, and looking always up at the dark face as though she fed on its clear lines. "My Dutchman would use you as he uses me for his game — the prize

is the Crown, and we Stuarts shall make way for a
Dutch King in England."

"That cannot be. You are as surely Queen of
England one day as you are now Mary Stuart by her
lover, James Stuart. How will he use me?"

She told him as brief as she could that when her
uncle Charles the Second was dead, — and that at
hand, — that William of Orange would loose him on
England to fight to make himself the Protestant King.

"He says you must fail," said the Princess, "and
having failed, you shall have trampled down the way
for another Protestant King — himself; and he will
drive out my father and rule, with me for his crowned
slave. And I shall so tempt you that you do my will
in all things and I carry back the news to him. But
now, he censured me because I blush when you come.
That was not in the bond, he said. It was not in my
bond with him; my blood has never run a heart-beat
the quicker for him; but for you, James, my cousin.
Feel it beat now in my wrist."

He felt the leaf-like tremble and kissed it.

"You have told me, heart's delight; and now I tell
you. I shall fight in England. Yes. Yes, for that was
fixed before. I have my mother's marriage lines, and
I am Prince of Wales if my father dare own me when
he dies. But be that as it will, I shall fight your father,
for I come before him; and only when I am dead can
he rule of right. You are not the Heiress of England,
sweet my heart, while I live. Do you weep for it?"

"I laugh for love to hear it," said Mary of England,
glowing upon him.

"And well you may, sweet heart of mine, for you are my Queen, and when your father is conquered I shall say this: Take great riches, my uncle, and be not only my uncle but my father. Break your daughter's marriage of the ditches and dykes, and give her to be my Queen and Queen of England, and so shall the Stuarts be one among themselves and happy."

"Can a Stuart be happy?" she asked, holding his hand. "Think of us and ask, is it possible? Look back upon our line in Scotland, and then in England. The terrible Tower is our palace, the block our pillow, and if not that, misfortune after misfortune. I am twenty-two, and what happiness have I known?"

"Do you not know it now, heart of mine?" He asked with his arms about her. "And knowing it for one day, is it not worth the seven years of wretchedness? See, I kiss your mouth. What is that worth?"

"A lifetime!" she whispered, and was silent.

It was dead cold, the grey clouds pregnant with snow; indeed a flake or two began to flutter earthward like a feather of Paradise.

"And if you fail, my lover?" she asked.

"It cannot be, with my Mary for prize. Yet, if I fail — the block. That is most true. But it troubles me least, sweet my heart. I am the more troubled about this poor woman with me — Henriette Wentworth. She has thrown all away for me, and I think I have not even my heart to give in return. Are you so much a woman that you will hate her, or so much mine that you will pity her when I go?"

This man could make men and women do his will

as no other, and with the love-light in his dark eyes,
like her own but more beautiful, who could refuse?

"I will pity," she said, "But O that you had not let
her follow you! It is the false note in our music. It
wounds me."

"There is no false note," he said caressing her
cheek with his. "It is the more harmony because you
love me and will do this thing. And now, my heart's
heart, we will go, for your Dutchman waits in the
Queen's Garden. Go you alone, and say we have met,
and when the sun sets, if it snows not, we will skate
in the torch-light on the Vivier."

"Yes, you beautiful!" she said, constraining him
to delay a moment. "To see your face in the torch-
light, with the bright flames tossing upon it, is a
thing to dream on all day. But yet I must ask you
this: Did you ever love Henriette Wentworth? Can I
think a great lady, a Baroness of England in her own
virgin right, had followed you unasked? Tell me
how much, how little, you loved and love her."

"Dear, how shall a man answer such questions?
You chill me in asking. It is certain this lady never
loved any man but me; certain also that I believed
I loved her. I have believed I loved many women.
If you will love a Stuart, you must know this of the
men of your blood. But O my cousin, my Princess,
your sweet eyes, your excellent red lips have dazzled
me! I am like a moth that flies to the taper. No,
no! I will hear no more. No questions, no reasons,
but love — love only. You shall not see her, but at
a distance be merciful.

Such beauty that from all hearts love must flow.
Such dignity that none durst tell her so.

That is you, my dearest delight. But I dare! I tell
you so now. I love — I love you!" His voice ceased
on a silence yet dearer.

Once more he kissed her lips, and slipped back like
a faun into the trees. She turned and went, warm
and trembling with joy, but as when a man leaves
the fire for the chilly outward air, the heat dies down
in him by degrees until he grow as cold as the bitter
air above and frozen earth beneath, so the warmth
died from her living eyes and lips, and when she
reached the Queen's Garden, where the Prince of
Orange walked hard up and down to bring some heat
into his starved body, she was cold as an ice-flower
on a frozen pane.

"Well, you were brief with him. Have you kept
him in play, Madam? I trust you have not been too
distant with him after your manner!"

"I have kept him in play, Sir."

"Then what news? Is he fixed for England when
the old debauchee his father dies?"

"He is fixed, Sir. But the King of England is my
uncle."

"Mine also, Madam. We too are cousins. I too
have Stuart blood and when I am tempted to commit
some folly, I say in my heart — Beware! That is the
Stuart blood and bound for shipwreck. Be thankful,
Madam, that you have married a man who can conduct you to prosperity. What else said the Duke?"

"Little else, Sir. His talk was of England and of
his hopes there."

"His hopes!" The Prince laughed, "He goes to certain death. I have my agents and know; but it will give the tree such a shake as will set the pear loose for falling into my mouth when I follow — as I shall."

She could scarce be whiter as she replied: "You speak of my father, Sir."

"Your father is a fool, Madam. He would lose England for a Mass. What is a man's soul that he should make such a coil about it? It is like a Stuart to stake a soul — and a worthless one — against a kingdom."

She said, looking straight at the ice of the lake, and not at him: —

"What shall it profit a man if he gain the whole world and lose his own soul? If that be a Stuart folly, it is at least a rare one — and a noble!"

"You are in a new mood to-day, Madam. I scarce know my silent Princess. But come in — the air is too eager, and a message has come that my Lady Wentworth, the woman who follows at Monmouth's heels, would speak with you."

"I will not see her. I cannot," said Mary of England, halting.

He stepped before and faced her.

"It is a peculiarity of this conversation, Madam, that you have never but once looked me in the eyes. Do so now."

She raised them and fixed their inscrutable darkness steadily on him. He spoke deliberately.

"The woman is a light-o'-love, or she would not be here with Monmouth. But she holds his heart in her hand, and it is my will that she shall stay here

when he goes, and from her I will have all his secrets.
It is therefore your part to expend yourself in civilities to her. You are to receive her as the English
peeress she is and as nothing else, but in our game
she shall be a handle by which we twist Monmouth
to right or left. The women they love have always
been able to befool the Stuarts. They have trusted
them like the fools they are. Have you understood
your part?"

"I have understood, Sir. And I will see Lady
Wentworth."

She curtseyed gravely and went off with slow feet
to the palace. William looked after her a moment,
and then with his gold whistle summoned Joost Van
Keppel, and they went together to drink schnaps at
the little pleasure-house in the wood.

But the Princess, returning, called her women and
bid them put on her her gown of orange velvet (she
often wore her husband's colour) and strings of pearl
in her hair and about her neck.

"Is my dress stately?" she asked when it was finished, and indeed it was magnificent, a blaze of
splendid orange in the dying day and firelight as she
sat in the black-oak chair carved and gilded for its
state. And again — a question she had never asked
yet: "Do I look my best?"

The women were full of honeyed assurances, even
the hateful Elizabeth Villiers, who was there always
to spy and vex her. But the strongest assurance was
the tall gilded French mirror in which she saw the
black chair raised on two steps, and the young pale

princess in it glowing in orange — an orange lily
with her flower-stem throat looped with the Stadt-
holder's pearls, and the clouds of dark hair like
Monmouth's, and the dark eyes — almondine also
like his. She had the great carved footstool drawn to
her feet and the velvet drawn in magnificent folds
over it. Her ermine was thrown over the high chair-
back and she took up her black feather fan.

"I am ready," she said. There entered, ushered by
her Chamberlain and making her deep reverence, a
woman as young as herself, dressed in a simple stiff-
bodied robe of primrose brocade, the sleeves decorated
with bows of black ribbons and ruffled with guipure.
Her neck, extreme long and slender, was encircled
with a black velvet ribbon and a throat-necklace of
large pearls, her fair hair arrayed in the formal ringlets of Charles the Second's Court, and the Princess's
first thought was that she was pale and insipid,
though delicately featured.

On one knee, at the second step of the chair, she
kissed the hand of the English princess and then
stood perfectly at her ease awaiting commands.

A chair was drawn near and she seated herself, and
replied to the chosen questions the Princess put her.
No mention of Monmouth. She was received as an
English peeress in her own right who had chosen to
visit Holland — no more. The ladies of the Princess
stood respectfully on either side and did not mingle
in the talk, though devoured with curiosity, since the
reports of her passion for Monmouth were known to
all and her presence there with him was damnatory.

"I have scarce seen you, Madam," said Mary, "since a day you may recall, when, at the Court of the King my uncle, we performed the ballet called 'Calista' before him. 'The Chaste Nymph.' I was Calista; you, I think, were Jupiter. My sister, the Princess Anne, also danced."

As she spoke the words she recalled that Monmouth had danced in the same ballet, and ended her speech abruptly. My Lady Wentworth continued it with composure.

"Yes, Madam, and the Princess Anne's Highness (your sister) was Nyphe. The Epilogue writ by Dryden."

It passed, and the conversation turned to other matters, the ladies still standing about, all ears and eyes. Near a half hour was passed when my Lady Wentworth said with outward calm: —

"Madam, may I venture a request to your Highness: a word alone? Be assured I should not ask so great a favour, were it not urgent. This must be my sole excuse."

Mary, playing with her fan, agreed; but beneath the splendid raiment of orange and pearls her heart beat to a rapid tune. She assented, however, courteously, and the ladies withdrew, headed by the dark-featured Elizabeth Villiers, who cast a keen eye on both as she went unwillingly. She had her orders and this frustrated them.

"We are now securely alone," said the Princess, adding — as she saw the other glance anxiously at the curtained door — "not a word can be heard."

Lady Wentworth rose at once and stood before the throne-like chair. At once the Princess was assured that the woman was not insipid, so completely was her air changed. Her pallor now had the appearance of an eagerness which had worn her so far that the very soul might be said to look from her blue eyes. Her very small hands were clasped so tightly before her that it seemed as though she wrung them.

"I am in great and terrible anxiety, Madam, though it is not for myself I ask your compassion. The Duke of Monmouth is your cousin, and though I disgrace him by my company, you will not be deaf to that appeal."

"I am not deaf," said the Princess with the chilly air she kept for her husband and Dutch courtiers. She had found it a necessary armour. It might be so now.

"Madam, I was deeply set against his coming here, for I knew he would be encouraged in his rebellion in England — "

"I will hear nothing against my husband," the Princess interrupted.

"I shall venture nothing against His Highness, Madam. I have word from England — as you know, my connection there is powerful — that the attempt is useless. It must end in his capture, and your Highness's royal father cannot pardon him if he would. His Majesty King Charles is dying as I speak. Even at this moment your father may be King."

"If this were so, the news would have reached me," the Princess replied coldly.

"I think not, Madam. The Duke and I have our means. What I tell you is true."

That she spoke of herself thus as one with him hardened the Princess, but, long accustomed to master herself completely, she said nothing, her eyes fixed and empty. The other continued in a passion of grief and fear.

"The news of King Charles's death is the signal for the Duke of Monmouth to leave for England and his own death on the scaffold. I think, Madam, if I ever had his heart, it is gone from me, but this will break mine. Will it trouble yours?"

"My cousin's death would certainly trouble me. How otherwise?" said Mary of England.

My Lady looked like a faded reflection of the other. Her primrose dress beside the glowing orange velvet, her fair hair against the dark beauty of the Princess, she seemed a fading moon at dawn. Only her eyes outmatcht the other's.

"I think," she said, with an earnest simplicity, "that there is one woman whose entreaty or command would hinder him, the more so as the rebellion is against her father. My whole soul would bless that woman would she but speak."

The Princess drew herself up in her chair.

"Madam, you are insolent. I have no such influence with my cousin, and, if I had, should be content not to use it, since, if it be true that he has his mother's marriage lines, he is now Prince of Wales, and shall be rightful King of England." And so saying she looked very keenly at my Lady Wentworth, knowing she had long been in my Lord Duke's confidence.

"He is certainly Prince of Wales, and it is believed that King Charles will declare this on his death bed. But as certainly he will lose his life if he go. O Madam — O your Highness, have compassion if you love him!"

"I have a natural affection for my cousin," says the cold precise Princess, her heart beating in her throat so that it caught sharply at her breath twice in this brief sentence. "If King Charles should decease, — but I pray God to be merciful to him, — I will speak with my Lord Duke and — "

But of a sudden Lady Wentworth fell on her knees before the princess and catching her robe, poured forth with tears wild words and sobs and entreaties.

"Madam, I love — I worship the Duke! When I look into his beautiful face I know I would die a thousand deaths to spare him one least pang. It will blot out the sun if he is slain. Beauty itself will perish. What are Kings, what are crowns, to his life? Do I not know that his heart is gone to you, and that I who was once something am now nothing, yet what is that to me in comparison with his life? O Madam, if your word, your love can stay him — love him, and keep him, and I will go away and bury myself in my ancient manor house in England and never more be heard of. To know his beautiful head at rest on your bosom is easier than to know it on the block — O me! my heart! Madam, save him and love him! And take him!"

Her wild words, her piteous tears a little thawed the ice about the Princess's soul. She pitied the desperate woman — a soft moisture like warm spring dews rose in her eyes. She stretched her white hand and laid it on the woman's shoulder who knelt before her, heaving with cruel sobs.

"I love him; I will keep him," she said; and the broken creature before her snatched her hand, raining wild tears upon it.

So they stayed a moment, for neither was apt at words, and the Princess drew the bowed head to her knees, and so sat still with a protecting hand on the pale golden hair, lost herself in a dream of love and pity and the power of a woman who has conquered.

"I will be good to you, Henriette," she said softly at length. "Him I needs must have, for he is mine and I am his — but beyond that I will be your friend indeed."

Now as she said this tenderly, the great violet velvet curtains of the door were parted and the Duke stood between them, stately and tall, his face full of urgent things mingled with dread.

"Henriette," he cried, "it has come! My father is dead. To-night I leave for England."

It seemed as though he did not see the Princess enthroned in splendours. All his eyes were for the kneeling, weeping woman.

"What is it, *ma mie* — mine own dear love!" he said, running to her and raising her so that she lay in his arms, her head fallen like a lily on his breast. "No, my Henriette, weep not, for you shall come with

me. Mary, my cousin, you promised me pity for her.
What have you done? Must women ever be cruel!"

Less in his words than in his face, the Princess
saw herself betrayed. His pretended love was policy.
She was a pawn in her husband's game, a pawn also
in the Duke's. She had been nothing else all her life —
would be nothing else to the close. In all the world
was no love, nothing to trust to but her own strength
and silence and the pride of a great lady. She had
no more at all. This she would hold.

She wronged him, yet was right. A man may love
two women, if it be not possible for a woman to love
two men. He loved her, yet loved better the woman
who had lost all for him. But such love a beggar
wench may scorn and a princess utterly disown —
even the truth that is in it. She sat still and waited,
with the lovers before her.

Recollection and her nearness, his unworthy
treatment of the two women, came back upon him
as he held Henriette in his arms. He looked up to the
pale Princess, despairing less for the vengeance that
must come of his insult than for himself and the ruin
his life had brought to many that had trusted him.
He little knew her, but who ever knew Mary of
England? Not even she herself. Her quiet eyes told
nothing. She rose sedately from her chair, and
stepped down the two steps to the rich carpet, her
splendid orange dress trailing after her.

"My cousin," she said, "you asked my pity for
the woman you love, my Lady Wentworth. I have
given it, ask her else! I recommend you to leave for

England instantly. If you should choose to leave your Henriette here, the Prince and I will have her in our keeping. If not, my ladies shall provide her with all things needful for her travel with you. We shall not skate by torchlight on the Vivier to-night. You will be on your way to the Brill to embark. Stay, I will see my husband. Wait him here."

She made for the door, trailing her velvet, and the Duke releasing Henriette, sprang after her.

"Mary, my cousin, forgive me — I scarce knew my own heart until I saw her weep. Your beauty drew me; it dazed me. Said I not I was a moth — no more? And yet it is most true that I loved and love you. Even now I know not my heart."

"My cousin, what is there to forgive?" said the Princess with extreme quiet. "I was a pawn in your game. One Stuart should certainly aid another. When you have conquered my father and dispossessed my heirship, doubtless my husband will acknowledge you as King of England. I will now say farewell, for you have preparations to busy you."

She tendered her cold hand. He knelt and kissed it with lips that might have thawed ice, but not hers. In that moment he knew not which beloved toy was the more precious, and, whichever he had chosen, must have thought the lost one his heart's desire. Such children are men! Women, the mothers of them, are older and wiser for all their youth, and in their eyes this folly is the very denial of Saint Peter at Jerusalem.

The curtain fell behind the Princess. He turned

to Henriette, who leaned against the wall, faint with fear. "We have but an hour more, sweetheart. I beseech you, do not vex it with tears. It is best I leave you here. The future is uncertain and my cousin, who is a very noble lady, has passed her word to care for you. My soul is perplexed, but I think this best. Will you obey me?"

"In all things, life of my life," she answered. He put his arms about her and so stood, looking over her fair head into the iron-grey frost of the wintry world without, silent — then kissed and released her.

"I must speak with the Prince," he said.

The Princess had already descended to the Prince's cabinet, where he sat with Joost van Keppel.

"May I speak with your Highness?" she said, with her usual reverence on approaching him in public. He rose, bowed, and dismissed van Keppel.

"Your Highness, during my interview with Henriette Wentworth, the Duke of Monmouth broke in with the news that my uncle, the King of England, is dead. It is a bitter blow for him. Had he been acknowledged legitimate, he had taken means to know it. He has not been acknowledged. He is nameless but for his peerage. My father is King."

William of Orange stood transfixed. The thoughts racing through his brain were almost visible in furrowed brow and clenched hand.

"What were your words?" he said presently.

"That he should hastily prepare for England. That — as your Highness desired — he should leave Henriette Wentworth in my care."

"Madam, you did well. I salute my true wife and partner and the future Queen of England!" For the first time in their lives he kissed her with warmth, upon the lips.

She was childless. The influence of Queen-mother could never be hers. She was his first and last step to the Crown of England. No more.

"If Monmouth needs money he must have it. I will see him," said His Highness. "Go you and rest, Madam. You are fatigued. To-night you shall not dance."

"Nor ever again," her heart said, as she watched him go. But still not a word, not even to herself. That was her life. That would be her life to the end. The fountains in the garden were frozen in the bitter March frost. So too, after a brief thaw, her heart.

She saw him once more and in her husband's presence, a stately figure, dressed and sworded for the road. She thought she had never seen him so beautiful, booted and spurred, with whip in hand, a most gallant slender cavalier. His face had the Stuart melancholy; there was no glow of knight-errantry, no brilliance of rash daring. He sent his heart into her eyes with pleading inexpressible, and had no answer.

The curtain had descended and would never be raised for him more.

The Prince of Orange attended him to the door.

"I must not wish my wife's cousin fortune against my wife's father, therefore I do not wish it," he said, with a smile that wrinkled his saturnine countenance.

"The Princess and myself will safeguard your lady. Farewell! To the Brill!"

'T was there the Duke embarked. William of Orange returned to his cabinet to write an obsequious and cordial letter of congratulation to King James II on his accession.

"Nothing," he writ to his father-in-law, "can happen which will make me change the fixed attachment I have for your interests. I should be the most unhappy man in the world if you were not persuaded of it and should not have the goodness to continue me a little in your good graces, since I shall be, to the last breath of my life, yours with zeal and fidelity."

He read it to Mary of England and she listened with grave attention.

Women indeed are difficult to decipher, but this one singular amongst the singular. 'T is to be imputed in part, no doubt, to the hard discipline of her young life, which taught her to expect neither joy nor freedom, but also to a nature and parts of strange force and endurance that must certainly have been implanted at birth.

She now turned back, seemingly unruffled, to the avocations of her daily life and the plottings of her husband. She shewed no disfavour to Henriette Wentworth, but rather a kind of cold countenance, and omitted not to send her — at Brussels, where she fixed herself — such news of the Duke as reached the Dutch Court.

When he was taken prisoner by King James at

Sedgemoor and committed to the Tower, she made it her duty to send for my Lady Wentworth and give her these ill tidings by word of mouth. The poor unfortunate woman entreated the Princess — on her knees, and with groanings that cannot be uttered — to plead with her royal father for the Duke's life. She entreated, and the Princess sedately but with extreme courtesy pledged herself so to do, observing that the Queen Dowager and the Queen Mary Beatrix had both been already beseeched on the prisoner's behalf, and she would add her voice to theirs; and so dismissed the agonised woman who dared make no warmer appeal, and indeed marvelled she had ever ventured it.

But Mary of England did not write on this to her father. Her husband forbade it and she obeyed him as always.

The world knows that the Duke expiated his Protestant rebellion with his head. Of this also the Princess informed my Lady Wentworth. The Bishop of Ely, commissioned thereto by King James, brought to the sorrowful lady a keepsake, wrapped and sealed, and this, with his last words, did bestow upon her in the Princess's presence; whereupon she swooned away, and, being recovered, said a strange thing: "Good God! Could not this poor man at the last find some better thing to think on than me?" And so wept bitterly.

And none but the Princess knew her meaning. When bishop and lady were gone, she sat with her chin leaned on her hand, looking out into the July gardens where the fountains played in silver merriment adown the long Dutch walks. She had dismissed her ladies and they wandered there with Elizabeth Villiers at their head, her husband's chief mistress, a woman of masterly mind and carriage. The Princess's eyes mused, not on them but on her life. Then very softly to herself alone she said two things.

"He loved her best, though she believes it not. She is a happier woman than I."

And, second: "I will never forgive my father for his death, while the breath is in my body." 'T is known she observed this vow to the full when with her triumphing husband she drove her father, a discrowned Lear, into France, there to live and die with his son, the Pretender, in exile.

Then, suddenly, wringing her hands, she broke into a wild and terrible weeping. "O, my love, my love, there was none like you! You have carried my heart with you into the grave!" As if her heart burst on the words.

The Prince of Orange complained no more, as he had no reason, of his dutiful wife. In all things was she his other self, as a wife should be.

When her father's resistance was broke and the Crown of England was secretly offered to her, she, being then still a young and beautiful woman in her twenties, carried the matter at once to her husband, observing that she knew not the laws of England were so contrary to the laws of God, and that for her part she did not consider that the husband should ever be supposed obedient to his wife, Queen or no queen, and therefore she promised he should ever bear the rule. This promise also she not only uttered but herein faithfully acted when he and she were joint sovereigns, in no way asserting her rights, but with a meek carriage towards him in all things.

For his sake (so it appeared) in silence she bore the soul-appalling letter from her father, received on her coronation morning, wherein the fallen King declared that hitherto he had made all fatherly excuses for what was done and had attributed it to obedience to her husband, but the act of being crowned was in her own power, and if she were crowned while he and the Prince of Wales lived, the curse of an outraged father would light upon her, as well as that of God Who had commanded duty to parents.

Even the Oranger flinched at this, declaring — like Adam with Eve — that he had done nothing but by her advice and approbation.

The Queen was dead silent; and so they went to their crowning.

Nor did she chide him concerning his amours, as most women — more especially royal women — are wont, but suffered Elizabeth Villiers about her person and made no complaint; and sure her letters to her husband are examples and models of conjugal respect and affection. For his sake she neglected her sister the Princess Anne, rightful heir to the crown at her own departing this world, and so fixed and justified matters that the Prince of Orange her husband should succeed her as King, which accordingly he did, to the great displeasure of a large part of the English people. So that she may be described as a conjugal heroine, and so her husband owned her, mourning the departure of her affection and great good counsel, even to the endangering of his own life when she deceased. Yet it may be owned as difficult to decipher this Queen's mind as it is easy to read and laud her wifely behaviour.

As thus: In the night, at Kensington Palace, when the hand of death was upon her, she rose from that bed where it had flung her down, and spent the night not in prayer, but in burning papers that she would not have any eye see: no, not the King her husband's. An awful vigil, sure, and one to excite strange questions. And this being done to her satisfaction, she took her pen in her dying hand and wrote to the King a letter — the last. And what she wrote was of Elizabeth Villiers.

Now this is known because it was delivered to his Majesty by the Archbishop with a stern message. But whatever else that letter held is not known. And it is indeed a part of this Queen's character that in life she made no complaint, and that she spoke only when she could no longer be answered, seeming as though even a word on the things that most concerned her peace was unendurable to her.

That she suffered much must be owned, from the people in great part misliking her lending of herself to her father's dethronement. On this were many ballads and pasquinades made that came to her ears.

"Mary the daughter," they called her, and there

too she had no reply to make — or made none —
when she and her sister were pictured as

> Mary, his false Regan,
> And Anne, his Goneril.

She had no weapon here also but silence — silence
that could scarce be deeper when the silence of death
took her, still a young woman and beautiful. Thus
this Queen died at enmity with all of her near blood,
and her works do follow her, if not her much speaking.

Monmouth, her cousin, lies in the church in the
Tower, St. Peter *ad Vincula*, or of the Chains. Of
Henriette Wentworth it may be said she died of a
broken heart the year after her lover — too long to
wait, alas! — and lies among the Wentworths.

'T was not long before death swept all William's
pawns from the board and left him master of the
game and King in England. And of them all, sure
the most pitiable was Mary the Queen.

Could she have writ her thoughts, they might run
thus, as a later poet[1] hath done it for her; but she
could no more write than speak when a matter pressed
deep upon her heart. Sure if she recalled those brief
bright love days in Holland she had thus writ.

> No one ever noticed when I danced my last,
> I go so staid and stately for all the world to see,
> And nobody imagines that I recall the past,
> Now the great grand future is awaiting me.
> You were light, you were disloyal, you were hard to hold,
> So you lie beneath the ashes of your hopes and aims.
> But my heart's grown cold to dancing now your heart is cold,
> Now you dance no more for ever, Cousin James.

[1]The verses are by Mrs. Evan Nepeau

I wear the Stuart crown you hoped in vain to wear.
I sit beside my husband on my father's throne,
A seat that's all uneasy and a burden hard to bear,
And I never loved but one man and I am his alone —
Princess Royal to win England, tool to break the power of France,
Pawn in all his princely schemings and his kingcraft games,
But he has no time to notice that I do not dance,
And I dance no more for ever, Cousin James.

But, even thus, as will be observed, with a reservation of her love to her husband the Oranger. For this Queen accounted her own heart her own secret, and both are now dust in the grave.

THE PIOUS COQUETTE

HENRY THRALE
1728–1781
MEMBER OF PARLIAMENT FROM SOUTHWARK
1765–1780

"IF he would talk more, his manner would be very completely that of a perfect gentleman," said Johnson of Mr Thrale. And of them both, Mrs Thrale writes that her husband could prevail on the Doctor "to change his shirt, his coat, or his plate, almost before it became indispensably necessary to the comfort of his friends." Again, where Mrs Thrale was powerless to curb the bitter tongue of the great man, Mr Thrale could quiet him quickly and peaceably. This seems an almost unknown side of the personality of the reputedly taciturn brewer.

As for Sophy Streatfield, Fanny Burney found her "a very amiable girl, and extremely handsome," but "not so wise as I expected." That she could cry at will, and very becomingly, we have reliable testimony. Mrs Thrale called her an "incomprehensible girl," "very pretty, very gentle, soft, and insinuating."

Mr Thrale died almost in Johnson's arms. Sophy, true to prophecies, "died an old maid — everybody's admiration, and nobody's choice." And Mrs Thrale, as we know, found greater happiness in her later years than her earlier, and celebrated her eightieth birthday by a concert, ball, and supper to some six or seven hundred guests.

Sir J. Reynolds pinxt   Dawson Ph. Sc   E. Scriven Sc.

Henry Thrale

IV

THE PIOUS COQUETTE

"Mrs Thrale was a lively lady." — BOSWELL

WHEN the coach deposited me at the office in South-wark in London, my first thought was to look about me for a public conveyance, that I might proceed to Streatham Place, the magnificent mansion of Mr Thrale, the merchant prince of Streatham, for less I can't entitle the eminent brewer who had married my cousin Hester Lynch Salusbury. I could not suppose that a lowly housekeeper, affable as had been Mrs Thrale's communications through Lady Corbet, could expect any higher consideration than the instructions for her journey from Wales. Not but what the cousin of Mrs Thrale and relict of the late Revd. Mr Sterne, Vicar of the parish of Llewenney (*not*, I beg to say, related to the Revd. Laurence Sterne, author of a book I could never understand and condemned by my venerated husband as the ravings of an unprincipled lunatic!) — But I have lost the connection. What I would say is, that the relict of that exalted Christian, and a Cotton by birth, need take no civilities however distinguished as beyond her due.

Still, when I beheld a coach drawn by fine horses and saw a footman in elegant livery looking about among the arrivals and welcomers, I own I did not connect his search with myself, and still stood gazing until the little crowd began to disperse.

What then was my surprise to behold a hand beckoning from the coach window, while a richly feathered hat surmounting a pair of piercing blue eyes nodded in my direction.

"Lord!" says I to myself, "it's me the lady means" — and advanced curtseying in a tremble.

It is not surprising that I did not recognize my cousin in the first blush, for I had never seen her since a girl of twelve, when we parted at Offley Place. A few letters had passed but the correspondence withered off and no notice on either side was taken of my marriage or hers. But I may affirm that though riches were wanting, I at least married a gentleman and a divine, which is more than could be said for my cousin Hester's match — one indeed very uncongenial to herself, Mr Thrale being the son of a family in mean circumstances in Offley Village, whose father had made his way to fortune in the astonishing manner distinctive of our beloved country. His son had followed in the parental steps, though a fortune made in beer can scarcely be congenial to the mind of a well-born female. Nor was it to hers.

I now beheld a lady dressed in a cloak of the richest damask, her robe of purple lutestring, and a chapeau turned up in the mode and covered with purple and black feathers. No beauty of the regular order, the features being too marked, but attractive in a high degree. Her face, broad at the brows as became her intellectual superiority, narrowed to the chin in a way which my lamented dear (a student in physiognomy) would have declared betokened rather impulse than a settled purpose. Her eyes were blue and beautiful, and though the cheek-bones were high, these eyes with finely marked brows and elegantly formed nose attracted attention from this defect. The whole was pleasing, and a clear complexion must not be omitted in this inventory. But her chief beauty was her lively, engaging expression. Gaiety and humour sat poised upon her lips, and this joined with the most agreeable manners, when she so chose, made her as much a Queen in society as a Queen of the Blues. Shall I be honest and add to these attractions the handsome fortune she dispensed in so unbounded a hospitality? It was admittedly no drawback to her pretensions.

"I'm sure 't is my cousin Anna!" she cried, as I approached. "I can't be mistaken. The description given by Lady Corbet is exact to the features. But what a thief is Time, that changes two old playmates so as neither could swear to t'other! I was on an errand to Mr Thrale at the Brewery, and joined the meeting of my expected cousin with it. Queeney, make room for Mrs Sterne."

Not judging it well to presume on the relationship in my new capacity of housekeeper, I curtseyed and expressed my gratitude, begging that Miss Thrale, a handsome-looking young woman about eighteen years of age as I judged, might not be incommoded, but at once and silently she complimented me with a cold bow and removed to the front seat. I learnt afterwards that she much disapproved her mamma's action in employing a relative in a domestic capacity, even though a miserable penury were the alternative. The steps being let down by the footman, I now ascended the coach and took my apologetic seat by Madam.

Greater affability cannot be supposed. She alluded to my reputation as a notable housekeeper, to the days of happy childhood, and her sincere confidence in my worth. She expressed the utmost satisfaction at our meeting and invited me to consider myself a member of the large family of relatives, guests, and domestics assembled beneath the roof of Streatham Place.

"I am not now to tell you, for you'll have heard it from Lady Corbet," she said, "that Mr Thrale's table is his boast, and there will lie your chief care. We are surrounded by perpetual and changing guests. The famous Dr Johnson, who was introduced into our family when I was twenty-four, is as regular a dish as the roast beef. Sir Joshua Reynolds, Dr Burney, his daughter, the authoress of *Evelina*, Miss Sophy Streatfield, Mr Burke — Lord bless me! I might run on all day and not have done. 'T is quite common with us to prepare for a dinner of twenty and have forty when we sit to table."

I said I was used to hospitable provision, and if I might have the advantage of occasional consultation with the mistress of so great a mansion, did not fear acquitting myself honourably. Never shall I forget the kind quick pressure of her reassuring hand.

"My dear Anna, Mr Thrale won't permit his wife to know the details of the kitchen, but any information your cousin Hester can give you is ever at your service."

I observed Miss Thrale draw herself up at this kindly familiarity, and resolved I would be circumspect to a degree in my manners, however invited by my cousin's goodness. That young lady (afterwards Viscountess Keith) will be admired, go where she will, but I doubt she inspires either the loves or dislikes that surrounded her mamma. A cold correctitude, almost insipidity, marked Miss Thrale and put me on my guard — a matter not difficult, for a solid education had trained my wild shoots of impulse into the fruit-bearing espalier of common sense. But even the space of the drive to Streatham Place impressed me with the good heart and almost masculine generosity of her mamma's character, and why should I blush to own that from that moment the fondness of our childhood returned upon me and strengthened later into a sincere friendship?

I will not attempt to describe the stately mansion, embowered in trees and seated on verdant lawns, which rose on my delighted vision when we entered the drive. Noble and inviting was its aspect! The sun lingered in its secluded bowers; the paddocks cropped by many sheep presented us with mutton not to be excelled even by my Welsh mountains; the peach houses, pineapples, vineries — never have I beheld the goodly fruits of the earth that excelled Mr Thrale's. The only difficulty in the way of the housekeeper was to control the cornucopia of plenty filled to overflowing with riches. No duke, no prince, provided more bounteously, though perhaps more ostentatiously, than Mr Thrale.

He himself was walking in front of the mansion as we drew up, with a lady on his arm clad all in virgin white, and, permitting the footman to assist his lady and daughter and myself to dismount, he advanced with a careless air to meet us, the lady smiling in the background. I have never seen a more perfect specimen of the florid massive Englishman. Well set-up, tall, and fully formed, his age did not prevent him from being a man remarkable anywhere for his good looks. I could see my cousin's keen eye on me to partake my first impression. A masterful handsome man, self-indulgent and passionate in all senses of the word — so I set him down in the unwritten tablets of the brain. I was not favourably attracted, I own, possibly because I recalled Mrs Thrale's remark to Lady Corbet: "Mr Thrale deigned to accept my undesired hand." Something — I know scarce how to express myself — of an underlying insult to women, as it were, connected him with that unforgotten speech. A little over-anxious to please those of consequence, a little slighting to those without pretensions, and therefore injurious to the sex.

She presented me genteelly yet kindly: "My cousin, Anna Sterne, Mr Thrale. A playmate of my childhood."

He bowed so coolly that I saw at once whence Miss Thrale derived her frigidity.

"Mrs Sterne will, I doubt not, justify the connection, however distant, by a close attention to my interests. Mrs Thrale's warmth of attention to other matters may render her a little inattentive to them," he said, and turned away to the lady smiling so sweetly in the background. His whole expression underwent a softening change as he did so, and became a genial sunshine. I merely curtseyed. The lady stepped gracefully forward.

"Pray present me, dear Mrs Thrale," said she. "I am by no means to be cheated out of the pleasure of an introduction to any connection of my kind hostess."

It was an elegant compliment elegantly said. I felt a flush of gratification mount to my cheeks, and Mr Thrale looked on with the pleasure a virtuoso may exhibit in admiring a beautiful picture.

"Miss Streatfield," said Mrs Thrale curtly, and turned away to give some direction to the coachman, while Miss Streatfield addressed some most winning attentions to me in the way of remarks on the length and fatigues of my journey, Miss Thrale staring at her coldly the while. It was felt by me to be a singular scene, though I scarce knew why, and I experienced relief when Mr Thrale offered her his arm and they promenaded down the lime walk, attended by Miss Thrale. I stood there to await her mamma's pleasure.

She dismissed the coach and turned to me in a moment more, and we walked slowly to the house.

"I fear from my master's manner it must be 'Madam' and 'Mrs Sterne' in public," says she, "but in private we will indulge our old affection and be 'Hester' and 'Anna.' I have secured his permission, however, for your joining us in the library and garden when off duty, though not at meals. 'T is a great regale to me to see a friendly face from Offley where I was a fondled favourite. I've never been that since, Anna — never again! My consolation is that here I have done my duty. If it were only for pride's sake I would not fail my handsome master, and, if he would, he must acknowledge that even in business I have been his head clerk and as staunch by his side in hard times as in good."

She looked down, frowning a little as though unpleasing memories crowded upon her. Then suddenly: "What thought you of Sophy Streatfield, Anna?"

There I could be fluent. I praised warmly her graceful and easy address, her caressing smile —

"Smiling Sophy!" she interrupted. "In the poem on the Bluestocking Ladies she is

"Smiling Sophy, ivory neck,
Nose and notions à la grecque.

"Yes, 't is an agreeable smile if ever it changed or varied from one to the other; but it never does. She smiles on little Burney, on me, on Dr Johnson and — yes, even on my master. All alike. I defy you to detect a drop of honey more or less dealt out to any of us. Unless in private — " she checked herself. Then resumed: "She is beautiful, is she not?"

"Undoubtedly. A classical style of beauty. The most exquisitely correct features and figure, and the ivory tint of her complexion with the tapering throat and bust gives her almost the air of a Grecian statue.

Surely, my dear Madam ('Hester!' she corrected),
she is as good as she is lovely?"

"The pious coquette!" she said laughing, but
without humour. "However, here, my Anna, is my
maid to carry you to your rooms. And if anything be
wanting in comfort, be so good as to order what you
will. The servants are naturally at your disposal."

She glanced swiftly away. Mrs Thrale's every
movement was swift, almost birdlike, and suited to
her small light figure, but I saw which way she looked
and my own eyes followed down the lime-tree walk.
Mr Thrale had laid his hand on that which rested
like a snowflake on his arm. His head was bent as
though to catch the murmur of her peculiarly soft
voice. The maid now appearing, I left my kind
cousin standing there alone.

I soon fell into the habits of the family and found
the life at Streatham Place congenial, even engross-
ing. 'T was a strangely different one from the quiet
Parsonage where all the poor visitors came to seek
either assistance or advice from my husband. I
moved now amid large florid men whose persons and
dress bespoke success in various walks, whose wit or
learning made them at first formidable, for whom my
chief concern was that they should eat and drink of
the best. The ladies were likewise striking — many
of them celebrated Bluestockings, some elegant and
beautiful. It was a world in miniature. Though I
had never then entered the theatre, I experienced
what I imagine a frequenter would describe as the
thrill of the play. It was a sensation indescribable,

as though unknown motives — not happy — played under the mask of riches. I was sensible of this in my cousin Mrs Thrale, who preserved a jesting, laughing exterior hard as enamel, though it could not deceive me nor any who loved her, had there been any such. Her warm Celtic temperament was not understood, however, at Streatham, either by her master or daughters, and from that and other circumstances she had so little true happiness that I could but marvel at the laughing composure with which she bore her stings.

Mr Thrale was what I have described him. I knew from Lady Corbet that he had been what is called a gay man at the time of the marriage, and that at first he kept his wife so secluded that Dr Johnson himself used the remarkable expression to her mother that she was as much shut up as a kept mistress, who may be supposed under lock and key. This ended when he entered Parliament and needed and discovered her genius as a hostess. I soon perceived, however, that he neither loved nor respected her. She brought him a son and daughters, but the son died and any little consequence she might have with her husband died with him. He never held up his wife's position. Such gallantry as he had was for others, and Dr Johnson and other guests knew well that they might slight their hostess with impunity and without resentment from their host. I have heard Dr Johnson cry — "Daughters — he'll no more value his daughters than — " he checked himself, but a hundred people might have finished the

sentence for him — "than their mother." His
daughters, having the example set them, slighted
their mother also and had no hearts to guide them
otherwise.

I studied Mr Thrale with interest. He needed and
repaid study, for it was difficult to imagine that his
handsome, dignified presence concealed the instincts
of low birth and the illiberal prejudices that so often
accompany it. He could not suppose for a moment
that a mere woman could deserve consideration
except in so far as she was one to be pursued, and
the consideration a bait. This made his manners
very different in the privacy of the family from what
he displayed in public. His tempers were sudden
and ungoverned and he was then careless of what
language he might use, whether violent or profane.
My cousin went in great dread of this, and it accounts
for her almost unbecoming endurance of slights and
small tyrannies in which her sex as well as herself
suffered. Yet in public all was genial good-humour,
and this procured him an easy popularity which her
restraint upon herself forbade her attaining. His
appetite at the table was ungovernable — indeed it
finally killed him — and in other matters of more
consequence to domestic peace it was the same. But
on what pleased him he would brook no discussion.
An odd expression picked up by my lamented dear
on his travels in (I believe) the Low Countries,
described such a one as Mr Thrale by the strange
term of "street-angel, house-devil." Certainly those
who knew him least admired him most.

Yet, as a public character, he filled his place and was a valuable man. This great nation is largely built up of such and we must condone the private miseries they inflict in consideration of the public confidence they inspire. It is indeed a type very congenial to the English mind — the male who rules his house as the lion does his den, with strokes of paw and teeth.

I was one day in the garden, gathering herbs for drying, and was hid by the lavender bushes, when Mrs Thrale came rushing in and flung herself on the seat by the dial in an agony of tears. I had never seen her weep. She wore her gaiety as a Roman soldier may be supposed to do his armour; and it inflicted a kind of horror on me now to see her so give way. Her condition was delicate at the time, a son hoped for, and she had been in agonies of rheumatic pain during the winter and a course of bark prescribed. Anxiety for her health was therefore my first thought, and I at once advanced. Without a word she caught my hand and drew me on the seat beside her, and sobbed as if her poor heart would break.

"Good God!" thought I. "If the world could but now see the rich, the radiant Mrs Thrale, could know the facts of her existence, how would compassion succeed to envy!"

After some moments she sat up and dashed the tears away.

"I'm a fool, Anna — a fool," she said. "You may well condemn such weakness. But sometimes — sometimes — " Her voice failed her.

"Madam," I began, and as a pressure of her hand corrected me, "Hester, my dear cousin, I am not sorry to see you weep. You need the relief. You take no rest night or day."

"Night or day," she repeated. "Anna, my dear, I dream of my room at Offley Place, the little narrow bed where no one came and I slept sound and dreamless. I hate my vast bedchamber here, and the great curtained catafalque, and Mr Thrale's head on the pillow beside me. I want solitude unspeakably. I want it — " she paused — "cruelly. Oh that I had wings — " There was a silence, and only the light fluttering of the butterflies in the leaves hard by.

"Look there!" she said, and directed my eyes along the lime-tree path where Mr Thrale walked, tall and personable, with Miss Streatfield. I could feel the wild pulses beating in her wrist as she laid her hand on mine. I looked at the couple with inexpressible distaste. Mr Thrale's age made the matter doubly repellent.

"Have you objected?" I asked.

"Objected? I? God knows I durst as well encounter death as disturb Mr Thrale's love affairs. I have tried it once. No — no!"

"But to speak to her? She seems all gentleness and piety and yielding civility."

She laughed bitterly.

"The pious coquette! Don't I know my Sophy? I did speak to her once, and she tenderly asked, Did I not know I could trust her? Surely I knew the principles she had imbibed from the great Dr Collier, her tutor and mine? What could I say?"

She waited a moment, watching them turn at the end of the long walk, absorbed in each other.

"She is all piety and conciliation, and I dare swear is at this moment virgin for Mr Thrale or any other man, and in my belief will remain virgin to the end of the chapter. Men don't love her; they love only to attack that soft resistance. She has no intellect, though she knows Greek like a parrot; no wit, is cold-blooded as a lizard. The only warmth she receives is gained from basking in the sun of the passion she rouses but never fully requites. From the moment she was admitted to my friendship she endeavoured to supersede me with Mr Thrale — no difficult task, for women have always been his object — and daily has grown dearer and more necessary to him. And she is perfectly secure if I keep silence. No one who knows her but relies on her piety and amiability. 'Sophy!' they exclaim. 'She is all sensibility and purity. She would not hurt a fly. The little grossnesses in Mr Thrale will all be purged by her companionship. Mrs Thrale herself should be the first to commend the intimacy.' Whereas —"

"What?" I asked; for she had flashed on in a kind of passion and the stop was sudden.

"Whereas," she said with vehemence, "it is more insidious, more dividing than any connection with a woman of easy virtue. She flatters him, she tantalizes him, she — well" (with bitterness), "I may die two months hence and then she can marry and make an honest man of him. But she could not. Let her step down from her pedestal and be accessible — "

She paused a moment, and added: "I scarce doubt her chastity. She was bred in the strictest principles, and had it been otherwise, Mr Thrale had tired of her by this. Well, is his preference surprising? She has ten times my beauty and grace of manner. Wit and knowledge she has none, nor he — and he likes her the better that she can't out-top him. What Gibson said of my Lady Elizabeth Foster he might say of her, that no man could withstand her, and that if she chose to beckon the Lord Chancellor from his wool-sack in full sight of the world, he could but obey. I should say no married man. The single are wiser."

Her bosom was heaving passionately, her hand in mine. I could discern the relief of this outpouring to her. 'T is a heavy weight of scorn and grief for a woman to carry in her bosom, therefore I would not check the poor thing.

"All last winter Mr Thrale was with her," she said. "Says Johnson to me, 'Why, he lives in Clifford Street!' and so he did — but left his carriage at his sister's door in Hanover Square, not to sully his favourite's reputation. She would desert him soon enough if he did that. His care for her is endless. His attendance at Divine Service is even more regular under her influence. Would not such duplicity drive a woman mad?"

"But," says I, "my dear cousin, Dr Johnson is a rigid moralist. If he have observed this attachment, as you say, would he not be apt to make reflections which would arrest Mr Thrale, who appears to regard him as a monitor?"

"Johnson!" with a laugh that wrung my heart. "He is all for man's prerogative. You may hear him say that, had he a daughter whose husband betrayed her, that fled to him for refuge, he would pack her back again. No, the men stand by one another as women do not. Hence their victory. If a woman suffer, her heart must break — that's all."

"Why should it, if she loves not her husband, my dear?" says I. "Your frankness emboldens me to enquire, Do you love Mr Thrale?"

For a moment she pierced me with bright angry eyes, then lowered them.

"Not before marriage. He never wasted five minutes on me that he could help. His doctor — Fitzpatrick — told me after, that he married me only because he could get no other woman — after trying several — to consent to live with him in Deadman's Place, Southwark, then necessary to his business. I did my best for him in and out of that, and I grew to love the father of my children. It's all over now."

There was a long sighing pause, the wind very gentle in the trees. The couple turned toward us again.

I marveled indeed how a woman of her quick and clear perception could ever have loved the solid handsome lump of humanity that advanced to us, looking down into another woman's eyes. Indeed neither he nor his Sophy troubled very greatly to conceal their tenderness from Mrs Thrale. Why should they? He was her master.

"To vex oneself for what is not valued — " I began, but was interrupted. Miss Streatfield appearing to think she had conceded as much as was good for her adorer at present, detached herself gracefully, and, with little lingering smiles and waves, parted from him and came toward the herb garden.

I had never seen her look more charming. She wore her favourite white robe, and a large drooping hat shadowed her delicate features and soft eyes. She rather floated than walked, so harmonious were all her movements. Her voice as soothing as a ring-dove's, so far different from the fashionable yell that bespeaks attention. Woman, I could still conceive what men must feel for that submissive beauty, yielding, yet always eluding: every day the hope of victory, every day the pitying disappointment — with the fresh hope for the next!

She glided on and seated herself between us. I would have risen but she gently constrained me.

"No, no, dear Mrs Sterne. I must go if I disturb your charming tête-à-tête. It is so hot under the limes that I came here to rest. Mr Thrale is gone in."

"Have you had enough of him, Sophy?" says Mrs Thrale, pulling her hat over her eyes and the smile over her lips.

"I never weary of his kind companionship, dear Mrs Thrale. I should think it a slight to his wife if I did. But I wished to show you the charming letter I have had from the Bishop of Chester."

She drew it from the muslin cross-over that draped her bosom. Mrs. Thrale read it as if in astonishment.

"Good Lord, Sophy! Another victim!" says she. "It's as tender and has all the tokens upon it as strong as ever I remember."

"It's but his goodness — the goodness I meet with is astonishing — I walk in sunshine. But you will see, dearest Madam, that he invites me to visit his lady in two months' time and she seconds the invitation. What I would say is this — Mr Thrale has begged me to stay over your confinement at that time. He dreads the solitude with his anxious daughters. You know I am ever guided by you. What is your pleasure?"

"My pleasure," says Mrs Thrale laughing, with her eyes on the ground, "is that you by all means forsake my Lord Bishop and please Mr Thrale. And indeed a woman should be very grateful to another who consents to fill her place when she needs must abandon it. By all means stay, Sophy."

"Indeed, Mr Thrale was so good as to say it would compensate him in part — but I well know it can only be in part — for your absence, dear Madam!" says the softly complying Vestal. And of all astonishing things ever I heard 't was surely the most astonishing to hear her boast to the wife of the husband's love-making. Yet is not "boast" the word. 'T was all done with a sweet disarming candour, as a child may tell its little gratifications.

"I know how his good heart loves me," she ended.

"I know it too," says Mrs Thrale. "I know the unusual and unrepressed delight my *caro sposo* takes in your society. I will try to secure Fanny Burney to enliven my own spirits, and make us a pleasant party of four. You will also no doubt keep Dr Johnson in good feather, and do all the honours."

Miss S—— either saw not or would not choose to see the raillery. She smiled charmingly. But on one occasion, I never saw that lady without her smile. It was as much a part of her as the mouth it adorned.

"But with regard to Lord Loughborough, of whom you spoke with some tenderness t'other day," resumed Mrs Thrale, "I counsel you, Sophy, to wait and see what turn my illness takes before you decide in haste, and — "

Miss S—— interrupted with an air of soft reproach. "My Mrs Thrale jests. She well knows how I honour Mr Thrale. He has never said a tender word that I have not joyfully repeated to her. But I must go in and write to the Bishop."

She rose with her gentle grace and included me in her parting curtsey as though I had been a duchess. Mr Thrale I saw waiting for her behind the great laurestinus bush at the corner.

"Is it assurance or innocence?" I gasped when she was gone.

"Lord knows!" said Mrs Thrale, the tears now dried in her eyes, and looking after her sardonically. "Good God, what an uncommon girl it is, and handsome almost to perfection. She half frightens me — she takes her own way so serenely. She knows Thrale would kill me if I offended her. I can only say the man that runs mad for the S.S. has nothing to be ashamed of in his choice, for I never saw another like

her. She'll die an old maid for all that! Mark my
words! 'T is the married men are after her. The
others fight shy."

Two days later Dr Burney and his celebrated
daughter came again to stay and I took the opportunity to observe whether Miss Streatfield would be
at the trouble to veil her conquest from them. Not
she! Her manœuvre was far more delicate. Without
letting Mr Thrale slide, bestowing upon him the
most alluring encouragement from melting eyes and
gliding fingers, she attacked Dr Burney with the
same weapons, to "Evelina's" indignation. Dr Burney, extremely amenable to attentions from the fair
sex, responded cordially, and truly the scene was a
comedy had not my poor cousin's heart been the
tragedy behind. Mr Thrale fidgeted; he hemmed, he
flourished his handkerchief. His "Sophy, you promised to walk with me," boomed across Dr Burney's
discourse, and not till the siren turned languishing
eyes on him, moistened with sensibility, was he
appeased.

Mrs Thrale cruelly interrupted.

"Sophy, of all your pretty tricks that's the oddest
and prettiest!" she cried. "I beseech you, show
Dr Burney how you can cry whenever you will!"

For a moment Miss Streatfield looked *caught*, if I
may so express it. She laughed a faint hesitating
laugh. "Dear Mrs Thrale — I can't. It is only
sometimes — it — "

"Oh, no, it's a charming, charming trick! Hark,
Sophy, I'll tell you my latest joke, to ensure you're

not in the melting mood. I shall be provoked excessively if you won't show off. Here it goes: A young clergyman known to us all told his mamma a while ago that he was fallen in love with pretty Miss Prideaux. 'My dear, you must see more of her,' says mamma's wisdom. 'More? Why I've seen down to the fifth rib on each side already.' 'Well,' says I, 'certainly the British beauties exceed those of every nation, and nowadays they utterly outstrip them.' Laugh, Sophy! Laugh all!"

All did laugh, she said it so comically, then she added: "You are all witnesses that she laughed. And now she shall cry! Come hither, little Burney, and see the S.S. cry!"

As I hope to be saved, it is true that Miss S—— raised her fine eyes first to Dr Burney, then fixed them on Mr Thrale, and that I saw two crystal tears rising and slowly spilling down her beautiful cheeks. I actually felt my own throat contract in sympathy until I saw the angry astonishment in Miss Burney's gaze and the malicious enjoyment in my cousin's. But Miss S—— knew herself safe. Dr Burney gazed at her enraptured, and as Mr Thrale rose and passed behind her chair, casting a look of fury at his wife, I caught his breathed: "Sophy! Don't suffer from her treatment! Walk with me. Why constrain your feelings?"

Each gentleman appropriated a tear! Lord bless me, the fools men are! Need women regret what they are pleased to call their heart? Sure a dog's is better worth possessing! The man can be flattered from you into folly at any moment; the dog's love not Venus herself could win.

Later she strolled away down the lime walk with both gentlemen, each casting disagreeable glances at the other; and says Miss Burney in her soft manner to us left behind: "I never saw the S.S. look more becoming than in that drooped hat. Sir Joshua should paint her so. She is ever the same, beautiful, caressing, amiable, sweet and — inexpressibly fatiguing!"

I noted her eye catch Mrs Thrale's with the last word. My cousin responded with her strange candour: "Now *I* find her interesting! I like to watch her. She's always flushed with new conquests; she collects hearts as other women collect Chinese monsters. But indeed you with your sisters must form a phalanx about your papa, little Burney, or he's lost. She will crunch his bones as she has the Bishop's and Wedderburn's and many more. How she keeps them all on a string — bishops, brewers, peers, directors of the East India Company — I know not. 'T would amaze a wiser person than me. I've known but one heart invulnerable."

Miss Burney bridled. In her heart she liked neither lady, in spite of her decoration of sensibility. I penetrated that little reserve. She must always be first, modestly resisting compliments to her genius but greedily devouring them. A very much cleverer lady with her acquaintance than she was willing they should guess her, outside her books! I considered her cleverer and more amusing than any fictional character she ever devised; an opinion for which I should have had no thanks of her.

"And who was this, my dear Madam?" she asked in a most soft manner.

"Why, Mr Crutchley, Mr Thrale's natural son. He declined courting the S.S. altogether. God knows why! Possibly he had seen too much of her tears and smiles. He's a very suspicious man."

Indeed, I thought my cousin too reckless here. I observed Miss Burney color high. She has a tell-tale face, with all her shrewdness. I thought — but no matter! Mrs Thrale had thought the same, but it was not to be. We could not foresee Monsieur d'Arblay, and Mr Crutchley was adamant.

Dr Johnson, attended by Mr Boswell, rolled into the library before dinner from a visit to Mrs Anna Williams, the blind poetess whom the Doctor sheltered so beneficently. We were surrounded by the famous portraits — Dr Johnson himself, Mr Burke, Mr Garrick, Mr Goldsmith and others — painted by the skillful hand of Sir Joshua Reynolds. Impossible not to admire them, but I maintain, with my lamented dear, that the modern touch falls far below the elder and that the solid genius of the immortal Kneller is sadly missed in these more *surfacely* brilliant works of art.

Dr Johnson approached, his linen far from spotless, a smear of gravy on the lapel of his coat, and somewhat disturbed in temper, and I observed the deep reverence, as to Royalty, with which the S.S. greeted him. This flattering distinction was the most agreeable incense to Mr Thrale's judgment, as could be seen in the delighted eye with which he regarded her, as with her own hands she moved forward the chair appropriated to Dr Johnson and adjusted the cushion. She left the room shortly after, and the soothed Doctor observed: —

"There is a pulchritude not only in Miss Streatfield's countenance but in all she does, which might animate a stone. All that may be supposed winning and ingratiating in the sex is to be there admired."

"She has that deference to male opinion which is the straight road to their hearts," retorted Mrs Thrale — for a retort I must call the animation of her manner. Alas, how she damaged herself with Mr. Thrale by a superior intellect which she was never at the pains to conceal! This gave Dr Johnson his opportunity also, who, I regret to say, was never unwilling to make his court to Mr Thrale by *downing* Mrs Thrale's pretensions to knowledge.

"Sir," cried Mr Boswell, thrusting his negligent wig almost into the Doctor's face from behind his chair, "we are not to suppose Miss Streatfield perfection. Have I not heard you object that a knowledge of Greek is as unsexing an accomplishment for a female as needleworks for a man? Now, I understand the lady has the language from her preceptor, Dr Collier."

The Doctor shot back at him a glance of the most severe displeasure.

"Would it not drive a man mad to be so taken up!" says he. "Sir, I would have you know that a general remark may be devoid of a particular application. I observed that Miss Streatfield has a pulchritude in all she does, and make no exception of her Greek, which is as much as becomes a lady and no more. Subtracting her Greek, she's as ignorant as a butterfly. She's a sweet creature and I love her much."

"And will you say as little for my Latin?" cries Mrs Thrale.

"Madam, I never compare two ladies when either is present," says he, bowing with a bearish gallantry. "Let each fair planet revolve in her own orbit and thus avoid risk of collision."

She smiled silently, with her eyes on the ground.

"No human creature may be assumed perfect, even where the visibilities flatter our expectations of the mind within," continued the Doctor. "And I would by no means become a sighing Strephon even for a lady so alluring as Miss Sophy; but yet it is certainly a lady with whom a man should wish to display his powers and to stand well."

Here, unfortunately, Mr Boswell, willing to give the discourse a humorous turn, intervened. "Why, Sir," says he, "the image of the great Cham of literature, the learned Dr Johnson, as a sighing Strephon, crook in hand and garlanded head, is one that provokes risibility and therefore — "

"Sir," says the Doctor, interrupting thunderously, "why am not I as well as another to be amenable to the tender passion if I choose? Inability in this connection argues limitations in which I refuse to be bounded. Because I have encouraged your company,

Sir, seasonably and unseasonably, I am not here for the purpose of being, before the assembled company, exposed to depreciation and insult!''

Heavens, what a blaze was here! I looked to see Mr Boswell sink through the Turkey carpet, and for what? He simpered and appeared abashed, but fortunately Mrs Thrale interposed with an apt quotation.

'' 'And like another Helen, fired another Troy.' Pray, gentlemen, let us not have Hector and Ajax at Streatham! Let an inflammation of the heart, not of the tongue, be the only ruin wrought by the fair mischief. Fortunate indeed are those who bask in her smiles and bathe in her tears. Nobody cries so pretty as the S.S. or smiles so sweet. And here she comes.

She came, and all faces smoothed themselves and concord appeared to reign.

Appeared, no more.

Mercy, what mischief may be done by a coquette, even if pious! My cousin lost her premature child and, it being a boy, Mr Thrale's disappointment took the turn of anger with her. Inoculated with the love of history by my lamented dear, I could but think of Henry the Eighth in the like case, when his flirtation with Jane Seymour destroyed his hopes of offspring with Anne Boleyn.

"You shall have no more boys by me!" he told the lady for a cordial.

My cousin made little outward complaint, but I knew her poor heart was sore. She spoke frequently of Miss Streatfield, and usually with a kind of mascu-

line generosity and tolerance wholly out of my reach.
I recall one day, as she sat — still weak and unable
for exertion — in the window looking out on the lime-
tree walk where the S.S. paced with Mr Thrale, how
I tried to divert her mind, and her reply.

"Anna, my dear, 't is useless. I can't tear myself
from the spectacle any more than the dram-drinker
from his dram that he knows is killing him. I don't
blame my master neither. Mr Thrale's preference of
her to me I well understand. She has ten times my
beauty, is not damaged in face or person by child-
bearing, and if she has neither wit nor knowledge of
life behind her Greek verbs — why, he likes her the
better for that and for her chastity that keeps him
ever in pursuit. Don't I know the S.S. is chaste!
She is and will be, for she is strict in her principles and
knows beside that as honesty is the best policy, so
chastity is a stock rules high in the marriage-market
where she is a seller. No, I can trust Mr Thrale in a
room with her. 'T is only his heart, his interest, his
compassion for his wife, she steals — and upon my
honour, I don't know that I ever possessed any of
'em, so where's the robbery when all's said? I could
like to see the cabinet where she keeps her spoils
docketed, — Dr Burney's quicksilver urbanities and
tender compliments, my master's sensual gallantries
tempered with sentiment, the Bishop's with the veneer of paternal interest in a charming soul, Wedderburn's, — oh, 't is a virtuosa's collection, but strange
— not a real heart among them. She 'll never marry."

"Not Dr Vyse?" I asked, thinking the S.S.'s
preference pretty certain.

"Not he! Men don't love her. They court her as boys the pastry with a window between. Her virginity of manner is more than half the attraction and each man knows — though he don't know he knows it — that half her attraction would disappear with marriage. Sophy is not made for a wife. She is the eternal siren. Once caught, the fish's tail is apparent. No, leave her singing on her rocks, just beyond reach."

Upon my word, I believe my cousin in the right. That lady promised heavens she could never realize. Is not this the true art of the coquette?

When Mr Thrale expired, awful as was the shock, I own a feeling of relief was topmost in my mind. The cynic might derive entertainment from some of the circumstances. The obituary notices were obsequious and certainly not one alluded to the fact that his death was brought on by voracity at the table. Yet Dr Johnson, himself a sinner in this category, warned him thus on the Monday before his decease: "Sir, after the denunciation of your physicians this morning, such eating is suicide."

However, let that pass. My cousin broke down for a time, for 't was not only his death, but was complicated with business in no ordinary degree; but she collected herself with the fortitude of a man rather than a female. 'T was this unusual quality in her nature, I have thought, that made her generally unbeloved by men, who prefer their own opposite and the position of commanding and soothing rather than that of the equality she aspired to and could never attain with them. They would not have it. Yet in kinder hands — but I anticipate.

I was with her when Miss Streatfield sent her name
in for condolence. She was seated at a table covered
with papers relating to the brewery and her own property, now returned into her control, Miss Thrale by
her, watching with a cold ambiguous eye. I never
liked that young lady.

"I'll see Sophy," says my cousin, pushing the
papers aside and sitting upright.

She looked extraordinary small and pale in her
weeds and weepers, her eyes glittering dangerously
bright.

"I think, Madam, if I was you I would decline that
horrid woman's visit," cries Miss Thrale, her tongue
now released from its politic silence. "'T is surely
not necessary she should intrude, now my father
is no more."

"Why so, Queeney? Your father's friend? No, I
will certainly see her."

"Then, Madam, I beg your permission to retire.
I am not equal to receiving strangers in the house
of grief!"

"Strangers!" says Mrs Thrale, with her odd smile.
"Nay, 't was mine own familiar friend — Direct her
to be shown in, Anna, and you can remain, if Queeney
chooses to go."

Indeed, Miss Thrale was already out of the room.
I partly sympathized with her here. Miss Streatfield
being introduced, I curtseyed and took my seat by
the window, in the shade of the curtains and as remote
as I could from their talk. She entered, most elegantly
attired in mourning, holding a handkerchief to her
eyes and the other hand extended to Mrs Thrale.

She rather swam than walked, so fluent were her movements, and in a moment was kneeling by my cousin's side, her head bowed over her knee.

"O dearest Madam!" she uttered, in a voice low and broken, and could say no more.

"You are weeping, Sophy," says Hester, disengaging her hand, and laying it lightly on the S.S.'s shoulder. "You are in grief?"

As if in amazement, in wounded reproach at the question, Miss S—— looked up, the tears flowing down her fair cheeks so charming that she appeared a weeping Magdalen by Guido, though naturally I impute nothing of the saint's characteristics in *any* direction by this remark.

"How could I be otherwise, my dearest Madam?" she answered with the softest sweetness. "When I see my kind friend departed, and all joy extinguished for his widow, what can express my sorrowing sympathy?"

The kneeling lady was motioned to a chair.

"My dear Sophy," says she, "let us be sincere. I am but thirty-nine years of age, and still hope for some days not entirely wretched. But your tears — are they for yourself, or for me, or meaningless as I have often seen them? In a word, do you feel anything? And if so, what?"

It must be allowed this was an extraordinary address in the circumstances and from a new-made widow. Miss S——regarded her as if half afraid her senses wavered under the blow. She hesitated, then replied gently: —

"Dearest Madam, when the kindness I have received from yourself and my dear departed Mr Thrale is remembered, what can I do but weep? My heart is not marble."

"That's where we differ, Sophy. I have long thought your heart marble. It will not, however, be a funeral urn for Mr Thrale. You have other uses for it. I believe, of the pair of us, I lament him more than you, strange as it may appear."

She paused a moment and then resumed, Miss S—— looking in her face as if confounded: "Tell me, Sophy, what was your object in winning his regard? You were admitted to this house as a friend, but were not long here before you espied, like others, that my lot was none of the easiest. You found your pleasure in making it harder."

Miss S—— faintly motioned toward me as indicating a listener. It was brushed aside.

"No — no, you can speak. My cousin knows the facts. While you were caressing me you were superseding me. Was it a necessity to you? Did you love Mr Thrale with such passion? He certainly desired you."

She drew herself back, genuinely shocked. "I? Love a married man — the property of another? No — a thousand times no, Madam! A tenderly reciprocal friendship — "

"Then you were not his mistress, Sophy? Yet you had many opportunities."

"May God forgive you, Madam! You were the pupil of Dr. Collier as well as myself. You know the principles instilled into me. I had sooner died at his feet than that such a thought should ever cross my mind."

I believed her. Her expression was attestation. My cousin resumed, looking strangely upon her: "I believe you. I may say I know it is true. Then let me tell you this: I had trusted you more — yes, honored you more, if, swept away by passion, you had sinned — flung yourself into the deeps of it, *drowned*, rather than coquetted about the shore, only dipping your feet that you might show off their beauty while you stayed safe on dry land. No, you never loved Mr Thrale. Don't I know it! Your object was coquetry, and to show Vyse, Crutchley, and the like, the prize others valued if they did not. But you made him desire you — his only notion of love."

Again she paused. Miss S—— stared at her as if fascinated, and was dead silent. I could almost see the words froze on her lips. Mrs Thrale resumed with an energy almost amounting to wildness.

"Shall I forget the Saturday before Mr Thrale's stroke? This you told me yourself — he pressed your hand to his heart, and said, 'Sophy, we shall not enjoy this long, and to-night I won't be cheated of my comfort.' And the first day he spoke after it, when you came to see him, 'Oh,' says he, 'who would not suffer even all that I have endured, to be pitied by you!' This I heard myself. Friendship? And in Clifford Street?"

"Madam," says Miss Streatfield, roused at last to defence, "if your marriage was not happy, was he to be deprived of a friendship yourself acknowledges harmless? He turned to me in loneliness for a little humble kindness, and — ''

But Mrs Thrale interrupted: — "Loneliness? A man wearies of his wife, he finds company more attractive and leaves her to solitude and sickness, and then bids for compassion from a pious coquette. Mr Thrale of all men — in this house where all the wits of London, men and women, congregated! Was he so deprived of company? No, be honest. You wanted his heart, and to triumph over his wife, and now 't is over and you'll turn elsewhere. My master had his virtues, however. I would remember them now, but you come between — you come between."

She paused, and resumed slowly as if in a dream, Miss S—— staring at her: "But no! There's something in marriage that can't be conquered. Even if it be unhappy, 't is a bond can't be destroyed. It clings — good God! how it clings! The roots are in the very veins of the heart. Memories cruel and tender, hopes, fears, shames, joys, all blend the man and wife in one. You never knew him, Sophy; you never won him. He would come back from feeding on your smiles and hoping for your favours, and with me he was himself, old, tired, violent, wearied, sick, frightened. You never had the real man — only the mask, that fell off when he came to die; and now it's gone for ever. You had run off in company with all the other toys he played with, had you seen him then. You virgins that have had neither man nor child, you know nothing, not even the mischief you did.

How indeed should you know? There, there — go now — I forgive you — and leave the dead man with his wife."

I saw Miss Streatfield comprehended not one iota of my cousin's meaning, which to me was inexpressibly moving. She rose, with a pensive sweetness of expression.

"Dearest Madam, you do me only justice in believing I meant no harm. Then my inadvertence is forgiven. Shall we meet? May Heaven indeed console you!"

"When and how you please, Sophy. The sting's out now. You're forgiven — if to forgive is to forget. The day will come I shall scarce remember your name. Now go. The thing is dead, done, forgotten. Dismiss it."

She also rose. Miss S—— took her hand and kissed it, dropped a graceful curtsey in my direction, and left the room.

I sat stunned, and which of the two ladies amazed me most I can't tell.

But I understood my cousin's heart. When the guest had departed, she stood a few minutes by the window watching for the carriage, then turned to me. "She'll never marry, Anna. Certainly not Vyse, who understands her well. Did you ever hear the old verses — they might have been written for Sophy —"

She repeated, keeping time with her fingers on the window pane: —

> "I do confess thou'rt smooth and fair,
> And I might have gone nigh to love thee,
> Had I not found the slightest prayer

That lips could speak had power to move thee,
But I can let thee now alone,
As worthy to be loved by none.

"Such fate ere long shall thee betide,
When thou hast handled been a while,
Like sere flowers to be thrown aside,
And I shall sigh, while some will smile,
To see thy love for more than one
Hath brought thee to be loved by none.

"Poor Sophy — an unthrift of her sweets!" she said, sighing. "Well, Anna, I must return to my Brewery papers, and leave romance. There she goes! See, she looks up and waves!"

She waved her own black-bordered handkerchief and returned to the writing-table. "The vanquished victor," she said, and resumed her work.

Later, when the world took upon itself to condemn my cousin's marriage to Mr Piozzi and spit its venom upon her, I was all of her side.

Miss Burney, who had been loaded with her benefits, spoke of her as the victim of passions disgraceful to any woman. Dr Johnson, that had ate her bread for many a toilsome year, forsook her. Baretti did his best to stab her reputation. Her daughters secured themselves in public opinion by slighting their mother on her marriage with a man gentle by birth and nature and in no way dependent on her fortune. You had thought the sky was falling, such was the hullabaloo. And for why? But I, who knew her heart, — difficult indeed to be known, — rejoiced in the marriage that gave her a kindness on which it might repose, and the amends it made her for griefs courageously borne and hidden.

The S.S. never married. In her diary, years after, Miss Burney writes: "We met Mrs Porteus; and who should be with her but the poor pretty S.S. whom so long I had not seen, and who has now lately been finally given up by her long-sought and very injurious lover, Dr. Vyse. She is sadly faded and looked disturbed and unhappy, but still beautiful though no longer blooming, and still affectionate though absent and absorbed. We had a little chat about the Thrales. 'Ah, those,' she cried, 'were happy times!' and her eyes glistened. Poor thing! Hers has been a lamentable story."

THE TWO AND NELSON

HORATIO NELSON
1758–1805

THE Admiral first won favor with the young widow, Frances Nisbet, by romping on all fours with her little boy under the drawing-room table. And — by common opinion — his position as a national hero attracted Emma, Lady Hamilton. As for him, his heart was soft both to childhood and to beauty; but where one woman sought to save him from the consequences of his vanity, the other fanned the flame, and even the wife herself could not fail to see which way the prize would fall.

However, in spite of her delight in personal display, in spite of her immoderate vaunting of power, so distasteful to many observers, Lady Hamilton — friendly biographers say — did come to love Nelson for himself, as Frances Nisbet loved him. And certainly Emma's daring spirit was more suited to the man's needs than that of the woman whose disposition and instincts were all unfitted for public enterprises. Says Lady Hamilton after Nelson's death: "Did I ever keep him at home, did I not share in his glory? Even this last fatal victory — it was I bade him to go forth."

"Too much emphasis on the I," we protest. But Nelson, supreme egotist and unusual possessor of the "gift of insubordination," might cry that these lines from *Cymbeline* were written for his goddess: —

> Mine eyes
> Were not in fault, for she was beautiful;
> Mine ears, that heard her flattery; nor my heart
> That thought her like her seeming; it had been vicious
> To have mistrusted her.

Horatio Nelson

An Engraving from the Portrait by Sir Wm Beechey

V

THE TWO AND NELSON[1]

A violent scene is said to have occurred between the two women.

- SICHEL

A FEW years ago I wandered through a little country churchyard in Devon, far away across the sea. It was an afternoon of golden silence, a very small breeze bringing the scents of clover and buttercups from the meadows about the ancient church, to lay them before the dim altar. So still it was, that life might well be in love with death and envy the dream of those quiet sleepers. And, even as I thought this, I saw a tomb beneath the trees, where the grass grew rank and luxuriant — a tomb old and forgotten, the lettering half filled with the close-coined gold of a little lichen, the shadows of the elm boughs coming and going. And this was the inscription: —

FRANCES, VISCOUNTESS NELSON
DUCHESS OF BRONTE

As I read, the deathless thunder of the guns of Trafalgar broke upon me in those thunderous names, and I beheld ships locked in death grips on the far-off coast of Spain, and a dying man, already more spirit than body, who whispered in agony: —

"Take care of my dear Lady Hamilton." And again: "I leave her as a legacy to my country."

But never a word of the woman who lay at my feet.

[1]With the exception of that purporting to be written by Lady Nelson, the letters quoted in this story are authentic. — THE AUTHOR.

And through the tolling of the great guns in my ears, I thought this: —

"In life this woman was scarcely less silent than in death; and because she would not speak, the world has called her harsh and cold; and as in life her lovely rival flung her from the throne, so it is also in death; and the fair face that wins all hearts from the canvas of Romney shows like a strong sun, in whose rays the wan star of this woman's memory perishes. Her silence is eternal."

The peace of the quiet grave-place was broken. I sat by the grave, dreaming less of great empires and dynasties than of one woman; and the shadows moved and lengthened, and the thoughts sealed within her buried breast thrilled in my own, and I heard — through the muffled thunder of the guns — I heard!

Now this is what I ponder night and day, the reason why I was not only cast off, — for that is a common lot of women, — but why, being cast off, I might not suffer in peace and with the decency of pity, but all tongues must call me harsh and cold, that they may find excuse for a great man and a worthless woman. She put it about that he never loved me and all the ardors of his soul and body were sealed until she came from the hands of many men to his; and at first this so stung my wounds that night after night I sat in the dark, my mind, like a wave that returns to break itself on a rock, resolving to overwhelm her with my wrongs, and again failing from the resolve, because

I must needs hold him up with her to shame, and I would not. And a voice said in my heart: —

"The time will come. Profligate and coarse in grain, she has but her beauty; and when that is gone, the world will see what it cannot now see, for dazzle. I have beheld the wicked flourish like a green bay tree, and I passed by — " And so it was; but, with it all, the world had no pity for me.

But he loved me — I swear it. Why not? Nelson's heart was easy won. He would have left the service and all for Molly Simpson at Quebec. Did not his uncle, Sir William Suckling, tell me he was ever in love, and his father say that he was ever open to the assaults of the tender passion? Then why not for the woman he made his wife? My misfortune was that I supposed marriage would fix his heart. A common mistake, but folly, not crime. But all was objected to me later — even that I was a young widow with a child. He felt it no objection then; but all I did and was must ever be in the wrong now.

I collected that the world entire, led by this woman, accused me that I did not take a wife's part in his glory, nor rejoice in it as I should. I have searched my heart and memory, nor can find this is so. If true, I might, I own, deserve what befell; but the truth is far other. It is this.

My Nelson, for once he was all mine, was fire, whether for the woman he loved, or the country he loved better again; but — was there ever a human nature perfect? I was of that disposition that where I loved I saw the faults more plainly than where they

concerned me not. It is so with many mothers; and
God knows that, though several years his junior, I was
always a mother to him, as a wife must with some
men be to the end. For he who conquered the world
at sea, was at home a very simple person, easy beguiled and accessible to flattery. Though I loved him
none the less for this, I knew it, and 't was needful I
should act answerably.

Flattery. Now here I touch a sore place — and
one I know helped to sever us. She who would hold
Nelson must choose to speak none but soft things to
him. His genius fed, as it were, on honey; it would
only expand its wings in a caressive sunshine. It
will then be said: What is a wife's part if not to
provide this, especially if mated with a Nelson?

The matter is not so plain. I knew he had in him
that spirit and courage to carry him to any point;
but knew also there was in him a love of flattery to
be traded on by the cunning. To myself I must add,
a boastfulness also in word at times, that set him at
a disadvantage with men unworthy so much as to
follow where he led. It is true that I have felt my
face redden when he would unloose himself in speech,
and tell of his great deeds. If I had not a value for
him above all earthly, would this have troubled me?
And his glory needed no words — none. They could
but lessen it. And I would see other men wink aside
and draw him on; and I own that, when I had tried
in vain to turn the talk, I would shed tears over this
in secret. I would not say this but to my heart. I
knew — I knew it was more than half of it eagerness

and the other half simplicity; but I thought it must increase as years came, and be unlovely. I broke it a little to him with delicacy that other captains did not so vaunt.

"Let them do the like deeds," was his answer.

An unpersuadable point. Whenever I touched him upon it, I had anger. Now, should I have encouraged this and fed it, as the woman did later?

It sickens me to remember that I was grateful for her obliging attentions to my husband and my boy when first they were at Naples. Josiah writ warmly of her; and Nelson, that she was a young woman of amiable manners that did honour to the station she was raised to. Then they left Naples, and for five years I heard no more of her than the talk of her influence over the Queen of the Two Sicilies, and her fine looks, and the power she had in that Court, and how she put forward to be noticed. Much of the talk displeasing to a modest woman.

Then came the victory of the Nile, and his sore wound, and his return to Naples; and again I must be grateful that these Hamiltons took him to their house to nurse — so frail and worn with wounds and hard service, and I so far away. Must not such a thing touch a wife's sensibility? But, on reaching Naples, he sent me a copy of the letter she wrote to him upon the victory, and 't was when I first read this my heart was heavy as lead. I saw she had fathomed his weakness, and I could not flatter against a practised hand like hers. She claimed her share also in the victory, making him credit (and I know

not if true or false) that she was the sole means of
forcing the Sicilian sovereigns to water and feed his
fleet. True or no, he believed it and all else she said;
and there was I — only his loving, far-away wife,
no more, and there was she with him, for a constancy,
the foremost figure, swelling with her own importance,
beguiling and flattering him as I think no man was
ever beguiled before.

From that time the tide of rumours flowed into a
torrent. What could I do? I knew every word I
wrote — and indeed I wrote feelingly as a wife should
— must seem cold water beside this bubble of intoxi-
cating champagne. She had all the beguilements of
the kept woman; I, nothing but honesty and love.

And this was how first he wrote of her when he
returned to Naples, and the last letter that carried
me anything of his heart. I never had another that
did. I may well prize that.

I must endeavour to convey to you something of what
passed; but if it were affecting to those only united to me
by the bonds of friendship, what must it be to my dearest
wife, my friend, my everything that is most dear to me in
the world? Sir William and Lady Hamilton came out to
sea . . . They, my most respectable friends, had really
been laid up and seriously ill, first from anxiety and then
joy. It (the victory) was imprudently told to Lady H ——
in a moment, and the effect was like a shot; she fell apparently dead. . . . Alongside came my honoured friends;
the scene in the boat was terribly affecting. Up flew her
Ladyship and exclaiming, 'O God, is it possible!' she
fell into my arms more dead than alive. . . . I hope some
day to have the pleasure of introducing you to Lady
H——. She is one of the best women in the world. She
is an honour to her sex. Lady H——intends writing to you.

I saw her drift in a minute, coupling it with what
was talked of. Modest Englishwomen do not so behave in public. But I saw also that this was the sure
way to her hand on the helm with him. On that letter
I might now endorse, "Here died all my hopes, and I
looked for no resurrection of the dead." It undid
the work of years, to say no more than that. It
showed me that she would hold him by a handle I
scorned to touch — his weakness, not his strength.

Can I express the agonies I suffered from 1798
onward! From his letters, from every word that
reached me, — and many, many did so, — I knew
his whole soul was now possessed by that bad woman.
My son was blamed for speaking his mind when, on
one occasion, her behaviour passed bounds in public,
and because it was the Queen's and the Admiral's
favourite he affronted, they put about the story he
was in liquor — he, that saved Nelson's life at Tener-
iffe, that would have cheerfully laid down his life
for him at any hazard, until he saw his mother insulted and neglected!

I think a son is scarce to be blamed that he takes
his mother's part, even if not so wisely as more years
than he had might have taught him. A boy is not
wise when he is angry, and he was little more than
a boy.

So, as the news came pouring in (and for all I
heard I knew fifty times more was kept back by
Nelson's friends and mine), the long and the short
was that I resolved I would know what her true self
might be behind the masking beauty; and to that
end I set myself to find out what was known of her

life — work very little fit for a virtuous woman, but
needful. My God, what a blackness met me! There
was no vile experience unknown to her. From hand
to hand she had gone, until the nephew Greville
passed her to the uncle Hamilton, as a pawn for the
payment of his debts; and because the dotard wedded
her, she was now to be received like an honest woman
and put where, by the aid of the profligate Queen of
the Two Sicilies, she could flaunt herself in a court
and draw more men into her net. A man of the world
might laugh and leave her, but my Nelson was never
that — he believed like a boy; where he trusted, he
trusted entirely. She would play on him as she did
on her harp. Indeed, I was horribly afraid, and it
made me the sterner, as they temper hot steel with
water to make it hard.

I visited the studio of Mr. Romney, and saw her
face on many a canvas, the man ranting of her beauty
and inspiration, and already unsound in brain, as
any calm observer might take notice. Except from
him I never heard a good word of her; and once, in
company with Mr. Charles Greville, though he spoke
not with me, I heard her name mentioned and saw
the summing-up smile he gave to her; and had I
known no more than that, it had been sufficient and
too much. Finally, when I had gained all I needed,
with testimony that fixed it for true, I writ thus to
Nelson: —

You commend constantly to my gratitude Lady Hamilton and her husband, and I am in a difficulty, because
what service is there done to you that I must not acknowledge with gratitude? But, as you know of old, I am not

quick to make friends, though, I hope, faithful when made.
I have made enquiry what like is this woman that I must
take to my heart, and this is what I learn.

I then plainly set forth her history; for what less
was my duty, seeing what I knew, and being informed
that Lord St. Vincent and many more were passing
jests on his infatuation, though of this I did not speak
as yet. I put the truth, however, before him, and
ended thus: —

Such a woman you would have forbid me in the old
days to take by the hand. Who so strong as yourself
condemned the women who make light of light behaviour
in their acquaintance? My own Nelson, I entreat you
that you would not lay such a command upon me. It
is more than flesh and blood can bear, and you yourself
would regret it later. You was never wont to encourage
such persons about our house and table. I hear great
talk and rumours I won't inflict, but believe me I don't
write without warrant.

And so concluded with fond talk of home and
meeting, and words of his good old father, that
trembled only less than me at what reached him of
the doings at Naples. More especially the high play.
Great God, what I suffered!

I had the misfortune to visit a friend of my Lady
Minto's, and thus to hear what her Ladyship writ in
a letter from Palermo, where the Royals and the
Hamiltons were now fled from the Revolution in
Naples, with Nelson. She writ that Nelson and the
Hamiltons lived together in a house he paid for —
the money running like water, and the gaming like
a gaming-house, and my poor Admiral sitting half

asleep, with heaps of gold before him, and that harpy dipping her hands in the gold without counting, and playing to the tune of five hundred pounds a night, she having the Neapolitan rage for play.

And this I might not have credited, indeed scarcely could, but that the dear Troubridge, his faithful friend, writ a letter to him remonstrating (this I had, with the very words, from a relative of Troubridge's), and my heart was cold as death as I heard.

Pardon me, my Lord; it is my sincere esteem for you that makes me mention it. I know you can have no pleasure in sitting up all night at cards; why then sacrifice your health, your comfort, purse, ease, everything? . . . Your Lordship is a stranger to half that happens or the talk it occasions. I beseech your Lordship to leave off. I wish my pen could tell you my feelings. I am sure you would oblige me. Lady Hamilton's character will suffer. Nothing can prevent people talking.

Lady H——'s character! That could not suffer. It was too sunk already. But Nelson's! I suppose there is not one that reads but would call Troubridge a faithful friend for his pains; but if the miserable wife made any objection, or ventured on warning, — she to whom it was her all, and her utter ruin involved, — then she was cold and harsh to a promising passion that she should take easy and no harm meant! O pitiless world to me and mine!

I saw where I should be, and writ instantly to my husband that I desired of all things to come out and join him — seeing we had been too long apart. Indeed, for many days I had neither eat nor slept for terror, while half the world envied my Lady Nelson,

wife of the greatest man alive. And he was that —
and I knew it, and I a poor trembling creature that
saw her all slipping from her.

He answered me thus — and I don't doubt she
leaned over his shoulder to bring the matter to bear
according to her liking: —

You would by February have seen how unpleasant it
would have been, had you followed any advice which carried you from England to a wandering sailor. I could, if
you had come, *only* have struck my flag and carried you
back again; for it would have been impossible to keep up
an establishment either at Naples or Palermo.

So I was successless and dare say no more on
that head, but asked when I might hope to see him.
He writ: —

If I have the happiness to see their Sicilian Majesties
safe on the throne again, it is probable I shall still be home
in the summer. Good Sir William, Lady H——, and myself are the mainsprings of the machine which manages
what is going on in this country. We are all bound for
England when we can quit our posts with propriety.

Good Heavens! — what had he to do with their
Sicilian Majesties and their affairs? 'T was a question
many asked besides myself. And "we"! I was too
sick at heart with dreadful alarms to say more, but
could only think that opinion at home might reach
and move him; for I knew through naval friends to us
both that there was anger at the Admiralty that
Nelson should so tie himself to a foreign king, more
buffoon than king, and a queen who deserved rather a
prison than a throne. But what opinion can help a
forsaken wife?

'T was about now his father came to me, very sunk in spirits, and to say he understood that publick and private affairs fretted his son, and his letters revealed his disturbance. I was shook to the heart by the lowness he could not conceal.

"Fanny, my dear," he said, "I do not like what I hear. You are aware that Horatio's heart is susceptible, and ever will be, to the tender passion. It will become you then to receive him with a cordiality that shall evidence his wife's heart is unalterably his own; and I am much mistook if that will not bind and seal his affections where only they should be fixed."

I promised with all love and duty, and he thus continued: —

"Horatio is still a comparatively young man and you five years younger, and long life and honours lie before you both if you behave at this juncture with conciliatory wisdom. If you consider, my daughter, that you have a right to complain in some points, yet do not exercise it. View your own knowledge of your husband and you will admit me in the right."

I knew it. Indeed, Nelson could be cruel to those that opposed him. Go with him, and all was sunshine. Go against him, and fierce anger broke out; easy bent, but impossible to break. I resolved to act conformably, bridling and hiding my terrors.

I sent to the Admiralty, to learn at what date and where I should expect him, and prepared to meet him and make a last struggle for him as well as myself, knowing well how deep his reputation was now involved with the loose-behaved wife and the doting husband.

Then came the news that, after all my agonies, all the long waiting, he was decided to make a tour across Europe by Vienna, dragged in their train. I had thought that even for decency he would take the straightest way. But no. And then came word that he enjoined me not to meet him, but to wait his return in London. Could he not be cruel — if to none other, to his wife? Let the world own there may be spots in the sun.

And still I thought, "When I see him — when we are alone!" Hope dies hard, it would seem. Mine should have been dead and buried by then.

The time came. I saw him. We were alone; and I, who had been used to the volcanic warmth of his affection, was now to know my day done. All his talk was of Lady H——.

She was the dearest, most beautiful of women, the most devoted of friends! A queen had sanctified her position abroad; all London would repeat the homage of Naples. Surely I could never have the foolish, ingrateful heart to repel one to whom he owed his life and also the glory of the Nile, for 't was she had procured the ships to be fed and watered, and thus made the battle possible! I would see how the good Queen Charlotte would honour and reward such merits! The country also.

His thin face, all worn with the sea, was flushed and strained as he poured out his story. It was a bitter taste in my mouth then that I had wrote to

Yarmouth a polite billet, saying I hoped at some future date to see them at Round Wood. I knew not at that time how utterly I was supplanted. He should not have permitted me to do this.

Good God, what was I to do? I would have fled from the room if possible; but his father's words rang in my ears, and I resolved to still constrain myself to silence. I believe I am blamed that I could not receive this with enthusiasm, and partake in the acclamation of a woman who had robbed me of my all and made him a jest for the vulgar. I think the wisdom of Solomon had scarcely carried me through.

My nature is a silent one, to my misfortune, and I was silent. At last, I said with gravity that it would not become me wholly to neglect his recommendation of Lady H——, and I would therefore meet her and form my own judgment of whether there was like to be mutual politeness betwixt her and me; and meanwhile, I begged not to be hurried, but to wait on events.

He shut his lips and his heart, and made his disappointment very manifest, but presently said the Hamiltons would wait on me next day. Was not this to hurry me? But still I said nothing. I only signified I would await them; and then, having no strength for more, I fell a-trembling with such a seizure of pain about the heart as I was forced to call my maid and go to my bed, and there trembled all night, distracted to think what was best to be done.

When I heard their step on the stair next day I thought I must have dropt — what wonder she could spread to all her party that I was stiff and ill at ease in manners? I own it. The very skin of my face tingled. Is there anything so disconcerting to a wife as to be in company, and know there is a secret understanding betwixt her husband and another? What shall she do?

She was a fine woman, I admit, but inelegant in her address, and full-blown as if with too generous feeding and drinking, which was indeed the case; her colour high but clear, her eyes blue, and auburn hair. But going off. Two years younger than me, but I knew I wore better. Her manners overblown like her figure. Her hands and feet large and coarse.

She stood a breath at the door, in her handsome pelisse, and then ran forward, both hands extended, very red in the face. Frightened, yet bold.

"Do I at last have the felicity to see my dear Lady Nelson — the lady of our friend of friends! We were Three joined in One, but henceforth it will be Four. Four hearts united to perfection."

I drew back and curtseyed. I could not do more — I felt it disgustingly repulsive. I believe I smiled, however. I saw Nelson's angry eye, but Sir W—— H—— came forward.

I shall never comprehend — 't is impossible I should — how a man of breeding could endure the woman. She said "'as" when she meant "has," and her voice corresponded to the spelling of the letters she favoured me with from Naples. A Wapping wench's spelling.

I beheld Sir William — a clean-faced old man of

aristocratic features, and marvelled. Yet of a bad
stock on the mother's side, she being the notorious
Lady Archibald Hamilton, mistress to Frederick,
Prince of Wales in George II's time. How shall a
woman ever comprehend? 'T is to be understood men
would have such a woman serve them a dram at the
tavern, and chuck her under the chin for her good
looks. But marriage — or love! Yet I was in presence
of both. Her proper sphere was in my kitchen; but
here she sat, and Nelson had no eyes but for her,
and Sir William the air of expecting my compliments
on such beauty and accomplishments. A virtuous
woman can't understand such things in men; but the
Moll Flanders that was Lady H——, she knows and
plays on them like a musician on the forte-piano!

It is very true I showed to little advantage, and so
made my own case worse. 'T is the wife's fate in such
cases. I must be conscious he compared the mistress
to the wife without pity, yet think he should have
made allowance for the agitating meeting that all but
overcame me. Still, I designed to do all in my power,
and sat to listen while, in her loud voice, she flattered
my husband to his face and mine in such a manner as
I could have wept for rage and shame. "Great Jove,"
she called him, explaining obligingly that his title of
"Bronte" signified thunder in Latin — Sir W——
mildly correcting her to Greek. She told of the fêtes
celebrating his victories at Naples: —

"And 't was I myself in effigy crowned our hero's
waxen effigy with laurels, my dearest Lady Nelson,
in the presence of their Majesties and all the people.

The only miss to our immortal triumph was your Ladyship's absence. 'T was not, for it could not be, worthy of the greatest of men, for never was such a saviour in the world. Her Majesty, Maria Carolina, said to me with her own royal lips, 'What can we offer, Emma, that's not dust beneath his feet? Alexander, Cæsar — what are they beside him? And I vow I don't think the upstart Corsican worth a snap of my fingers when I think of the immortal Nelson!' Indeed, your Ladyship, her swollen heart would scarce admit her to speak. She 'as a noble sensibility, though it don't surpass my own and Sir William's."

'T was a dose that had been too strong for my husband a few years since. Now he sat, all ears and eyes, feasting on every word she spoke. I knew not which way to look. Surely, I thought, Sir William must check her. He sat leaning his chin on his cane, and not a word but this: —

"Indeed, Lady Hamilton does not overrate the occasion, Madam. It was beyond expression splendid, though far below our invaluable friend's deserts. I can show your Ladyship an elegant print of Lady Hamilton as Victory. The classical robe was judged to become her. It is the general opinion that she appears to greatest advantage in the dress of Greece or Rome. I have called her my Modern Cameo, and the name is not misjudged, as you 'll allow when you behold her famous Attitudes."

"The robe was white and I held a wreath of laurels in my hand," she interrupted. "The laurels was decorated with dymonds, with which His Majesty later crowned our glorious hero. He also placed laurel wreaths on Sir William's head and mine, and we all wore them during the entertainment. Your Ladyship can't conceive anything more splendid and heart-raising. Was you to have been there, you must have died of joy."

"Then it is possibly fortunate I was not present" — the words came before I could restrain them; but indeed I was near dying of shame to see her so puff the incense in his face and he accept it. Can even such glory as his — and there is none, none like it! — be made to appear foolish? I could picture Sir William and the woman flaunting in their laurels, but not him — not my husband. Indeed, I thought us all mad together, so were things reversed from the right. She it was that owned and showed him off to his wife, and me that was but a listener on her sufferance. And to all this Sir W—— and Nelson subscribed. I know not which or what bewildered me most. 'T was like seeing things upside down in a looking-glass, enough to make a woman giddy. I felt I could not bear it longer, and should not be present, and half rose.

Sir W——, mistaking me, rose also, politely.

"Pray do not fatigue yourself to rise, your Ladyship. I will bring the print to you."

And did, laying it in my hand, while she stared, all uneasy smiles. 'T was as he said — a wax effigy of Nelson on a plinth, and she, in a Grecian habit, extending a wreath over his head. The artist had

softened the outlines and gracefulised the big hands
and feet I noted ere she was five minutes in the room,
so that I admit it beautiful. But, oh, when I saw
the drawn cheeks, the worn face — the tears blinded
me that they should so strip him of dignity. A woman
of bad life to crown him — she the cast-off of many
men! And he what he is!

What I experienced then was not selfish; my own
soul knows it, if no other. 'T was the passionate desire
to rid him of these sponging parasites, even were I
never again to see him — that he might stand alone,
great and simple as he truly was. But I constrained
my lips.

"Indeed, a graceful picture, and the robe becomes
her Ladyship — "

"Graceful! Becomes!" cried Nelson. "These are
cold expressions, and worthy only of woman's envy.
It's divinely beautiful, and to be crowned by that
hand greater honour than the King's crowning. I
should have supposed," he added with bitterness,
"that my wife would be grateful for the distinction.
But I was mistook, it seems."

Indeed I almost despaired. How could anyone
compete against her floods of honey? She had spoiled
his palate for simple fare. She spoke apart with him
while Sir W—— addressed me; and his brow then
cleared — at her bidding, not for me.

"I must not be hasty, Fanny," he said. "It's not
every woman has Lady Hamilton's political genius,
nor comprehends what my victory of the Nile has
accomplished for the world. I am aware I am

undervalued in my own country and 't is not singular
a woman should share this ignorance — "

I protested, with beating pulses, but he went on: —

"The saviour of Europe is better treated anywhere
than in his native land. I could wish never to have
set foot — "

She leaned towards him.

"Indeed, you say true, Nelson. Your statue in
pure gold should be in every part of London, had I
my way, and the Admiralty compelled to salute it,
and the niggardly politicians to lick its feet. Never
was so great a soul as yours; and if they don't know it,
we'll despise them together — we three."

By this time the room was going round with me,
and I did half believe I must sink where I sat, so
much was I made an intruder. I knew not where to
look, while she overwhelmed me with loud professions
of regard and service. Luckily, the carriage was
shortly spoke for, and they went, and he with them.

So of all our meetings — need I record them to
myself? At dinner, it was she who helped him, saying
she must do it, "until your Ladyship shall learn his
likings"; and in all things, little and great, I was
supplanted. Will it be believed that he spent his
Christmas with them at Mr. Beckford's palace of
Fonthill Abbey, and I left to my melancholy
thoughts? And so in everything. When the world
blames me as harsh and cold — I ask, was it in my
power to seem free and content, and cannot tell.
Let the world judge honestly, as it has not yet done
of the sad case of an openly forsaken wife.

I had also to endure that my husband's family, his brother, his sisters, betwixt whom and myself there had been kindness, went over to her party in a body, and paid their court in the face of day. They knew how to keep well with the risen sun, and that they might lack their share of his bounties if this was omitted. Only his old father showed me kindness. She and the others nicknamed me and mocked my sorrow. He remained kind.

The night my eyes were finally opened, and that ended all, was at the theatre. My husband had commanded me to be present in publick with the Hamiltons, and I sat, enduring the stares of the fine company. There happened an allusion in the play to a secret birth; and as it was spoke, I saw her redden up and go dead white. Nelson leaped up, and Sir W——, for she swayed aside, and her head fell on the arm of Sir W——'s chair, and she fainted. The two helped her out of the box, and I sat dead still. He did not return, nor did I expect it. I knew now. I understood. After a decent interval I left the play and went home.

I won't recall my feelings that night, tossed on a sea of despair. What profit to dwell on my sorrow and shame that I had given him no child? That was the hidden sore that had bit into my soul before she came. There are some men — I think not many — that desire a child with as strong a longing as any lonesome woman, and he was so. I would see his eye soften when it fell on the boys of twelve aboard his ship, so proud and strutting with their dirks and gold buttons; and I knew too well why. Never a harsh word to me of it. And he was kind to my boy. He was never harsh until she stole him; but it came out in a thousand ways I could but feel in the inmost veins of my heart. It possessed his spirit and mine, and once I thought to speak of an adoptive child, and dared not raise the sleeping grief.

And now this was upon me! It would make bonds unbreakable betwixt them. I knew it imaginable 't was not his, for with such a woman what cheat might not be possible; but the thunder of God would be powerless to oppose her if she so told him. One who knew her well said later: "Nelson was infatuated. She could make him believe anything."

No. I pass over that night.

Next day, I sitting alone, the door opened, and she came in unannounced, as she had done of late. Unbearable, but I had borne it as best I could with much else unbearable.

I rose instantly. Her colour was high and fixed. She had the appearance of having slept ill, which I could credit. Now I saw her with open eyes, I marvelled I had been so blind.

"Your Ladyship gives me no invitation to sit," she said boldly. "If my visit is inconvenient, I'll do myself the favour later. I come to enquire of your health after the alarm I gave you last night."

"Your visit," I said, cold as death, "is and will be unwelcome. It is what your own conscience should forbid you to inflict upon me."

We looked at one another a minute. Finally she spoke as a woman of her class must do.

"If your Ladyship means any slur on me that have been the companion of your betters, speak it out," she cried. "I don't know what you hint, but I don't fear to face it, whatever it is. The bosom friend of a Queen, and an Ambassadress myself, I need n't shun to look any woman in the face, even if she does wear titles she never did a hand's turn to earn."

As she spoke, I hardened and took courage. I believe I now dreaded only that Nelson, that Hamilton, should come in before I could speak once for all. It was the locked-up things that ached in me, and I yearned for delivery like a woman in travail.

And first I turned the key in the lock and pocketed it, and she looked at me, furious and trapped. Then I stood with the table betwixt us.

"Lady Hamilton, before ever my husband returned to England, I knew your character. Did you credit that, because the profligate Queen and Court at Naples did honour to a woman of their own kind, it would be the same in England, where decencies are still respected? You are much mistook."

She choked with rage, interrupting: —

"What — my Queen! The daughter of emperors! And you dare — a miserable doctor's widow that Nelson stooped to — to belittle Her Majesty and her condescension to me. If I was good enough for her, I'm good enough and too good for you."

"Madam, apart from my own cruel wrongs, one who is not good enough for my virtuous Queen Charlotte is not worthy of my own reception. I decline your acquaintance. She whom my Queen refuses is no fit company for the matronage of England. She sets an example in all things to be followed."

For it was now known that Sir W—— was forced to go to Court alone, the Queen entirely refusing to receive the woman. Indeed, she was livid with passion, to hear this on my lips.

"You had best heed what you say," she cried, losing all restraint. "I have it in my power to make Nelson kick you from the house, without a penny but your hoardings to keep you. And I promise you I will, if you insult a woman that saved the fleet for the Nile, and helped your glorious husband to his glory, as he owns daily. You miserable upstart — that dares — "

"Madam, it does not need your admission that, apart from the Service, you rule my husband. That unhappily is known. But you do not rule me."

"I'll make you crawl to my feet for pardon. I'll have you stript of all but the name he gave you, and with good luck I'll strip you of that, too. You don't know — a dull fool like you — what is the due of one that acts on a great stage with queens and kings and great men. There's nothing between him and me that all the world may n't know, and I glory in. You could not hold him, for you never knew what he was. Don't blame me if you've lost his heart and know its worth too late."

I grew colder as she hotter. 'T is the effect rage has on me always — it had served me better with him could I have wept and pled.

"I know your secret. I am well aware you'll turn

it into a weapon for cutting the last bond betwixt my husband and me."

"What secret?"

"One I disgrace not myself to say. Let me be plain with you. I know not only this, but a former secret of the like sort that I had from a cousin of Captain Willet-Payne's."

She shrieked at the name. "It's a lie — a lie!"

I closed the window quietly, that her violence be not heard in the street. She made at me like a wild-cat — then drew back, glaring, her breath coming and going quick. So we stood what seemed like minutes, and then she fell back into the sopha.

"Go on. I'd best know what you mean. I won't part with him — if that's your price. I'm an innocent woman, but there's few of us can stand mud-throwing at us without some sticking. What do you want?"

"Only that I may never see you again. And one thing more."

"I'm sure I have no hankering to see you again; but if you want to see Nelson you'll have to take me along with him, for he'll have no scandal and won't break a friendship as does us both honour. But I don't desire you should carry your tales to him, though he won't so much as hear them if I give the word."

I said nothing awhile, and she sat there, big, sullen, handsome, with dangerous eyes, but did not frighten me any more. Oh what a fate was mine! A man may face the guns and all applaud his courage; but who values a woman fighting against all odds, desolate, no refuge, her own hearth shut against her? I tried to gather a final strength to end it all and face Nelson's wrath after.

I sat, as I think it must have been, a few minutes, for I had need of silence to recollect myself, for I had still a thing to say and I conceived there could be no woman so vile but she must hear. She now was as if revolving some hidden thing in her mind — as turning it over and over. And I feared her once more, — I could not say why, — she sat so brooding, and a hid thing in her eyes. Presently she spoke again.

"For my part, I don't see why all this fighting and abusing is needful. There's better ways by far. His Lordship praised you as a wise woman when first I met with him. 'A very valuable woman,' was his words. Why not be friends? And if not friends, see we have a mutual interest. The way you're going, you'll ruin yourself and drag him in. Why not have a little sense? I'm apt to blow out in a temper, but I cool as quick, and a thought comes in my mind that we're better friends than enemies. I'll not be wanting to my part if you won't neither.

"You're right about my secret, and I can tell you as much as that I'll guard it safe from the world. No fear of that. I now desire your opinion whether you won't do wiser to meet what can't now be helped and turn it to your advantage. If you was to act the part of a friend and acknowledge the child for your own, you would give him a child he loves with passion already, and take his undying love and gratitude,

and my faithful service to my life's end. There's no
heir to his glorious honours, and 't would give him his
heart's desire. Consider of it. Here's your way
straight back to your husband's heart, and not a soul
the wiser."

I sat still, listening. Her hands spread out, she
continued, as eager as if the first part of our interview
had not been.

"Here is us two women that have cause to think
of him before ourselves; for look at it as you will, he's
the world's hero. This notion of mine will give him
comfort and quiet, and he'll never think of you but
to bless you when he sees his own flesh and blood
grow up under his own roof. And if you'll come so far
to meet me, I'll swear that for the future I'll be no
more to him but an honest friend. You won't grudge
that much? And indeed this was a thing entirely
unforeseen, and — "

She went on, but now I did not hear. Was it a
temptation? Could I endure such a situation, if it
gave me back his love and confidence? If I be thought
even baser than she, I own for the moment it tempted
me. My soul had ached for a child, but fate denied it
and flung him into another's arms. Should I hate it
for her sake, or love it for his? She said true. I knew
he would worship that child — and a child is sweet
even if found in the gutter. She saw and spoke with
frantic eagerness, while the two passions fought in me
of love and hatred. She continued, her face working
convulsively.

"Forget our hatred, and give him the child he'll

bless you for with all his heart. If you did this —
't is but to affect a friendship (that we may feel one
day if this should be), and you and I go off later to
Italy or elsewhere, and the thing is done. Oh, if a
son, he'll worship you, or a girl cling close about his
heart; and then, with his soul at rest and seeing the
babe in your bosom, who's to say he won't forget me
except as a friend, and I'll help him to it. And Nelson
yours once more and a babe in the house, my dear
Ladyship, I'll give you leave to forget the unhappy
mother while you go on your way attended by the
respect of all. Don't value me in the matter, but
think of his Lordship and yourself. Surely Sarah
and Rebecca did the like, and took the children of
their husbands for their own. Consider of it, I
beseech you."

Much more she said. I was like a woman drugged.
Through her talk I could see my husband — I could
hear him: "Fanny, my angel of forgiveness, my
child's more than mother!" I could see a hearth,
with a man, a woman, and his child beside it in
great contentment.

Then sudden, like the sun bursting from a cloud,
the truth. He knew nothing of it. This was a trap —
another of her Attitudes — a plot to save herself and
lower me to a baseness that, if I accepted, neither he
nor any decent person could look upon me more.
Why, what should I be? — and if he choose such an
offering, what would he be? She had dragged him
down in all she could touch, though the spirit in him
escaped her and will for ever; but this, if done, would

complete her triumph, and never again could he hold
up his head with the rest. And if he refused, — and
he would, — I had flung myself in the mud in vain,
and then indeed he might say, "Let me be rid of this
plotting woman." No, better loneliness and misery
than crime. The secret ways of vice were familiar to
her, but I had never trod in them, nor would. Better
he should hate and honour me, than love me with a
shameful secret for bond betwixt us.

"Madam," I said, "I refuse your offer. But not
with the rage and scorn I felt awhile ago. It would be
impossible to explain to you why this is so, and how
you have opened my eyes to another view than my
own wretchedness; but so it is. Your proposal, however leads me up to the last words I shall ever
utter to you."

"Your Ladyship needs but time to consider," she
exclaimed, evidently believing she had made an
impression that might be turned to account later.

But I continued calmly: — "I comprehend your
motives, and refuse. But to the mother of Nelson's
child, I say one word. His name is, as you justly say,
very glorious. You proclaim aloud that you value
his glory — "

"As you with your blood of ice can't never know.
He and I are fire, and you freeze him at every turn."

"If this intrigue continues, you will cling to him in
life and death — "

"In life and death," she repeated proudly.

— "as a deadly shame and disgrace. When men
speak of his glory, they must remember it clouded.

A man can't cut his private life from his publick, and he least of all who is so open to slights and griefs. Oh, set him free — have pity on him! Set him free — not to come back to me: I see that's done for ever, but to a loneliness that's honourable, and where he can devote his undistracted heart to a love that's more to him than you, or any woman. You know what it is. If you do indeed love him, spare him."

It had all turned so different from what I meant at the outset. I pleading to her, and after a shocking insult! Oh, what are we but the thistledown blown in the wind and dropt, we know not where — but in strange, strange places. She did not, however, understand me — not at all.

"Is it your meaning," she said at last, "that you would have done with him if I promise the same?"

"It is my meaning."

"My poor Nelson is certainly unfortunate in a wife that loves him so little as she can offer to part with him to gratify her spite, and sever him from one that loves every hair of his head and that he adores. No, Madam, you can't part us at that rate, nor at any other. I was a fool to make the offer I did. You have it not in you to love any man, nor make any sacrifice for him. You'll respect my secret, for you can't ruin your own husband, and it's as much as your position's worth to offend him. Let me tell you you've lost a chance to show yourself a true woman and wife, and now you can do your worst. I told my poor hero long since that his cold wife did n't know what love is, and I don't need to tell him again what all the world sees now. You think of yourself only. I that you scorn have risked all for him, and you not so much as your little finger. Take your own way, alone in life and death. My generous heart gave you your chance, you cold coward!"

She said much more, but I did not hear. I took the key from my pocket at last. She stretched her hand for it and, unlocking the door, went out without farewell. I sat down and hid my face, weeping for the temptation I had resisted, yet knowing I had with me the right. Does this console a woman?

I tell my story as lame as I lived it. But I have suffered. God knows it!

The passionate voice in my heart had ceased. The shadows were long and cool. Even the breeze had nearly dropped asleep in the quiet. I sat musing.

The world knows that Lady Nelson left her husband's house after sufferings unbearable. One may well understand the wife's position — her longing was for him. She heard, what the other kept from him as far as possible, the injurious reports, the ridicule that his serious attachment to a woman so well known drew on him. She trembled for his imperilled glory and hugged it to her barren bosom.

Therefore she implored a reconciliation. But it was too late. He would have none of her. He wrote that he had amply provided for her during and after his life and desired only to be left to himself. After the death of Hamilton he shared "Paradise Merton" openly with Emma. It cannot be known how he thought of his wife and past tenderness — the other so possessed him. He spoke of her bitterly. Emma mocked, with his sisters, at the forsaken wife, and, at his bidding, handled and returned her poor belongings. A petty triumph, we may think, but Emma's heart also is veiled. In the last days at Calais, when Trafalgar was for a time forgotten but by a few, and the country had rejected her claim to shine, a twin star, beside her Nelson, she must have owned to herself certain things at last. Certainly she sought refuge in the bosom of that Church which absolves only on condition of full confession and repentance.

I have imagined the scene between the two women, for none but themselves were present.

But a far wider question than the heart of either arises. How hold the balance between these two?

The one was all chastity and virtue. With all her purity and cold passion she sank the man she loved into such cruelty to her wifehood and womanhood that she hovers for ever about his great name a weeping cloud, dimming its radiance, protesting mutely and justly against a bitter wrong. Was she to blame? Shall we judge her by her virtues or their result?

And the other, a rose of the gutter, of whom her lover declared that without her aid and inspiration he must have failed at the Nile? "If there were more Emmas, there would be more Nelsons," he cried, believing it in his inmost soul. Without her fair face it is therefore conceivable that England might have perished. Yet she it was who tarnished England's uttermost glory in her son. Must she be judged by her vices or her attainment? Has the one woman earned the wreath, the other mere shame? Life is inscrutable. We cannot tell.

And the man? It is certain only that if England must have her hero she could not have him otherwise. Pure fire and black smoke rise from the same burning, sunshine between rifts of ruining storm. There are moments when Justice veils her eyes from him, days when he stands a shining and eternal splendor.

Of the women it may be said that each was most pitiful in the ruin she inflicted and endured. The man is least to be commiserated, for his work was accomplishment and he stands above them both, passed utterly from their keeping into his country's.

The riddle is insolvable.

But there, by her tomb, in the sunset and its golden calm, it may well seem that, in the cloudland of all the faiths, where the guns of Trafalgar are forgotten and glory is an outworn toy, a very wearied man may dream that all love is reconciled in a divine unity.

And, as I rose to go, the breathing air gathered the faint sweetness of the meadows and laid it upon the unseen altar.

THE BEAU AND THE LADY

GEORGE BRYAN BRUMMELL
1778–1840

"Why, sir, the Prince wears Superfine, and Mr
Brummell the Bath coating; but it's immaterial
which you choose, Sir John, you must be right;
suppose, sir, we say Bath coating — I think Mr
Brummell has a trifle the preference."

Thus the tailor to the prospective purchaser of
a coat, in the day of the *arbiter elegantiarum*. And
't is said that when Madame de Staël visited
London, she considered her failure to please
Brummell the greatest *malheur* of the experience
— the next being that the Prince of Wales did
not call upon her.

There was jealousy enough on the Prince's
part and resentment enough on the Beau's to
furnish food for many a quarrel, and Brummell's
consummate impudence was displayed on more
occasions than those of the "Wales, ring the
bell!" and "Who's your fat friend?" incidents.
But when it came to the point of interfering with
his debts and his marriage, the First Gentleman
in Europe was not inclined to excuse it, and the
last quarrel was fatal, both for Brummell and for
Mrs Fitzherbert.

The Beau — who preferred to "be genteelly
damned beside a Duke rather than saved in vulgar
company" — met a miserable end in the asylum of
St-Sauveur, at Caen. The story follows the course
of the Prince's life. And the Lady, after all, had
perhaps more happiness than either of these.

George Brummell
From an Engraving at the British Museum
By J. Cook from a Miniature

VI

THE BEAU AND THE LADY

A BALL at Carlton House was certainly one of the most splendid sights of the day in London. No more magnificent host than the Prince of Wales, later to be Regent and latest King George IV, and the palace itself was designed and decorated with all the grandeur that gilding, marble, and mirrors could bestow, lavished by a taste which considered gorgeousness the utmost reach of regal dignity. That a great part of this splendour was still unpaid for, that the Prince was heavily in debt, and that his royal father, wearied of his dissipations, refused to be responsible for them, made little odds to the enjoyment either of host or guests, any more than did the question of whether an appeal to Parliament would produce the power to continue in his mad career of pleasure. It was vain for Charles James Fox or the other politicians of his party to endeavour to fix his volatile mind on the danger of his growing unpopularity, for his levity could never be induced to believe that anything but the pleasure of the moment was worth consideration. At this time the beautiful Mrs Fitzherbert, his canonical though not his legal wife, — in consequence of the solemn ceremony which a few initiates knew had taken place between them,— acted invariably as hostess at his entertainments, and thus received and was received by many of the greatest ladies in England — an ambiguous position deeply resented by the King and Queen and indeed by the whole nation, not only because of its ambiguity but because the lady was a determined Papist, and the alliance thus put the Prince in a highly dangerous situation with regard to the Act of Succession. But what cared he? If to take no thought for the morrow be a virtue, the Prince was the most virtuous of men. He was as gay, as care-free at this moment as the youngest débutante at his gorgeous entertainment should have been — and was not.

For a very elegant girl stood beside the ballroom door with her mother, the Marchioness of Stanstead, her features cast in the classic mould of beauty, a Grecian nose and mouth softened into English loveliness, the dark ringlets waving around her fair brow in the style that the famous Sir Thomas Lawrence, now the fashionable artist, had made the mode. Dress, beauty, fortune, and distinguished family all singled her out as one of the most desirable partners in the room. His Royal Highness had given her a truly gracious reception, and yet she stood shrinking by her mother as if some dread and anxiety weighed upon her young heart and overclouded all the brilliant scene for her. She had just refused an invitation to dance, and was looking about her with anxious expectation.

"Mamma, mamma, Mr Brummell's coming this way!" says Lady Georgiana in an agitated whisper. "O do you think he'll speak to me? When we met him at Lady Spiers's he never said a word — only bowed! Surely here at Carlton House — "

"My love, be very quiet. It looks better bred and he will be seen with no one flurried or hurried. We can't tell, but I trust he may, for if he takes any notice of you we need have no more anxiety about your introductions. Perhaps as the Prince has been so gracious — and here's the sweet Mrs Fitzherbert approaching. Mind, Georgiana — be absolutely obsequious to the uncrowned Queen."

The Marchioness of Stanstead makes her deepest, sweetest curtsey to the lady whom the Prince of Wales delights to honour. It is most gracefully returned, and Mrs Fitzherbert glides into the seat at her elbow.

"Indeed, Madam, you confer a favour on us by introducing such a lovely young creature into company," she says softly. "And her dress is perfection — that blonde over *bleu tendre* falling off the slope of the shoulders is exquisite indeed. Fairy-like. I see nothing to-night that I like so well. His Royal Highness remarked it to me at once. Mr Brummell, you know Lady Stanstead. Have you been presented to Lady Georgiana Hotspur?"

The Beau bowed, but with a coolness which evidenced that he preferred to choose his own friends. He did not consider Mrs Fitzherbert one of them and objected to her influence with the Prince in social matters, of which he considered himself the sole arbiter. Charles Fox might guide the Prince in politics, Sheridan in matters of gaiety, but in the realm of fashion Mr Brummell and he only was to be the guide, and that a mere woman should presume —

But his bow to all three ladies was the perfection of genteel silence, as he turned away to the *riante* and lovely Duchess of Devonshire, who was enveloping the Prince in a fairy glitter of coruscations of toilette and laughter.

"O mamma, he never spoke to me!" whimpered Lady Georgiana, the tears welling into her eyes, mamma looking to the full as disturbed as her daughter.

Mrs Fitzherbert kindly interposed.

"Don't be disappointed, my dear. He seldom speaks to anyone until he has ascertained all about them and watched them for a time, and I was not the best sponsor, for I have never been acceptable in that quarter. See, the Prince comes this way. I will drop a word about Brummell."

The Prince's celebrated bow equaled that of Mr Brummell, but his neckcloth was not so finished a performance. There was the mischief. Day after day for months he had assisted at the Beau's toilet, that he might fathom its exquisite mysteries and the surprising simplicity, concealing perfect art, which made Brummell the best-dressed man in the world. He had sat by with his own valet in attendance, while Brummell's brought in a light hamper of neckcloths and the rites began. It was easy to study such details as that the collar attached to the shirt completely hid the head and face before folding down, and that the neckcloth must needs be twelve inches in width, but the deuce was in the finishing twirl of the wrist! One who had the distinction of knowing

the Beau personally, informs a listening world that
the *coup* was made with the shirt-collar, which he
himself folded downward and then, standing before
the long glass with his chin pointing to the ceiling,
by the gentle declension of his lower jaw creased the
neckcloth to the perfect dimensions. It is certain
that perfection can be reached only by repeated
failures, and the crumpled ties, often nearly filling
the hamper which Robinson carried off every day,
were the wounded in a great cause. That was where
genius distinguished itself from mediocrity. The
Prince made more failures and never attained su-
premacy until years after, when Brummell was in
France and no longer a competitor.

His dress to-night was a replica of the Beau's.
Each gentleman wore a blue coat and white waistcoat, black pantaloons buttoned tight to the ankle,
and striped silk stockings. But whether it was the
star on the Prince's breast which was the shade too
much, or a figure of rather too full outline, is difficult
to decide. The fact remains that Brummell, supremely light, easy, and graceful, the darling of his
tailor, looked elegance personified, and his Royal
Highness was merely a stout gentleman in a carefully
thought-out costume.

His bow, however, was perfect, and the compliment he paid Lady Georgiana made her flush and
tremble.

"Do remind me, Madam," he said to her delighted
mother, "if there is any connection I have forgotten
between the Hotspur family and the Spencers, for

Lady Georgiana has such a strong likeness to the lovely Duchess of Devonshire that anyone might take them for cousins."

Here was indeed a Prince to whom a lady might be loyal without effort. Mrs Fitzherbert intervened.

"Mr Brummell has just greeted us, Sir, and Lady Georgiana is distressed that such a distinguished man spared us none of his time. Like all young people, she has a fancy to meet those who are talked of."

"What, Brummell? O — ah! Yes! Of course he must talk to Lady Georgiana if she desires it. He dances well too. I'll fetch him."

"Brummell!"

"Your Royal Highness?"

"Lady Georgiana Hotspur wishes to dance."

"Indeed, Sir?" A pause. Then, with consummate impudence, "I believe Alvanley is disengaged."

The Prince reddened angrily. He was already flushed with drink.

"Damme, Brummell! When I say — "

"Allow me, Sir, to admire your coat to-night. The cut is good. Who made it?"

Royalty softened and unbent immediately. Praise from the Arbiter! The compliment was irresistible. It recalled Moore's verse, of which the Prince would have given worlds to be the subject: —

Come to our *fête* and show again
That pea-green coat, thou pink of men,
Which charmed all eyes that last surveyed it,
When Brummell's self enquired, "Who made it?"

"You like it? Meyer. I'll tell him what you say. He'll be damned pleased to hear it."

Lady Georgiana, shrinking back, was forgotten, and Mrs Fitzherbert slightly, almost imperceptibly, shrugged her lovely shoulders as the two men strolled away, the Prince thrusting his arm through Brummell's, and all eyes on the pair.

"Never mind, my dear. You will have plenty of opportunities," she said kindly. "It is no slight. The man is not altogether unamiable. It is only that he asserts his importance in this way. He has no other. I own it difficult to understand why people of fashion endure it— but so it is."

"O but, Madam," whispers poor little Lady Georgiana, almost sobbing, "what a situation am I placed in! Half the world was listening when his Royal Highness spoke! O my mamma, take me home!"

"What shall I do, Madam?" enquires Lady Stanstead, much perturbed.

"Why, let her choose another partner, of course. Don't let the insect see his power to sting. Here's the Duke of York — good nature itself. Your Royal Highness, we want an immediate partner for Lady Georgiana Hotspur."

"Then I'm your man, damme!" cries the jovial Duke. "I wanted the best-looking gal in the room and here she stands!"

And with a bow and a flourish, the Prince's brother led off the pretty shy damsel. He always treated Mrs Fitzherbert *en belle-sœur* and she could count on him.

She moved to the next group and Lady Stanstead, somewhat comforted, watched her daughter revolving in the newly introduced waltz, which was permitted at Carlton House but never countenanced at Queen Charlotte's stiff and decorous Court.

She could not be certain that it was agreeable to her to see the Duke's stout arm encircling that fairy waist and his hot face pressed as near the delicate features of her daughter as possible. His dancing too was more on the romping order than she could approve, he reeked of wine and snuff, and his reputation with women was of the worst. But there was not a girl nor a matron in the room who would have refused his hand. In short, he was Royal. There was no more to be said.

Mrs Fitzherbert was at this time in the full bloom of the surprising beauty which had won her the hand of the Heir Apparent of England and a life so unquiet, both publicly and privately, that she never dared consider the morrow, having her mind so overcharged with the present. Indeed her loveliness and good nature deserved a better fate. Her charm was of an unusual order. Masses of pale golden hair, shimmering in an unpowdered aureole about her head, gave her the fashionable width of coiffure which most of the fine ladies must attain with the help of art. Blue eyes would be naturally expected with such a hedge-rose delicacy of colour and the bright pale hair, but no — her's were the deepest, most tender hazel-brown, shaded with the silkiest lashes that ever woman sighed to possess. Her mouth and smile were sweetness itself, and if a fault could be so much as hinted, it was only that the nose was a trifle aquiline for such a charming gentleness of demeanour.

Alas for the lady! No beauty could secure her from the fact that her Roman Catholicism made her dangerous even as a mistress for the Prince, not to mention a wife; indeed, as if to heap every impossibility on her devoted head, she was some years older than her royal husband, had already been twice a widow when he married her, and though of good family was originally a Miss Smythe — a name which had it been Howard, Russell, or Spencer, had served her turn better with the multitude.

Her position was indeed most peculiar, tacitly acknowledged for a wife by the Prince's party, though few knew the circumstances of her marriage, received by the ladies of highest fashion on the Whig side, almost universally respected, and yet sternly ignored by King George III and Queen Charlotte, her very name forbid to be spoke before them, and viewed as a public danger because of the Prince's attachment to a Papist.

There need not have been so much anxiety. A descended archangel could not have given him a religious turn of any kind, and bets flew freely already at Watier's and White's as to how many years his attachment to the lady was likely to subsist. The outside gave her two.

When the company was departed and the happy hostess relieved of her fatigues, she stood awhile looking round her at the empty gilded saloons, where the roses and garlands were beginning to droop a little in the excessive heat which the Prince always commanded, and which caused Carlton House and the Pavilion to be known as the Royal Ovens.

The rooms themselves had a dissipated air, especially the great supper-room with the mounds of melting ice, plundered fruit, and sandwiches left as they were, half the weary lacqueys having gone off to snatch what sleep they could before the fatigues of the morrow, while the few that were left were yawning miserably as they made the needful preparations for what remained of the night.

"Madam, your carriage waits!" and she drew her roquelaure round her shoulders, looking about her for the Prince. He had disappeared, and with a patient sigh she went down to her carriage attended only by the majordomo, and drove off to her house in St James's Square.

She had made it a condition that she should never live under his roof until the marriage was acknowledged, and often had reason to be thankful for that choice, for it enabled her to escape some of the worst carouses of his wild companions, though by no means all. People in society who knew the facts declared that the Prince would have gone to the devil altogether before this if it had not been for her gentle influence upon him. She was passionately fond of amusement herself, — and no one who was either grave or straitlaced could have been endured by him for a day, — but she liked elegance and refinement about her, which were the most difficult of all things to impress upon him and yet in his position the most needful to be observed. She detested the pinchbeck ornamentation of Carlton House and the Pavilion, and her own mansion was a model of taste and discretion, which he described as niggardly but was pleased to hear commended by others.

Now, arrived in her own drawing-room, the lovely Fitzherbert threw herself into a chair to wait with what patience she might until her royal husband came home. This was an invariable custom, because she believed it might cut off an hour or two of drinking if he knew she was waiting and deprived of rest. As she sat there, her chin leaning on her jeweled hand, the weariness on her face was not only bodily. It flowed from a far deeper source, as well it might when the anxieties of her position were considered.

As to the Prince's especial set, she would have given her all to detach him from it and see him surrounded by men more worthy of his rank. Fashionable people might sneer at the old King still mourning the loss of his American colonies, at the starched decorum of Queen Charlotte, and the strictness with which her sweet Princesses were brought up, and Maria Fitzherbert relished dullness and tedium as ill as any. But when she saw the steady deterioration of the Prince, her very heart misgave her, and with an inexpressible solicitude she yearned for the dignity and rectitude of the elder Court. The countenance of the Queen, her sympathy with her hopes for the Prince, would have been balm to her wound, and yet were unattainable. It was for this reason, and this only, that she bore the sneers of people who did not understand her case — people too unfashionable to enter the gay portals of Carlton House, yet who made up what is called English opinion.

As she sat, sorrowfully revolving this and other matters, her maid opened the door and curtseyed.

"Madam, Williams says Mr Brummell is waiting below, and asks if he may see you for a moment."

"I can't see anyone now, Fletcher. Tell Mr Brummell I can see him on Wednesday at my reception in the evening."

Fletcher disappeared and returned. "If you please, Madam, the gentleman says it is urgent!"

She hesitated. Her dislike for Brummell and a natural contempt for what she thought his effeminacy made him always unwelcome and now doubly so, wearied and dispirited as she was; but such a close friend of the Prince's she dared not offend. She looked at the crystal timepiece on the mantel — half past two — and sighed again.

"Ask Mr Brummell to come up" — then sprang to the glass to arrange her coiffure and the rich fall of Brussels point about her bosom. It was a very stately bright-eyed madam who curtseyed to his bow when the door opened.

"Wait in the anteroom, Fletcher," said the Uncrowned Queen, as the great Whig ladies called her. And indeed no queen could have a more delicate distinction of manner.

"It is so late, Mr Brummell," she began, scarcely indicating a chair, "that I am persuaded your business must be urgent indeed to bring you here at this hour. Perhaps it was the Prince you wished to see?"

"By no means, Madam. I wished to have a word of the utmost importance with yourself. I flatter myself that it will not be unwelcome."

"It is difficult to imagine what it can be," Madam responded with some hauteur. Brummell knew as well as she the *froideur* between them, and his cavalier treatment of her introduction in the ballroom that evening had not improved matters. It really astonished her that he should have had the impudence to approach her in this way, though his impudence was more or less his stock in trade.

"Why, Madam, there are circumstances present and approaching in which you and I have a mutual interest, and as I have only just heard of them from a source that must be nameless, I conceived that your influence with his Royal Highness might be valuable in more ways than one. But permit me before I proceed to express regret for the little *contretemps* of this evening. Lady Georgiana Hotspur is a pretty gal, but did you not observe that she has by no means the *bel air?* The mésalliance of her grandmother on the mother's side, who was the daughter of a wealthy merchant of St. Mary Axe, probably accounts for it. One could not be seen standing up with a gal who moves like a linen-draperess!"

"I am a poor dissembler, Sir, and must say that I noticed no difference in your manner from its ordinary assurance. Perhaps you will now proceed to business — if business you have with me."

The Beau's eye shot a flash at the lady on this rejoinder, which he instantly subdued into its usual languor.

He laid his opera hat on the table.

"That is a compliment, Madam, which I cannot bring myself to refuse. Assurance is the indispensable outfit of the gentleman in the social world. However — you are aware that the question of the Prince's debts is urgent and — "

"Mr Brummell, I will not endure this," she cried, half rising. "Anything I hear on that point must be from his Royal Highness, and — "

"From his sincere friends, Madam. The Prince is at this moment at Mr Fox's house, meeting the inner circle of his political friends and consulting whether his debts shall be brought before Parliament or no."

"I don't believe it. The Prince himself would have mentioned it to me. How do you know this?"

"Through a friend to whom I have been useful, Madam, and who therefore obliges me with useful information."

"The Prince would have mentioned it."

"The Prince does not mention everything, and there are reasons why it is very unlikely that he will mention this at the present stage. But it is convenient you should know it. And there is more. I have also a piece of information, unknown to the Prince but extremely important both to him and to you, which I am prepared to lay before you — for a consideration."

"Money?" she said, with the most frigid contempt in her tone. "Well, Mr Brummell, I confess I have not had a high opinion of you, but I never supposed you were to be bought and sold in this manner. What will his Royal Highness think when I tell him of such a hateful proposal? Is it not what the world calls — blackmail?"

Brummell still preserved the coolest composure.

"Money? who spoke of money? I must really request you to preserve the serenity of a gentlewoman. Money is the last thing I desire, Madam, or would accept in such a case."

His florid well-kept face had a touch of languid anger — no more, but in such a man a danger signal. Mrs. Fitzherbert, accustomed to the uncertainties of her position, felt the need of conciliating him, and indeed the whole matter puzzled her considerably.

"I apologise, Sir, for an unworthy suspicion. What is it you wish?"

"Madam, it is not needful to apologise. One does not expect reason from your delightful sex. I have been well aware of your prejudice against me and the mischief you have done me with his Royal Highness in consequence. Now his countenance is valuable to me from several points of view. I wish it continued."

Mrs Fitzherbert flushed hotly. She felt danger and could scarce tell why. Possibly it lay in the emergence of anything that marked feeling or character from beneath the veneer of Brummell's masking face and preoccupations. It was as when the water of some stagnant pool is stirred and strange living creatures of the depths are brought to the surface.

"I am sure," she said, stuttering in her nervous haste, "that nothing could be more conciliatory than the Prince's manner to you this evening. He promenaded the saloon for quite ten minutes with his arm through yours."

"Undoubtedly, Madam, but you are as well aware

as I that no one is his equal in keeping individuals he dislikes 'in play,' as he terms it, by the most winning courtesies, while he is preparing to trample them underfoot. I should regret to state, unless you knew it very well yourself, that not a word his Royal Highness utters can be believed unless it is otherwise supported. He is certainly the prince of dissemblers."

She bit her lip almost to bleeding and was silent. No one knew this better than she, no one dreaded it more, and no one would less admit it.

"Consequently," he went on, "when I hear a tale at Watier's of the Prince having said that I was lately guilty of the solecism of saying to him 'Wales, ring the bell!' when he and I were in company with one or two friends, I know what it means. My day is done."

"Did that not take place?" she said, startled into candour.

"You see, Madam! No, of course it never took place. Is it likely that a man of my breeding would, even for his own sake, commit such a vulgarity? But we waste time, and the Prince's conference would break up about four. Do you wish to know what has occurred, and shall I have your support with his Royal Highness as my price?"

The poor woman was much agitated by this time. Her position had entailed and prepared her for many discomforts, but this one came from so unexpected a quarter that she could not tell how to receive it. Yet if the information were important how could she dare pass it by? Her features relaxed and she did her utmost to be calm.

"I will hear you, Sir. And let me be perfectly candid before I do. My word, at least, you will accept."

"Mrs Fitzherbert is known to be as complete a model of truth as she is of discretion."

Was it a sneer? His face was the dandy's mask again, indolent, imperturbable. He took a pinch of snuff languidly.

"Then, Mr Brummell, I have disliked your influence on the Prince. Not that you led him into debauched habits like others I could name, but surely for the Prince of Wales to fix his thoughts as you do yours on the mere niceties of attire, of manner, of appearance, of gaming, is most unworthy and a lamentable waste of time. He cares more for the set of a collar — "

She paused. There was not the flicker of an eyelash to show she made any impression on her hearer.

"I waste breath," she said. "No, I can't bring the grave charges against you that I could against some. I will do what you wish. I promise. Tell me your news."

No one ever doubted this woman's truth. Certainly not Brummell, who had had plenty of opportunity of watching her.

He continued without more comment.

"Then the facts are these. If the Prince's debts are to be brought before the House of Commons, the other side intends to raise the question of his marriage."

"Good God!" cried Mrs Fitzherbert, turning pale with terror. It was the one thing she dreaded more

than any other. The Prince's position at this time
was so perilous, owing to his own debauchery and the
King's inflexible animosity, that she knew perfectly
well the discovery of their marriage must mean ruin
to him; and whatever she might face for herself she
could not face the fact that his passion for her would
be his downfall.

It was not only that the marriage was far beneath
him for reasons already mentioned; not only that the
Royal Marriage Act made it absolutely illegal; not
only that popular opinion would never forgive the
marriage of the Heir Apparent with a Papist; it was
the terrible clause in the Act settling the Succession to
the Crown! She knew every word of it by heart: —

And whereas it hath been found by experience that it is
inconsistent with the safety and welfare of this Protestant
Kingdom to be governed by a Popish Prince or any King
or Queen marrying a Papist, the said Lords Spiritual and
Temporal, and Commons, do further pray that it may be
enacted that all and every person and persons that is, are,
or shall be reconciled to or shall hold communion with the
See or Church of Rome or shall profess the Popish religion,
or shall marry a Papist, shall be excluded and be for ever
incapable to inherit, possess, or enjoy the Crown and Government of this Realm and Ireland, and the Dominions
thereto belonging or any part of the Same. And in all and
every such case or cases, the people of these realms shall
be and are hereby absolved of their allegiance, and the
said Crown and Government shall descend to and be
enjoyed by such person or persons as should have inherited
in case the said person or persons so reconciled, holding
communion, or marrying aforesaid, were naturally dead.

Here was her terror exposed to the light of day.

The Prince of Wales had so married, for never a stronger Catholic existed than Mrs Fitzherbert. She loved her faith, was incapable of denying it for any earthly advantage; but she also loved her husband, and had pledged herself never to reveal their marriage in his lifetime without his consent. She held the certificate which the Prince had written in his own hand: —

We the undersigned do witness that George Augustus Frederick, Prince of Wales, was married unto Maria Fitzherbert this 15th of December 1785.

> *Signed:* JOHN SMYTHE   (her brother)
> HENRY ERRINGTON (her uncle)[1]

But if this paper had been the witness of her dishonour instead of honour, she could not have kept it more carefully hidden. She had even in a moment of terror cut off the names of the witnesses, lest she should expose those men of her own blood to the terrible penalties allotted to those who witnessed or aided such a marriage, though she afterwards regretted this haste, and kept, to correct its rashness, a letter of the Prince's couched in these words: —

Thank God my witnesses are living. Your uncle and brother, besides Harris, whom I shall call upon as having been informed by me of every, even the minutest circumstance of our marriage.

But how she hid it! How she endured aspersions, slights, and the loathsome comment that her position with a man of such known character as the Prince must bring upon her. And this not only because she

---

[1] Following the signatures of "George P." and "Maria Fitzherbert."

loved him, but because of the natural terror that such
an upheaval must inspire in the woman who was the
cause of it all, her sole consolation being that she
knew herself a wife, not only according to the laws of
her own Church but even by the canonical law of the
Church of England.

It was known that the King and Queen had no love
for their eldest son. Their affections were centered on
his next brother, the Duke of York, who however
licentious, had not affronted public opinion like the
Prince of Wales and was perfectly prepared to make
such a marriage with some honest homely German
Princess as should commend itself to King and
Nation.

The Prince then, had run the risk of a frightful sacrifice to her scruples, though neither he nor she had
ever imagined it would be brought to the test of
enquiry. Who would dare to start the stone that
might bring an avalanche in its wake?

It will thus be understood what horror seized her
when Brummell — Brummell of all men, the dandy,
the irresponsible, uttered those words.

He gave her a moment to recover, and then continued: "Yes, Madam, this is the absolute truth.
The man who is to bring forward the motion when
the question of the debts is raised in the House of
Commons has informed me of the settled intention
of Mr Pitt's party. That is to say, he has not himself informed me, but I have it from a person who
knows all the circumstances intimately. There is
no questioning my information."

'Mr Brummell, it cannot, must not be!" she cried
in an agony and with clasped hands. "That you have
warned me, is a service I can never forget, but you
must go further, you must give me the name, that he
may be approached and this frightful mischief nipped
in the bud. You need not have made me promise to
aid you. The man who has acted as you have done
must be valuable to the Prince for ever. Give me
his name."

"Madam, I would never withold it from you. I
am one of the group of persons who know that your
promise is inviolable even to your own hurt; but the
Prince cannot be trusted, and if he sets Fox or Sheridan on this person, irreparable mischief will be done.
No, it is you who must find agents to approach
this person unknown to the Prince, and induce him
to let the question of the debts stand alone. Better
still, get the King's assistance and carefully avoid
bringing them before Parliament, lest the other matter
be dragged into the light of day."

She sat, a drooping figure of misery, her mind so
ranging over the terrible possibilities that she scarce
heard what he said. The debts — something most
certainly must be done, for the Prince's coffers were
all but empty. Many of his tradesmen refused to
supply him; the Jews were relentless in the face of
many broken pledges; and it was known amongst the
wealthy that those who lent money to H. R. H. were
rewarded only by his dislike and suspicion. All in
society were in possession of these facts. She broke
no seal of confidence in her next speech to Brummell.

"You knew the Prince on the verge of ruin —
what then is your object in desiring his countenance?
What can you hope to gain? There must be some
motive I can't fathom. Be candid with me, if
you can."

"A simple motive, Madam, though one I can't
expect you to appreciate. The Prince, whatever his
difficulties, is Arbiter of Society and King of the
Clubs. Those two things are all that concern me —
the only elements in which I can exist. If he turns
against me, I can make him ridiculous, and you know
there is nothing on earth he so dreads as ridicule.
But" — his face even now was a mask of languor —
"he can ruin me. My small fortune is near gone. I
live by gaming and invitations. If these disappear,
it is a case of Calais — and extinction!"

He slightly shrugged his shoulders and sat looking
at her.

The tears welled into her eyes and began to trickle
down her face. She stopped them with her richly
laced handkerchief, her lips trembling so that she
could scarce speak.

"I see. I know not that your aim is more worthless
than his, than mine, than anyone's. We all alike
seem to me like shadows in a world of shadows, pursuing shadows as useless as ourselves. Well, sir —
you have my promise to forward your aim, such as it
is, and I am to request you will favour me with any
further information that comes your way. Application to the King is hopeless, but what I can do, I will.
Is it better I should or should not know the name of

the person to bring forward the motion of enquiry as to the marriage?''

"Better not, Madam, for the moment. I am advised that what you should concentrate on is gaining the King's ear and getting the debt settled without application to the House of Commons. If that fails, let me have a message and I will consult the principals. Meanwhile, I count on your good offices with H. R. H."

"They are pledged to you, Sir," she said firmly, but without any motion of cordiality.

She rose, and he of course did so instantly.

No person looking at the famous Beau, the ornament of the clubs and gilded saloons of Carlton House and Almack's, could have supposed him the messenger of anything more serious than some elegant dissipation, and there was certainly nothing in his expression to speak him more. A well-bred suavity was the most it bespoke.

And as little might any observer guess that the beautiful woman, dressed in the highest splendour of fashion and taste, surrounded by the gifts of Royalty, shed tears for anything more painful than the death of a pet bird or the loss of a jewel. Both, trained in the world's school, responded to its tutoring and parted with a bow and a curtsey that might have admitted a hundred spectators to their advantage.

He turned at the door for one more word.

"The matter is so delicate, Madam, that it had better be left in this way. If you hear no more privately from me, conclude that the determination to bring up the marriage is discarded as too dangerous. In that case there will be no danger in placing the debts before the House. If there is persistence I will warn you at once. Act accordingly, and keep all this religiously to yourself. It is as dangerous as gunpowder."

"Sir, I understand you completely. I thank you gratefully."

Left alone she sank into her chair and endeavoured to fix her weary mind on the essentials.

Never a woman sought more anxiously to substantiate her honour than Mrs Fitzherbert to conceal hers. It is true she eagerly desired the good opinion of men and women, — especially the latter, — but to please her it must subsist without testimony to support it. They must accept her because they believed her a woman incapable of unchastity, not because they knew her so. They must say, "See, she attends all the rites of her Church. She confesses. She receives its sacraments. All must be well, though we cannot tell how."

Beyond that they must not go. She dared not have any inquisition — least of all, that of His Majesty's faithful Commons. Therefore the debts must wait. It could not be risked.

And as she sat, lost in the intricacies of doubt and fear, there came a noise of drunken shouting in the quiet square, as of a rabble singing, laughing, making for her door, a thunderous knocking, the trampling of feet in the hall, and in an outburst of terror she flung herself crouching behind the sofa just before the Prince, the Duke of York, Lord Barrymore, and several other gentlemen, all wild with drink, broke into the drawing-room.

"Where is she? Have her out!" shouted the Prince, and all began searching behind the curtains and chairs.

"Maria! come out! I'll wager you're here in hiding!" he shouted, and then, drawing his sword and flourishing it wildly, "Come out, or it will be the worse for you!" He flung the sofa aside and dragged the trembling victim out, roaring aloud with laughter.

"You little vixen! Were you gone to earth? See here, my Lords, did n't I tell you?" holding her by the cold and shaking hand. "This is what happens when a man's wife sits up to keep a watch on him, when she should be in bed and asleep."

He was too far gone in drink to heed anything, but her misery half sobered the Duke of York, who had a kind heart under all his dissipation.

"Let her go, Sir. Let her go, George, I tell you! Come, Madam — I'll see you to the door. George, if you don't let her go, I'll force you to!"

She was half fainting when he got his burly arm about her waist and dragged her from the Prince, then supporting her to the door, he opened it and thrusting her out, set his back against it.

"Now, gentlemen all, there's punch downstairs. Come down and drink a good woman's health — Mrs Fitzherbert's, and then get home quietly. You're all bosky enough already. There's the dawn!"

He tore back the curtains and let the grey light

in on the flushed drunken faces. The Prince crumpled up in a velvet armchair and began to snore where he sat. The rest, led by the Duke, stumbled downstairs.

Watier's, the Dandy Club, — so called because Brummell, Lord Alvanley, Mildmay, and Pierrepoint, famous dandies one and all, were the four leading spirits, — was the home of much talk and speculation a week later, for it was rumoured strongly that at a meeting of many highly influential supporters of the Prince it had been decided to bring the Royal debts, amounting to some £250,000, before Parliament. The talk at Watier's was of importance because Fox, Sheridan, and others of his partisans made the place their night resort after the debates, and, over grilled bones and to the music of the dice, State secrets were freely discussed and amid the vinous excitement by no means so carefully kept as they should have been. The Prince himself was a frequenter.

That afternoon Brummell, exquisitely dressed, was standing by the window looking into Bolton Street, displaying his Hessians and pantaloons, with blue coat and buff-coloured waistcoat, to the admiration of the passers, some of whom indeed stopped to have more than a glance at the supreme dandy. The Prince's carriage drove up to the door, and he got out with the assistance of one of the footmen, for obesity was increasing upon him so rapidly that he had become nervous of getting in and out unaided. A slightly sarcastic curl of Brummell's lip, as he looked on, attracted attention and one or two

more men lounged up and watched also — Creevy,
a well-known man about town, among them.

"Prinny's rounding apace!" says he. "No more
sympathy for him on the Florizel lines — the gay and
beautiful young Prince. Eh, Brummell?"

The Beau shook his head, slightly smiling, and
Creevy went on.

"This debt business is going to be a very difficult
matter for Pitt and the King if Prinny persists in
bringing it up in the House, and a far worse one for
Prinny himself. I heard on sound authority that
when he submitted a schedule of his debts to the
King there was an item of £54,000 for plate, jewellery
and so forth for Mrs Fitz, and that the King swore
then he would see the matter through and face him
with the consequences of his follies. Mrs Fitz is the
most dangerous of them, eh, Pierrepoint?"

"I fear our friend's in the ditch!" says Pierrepoint,
taking snuff. "But for all that I can't see what he's
to do. The Jews laugh when they see his name on
paper now. He's offered an Irish peerage and
£10,000 when he succeeds, to anyone who'll advance
him £5,000 now. A nice House of Lords that would
be yonder!"

"Sh — sh! Here he comes," says Brummell in a
whisper, and the Prince advanced into the room,
looking urbanely about him, and scattering greetings
to all — but Brummell! The Prince cut him deliberately. As great an adept in that noble art as Brummell himself, his eye wandered over him negligently,
almost affably, as though he were a stranger to be

pleasantly considered before forgotten. A look of the serenest unconsciousness — studied indeed most carefully from Brummell in the days when to walk together from White's to Watier's, both dressed in the perfection of dandyism, may be said to have been the Prince's highest, most harmless pleasure. The insult was gross and direct.

It was a moment before the room full of men realised the situation, and as they did so, a most distressing silence succeeded. Brummell slowly stiffened; not for a moment did his presence of mind forsake him. He followed the Prince's example to the lift of an eyelash, then turning to Lord Moira who stood, bowing, beside him, he dropped one sentence and one only into the silence: —

"Moira, who's your fat friend?"

It was irresistible and sufficient. It fell like a stone flung into a pond and its circles were as endless. The Prince glared in speechless fury, turned, and walked quickly out of the room, for the moment a vanquished man. In the general consternation, Moira said loudly: "Damme, Brummell, you've done it! The Prince will never forgive you: What in the devil's name possessed you?"

"What in the devil's name possessed him to cut me?" says Brummell, with a slight quivering about the mouth, but laughing all the same. "Is a man to come into this club and cut one of the members without any reason given! I won't stand such vile bad manners from any man in England. Certainly not from our friend Big Ben!"

All present knew that the magnificently colossal porter at Carlton House went by the name of Big Ben, and that Brummell with his usual assurance often alluded to his master by that name, and had even gone so far as to call the lovely Fitzherbert "Benina," but to hear it thus and then was too much for the assembled gentlemen.

"As a matter of fact he'll probably repent it and make some sort of an excuse to-morrow," Brummell continued, coolly looking about him. "The man has enough on his mind at present to overset his manners. The question with me is whether to accept it. Serve him right if I cut him, and make the old King the fashion! As easy done as said!"

Pierrepoint shrugged his shoulders at this consummate impudence and muttering something about the card-room, went out. The others, all but a man named Sellers, quietly disappeared. He remained, facing Brummell.

"What's at the bottom of all this? You and he were hand in glove the other night. All he does must be political in its effect sooner or later, yet I know you're not such a fool as to dabble in politics. This seems rather a serious business."

The other, very white about the gills, answered with a forced laugh.

"By no means political — not such an ill-bred fool, Sellers. Benina's at the bottom of this. Nothing less will serve the lady than to identify herself with the Crown of England and that's a matter that Big Ben's friends can't well recognise. I owe this to her.

I gave her her chance once, and damme if I don't repay her now!"

He turned and walked off, noticing as he went down that the report had spread through the club. Even the servants suspected that something of consequence was in the air, and the very porter being in talk with the man who received the letters, the Beau was allowed to pass out without the information that there was one for him. There were more: *billets-doux;* verses written in fair Italian-sloped handwriting for his famous album; invitations by the score, many of them hopeless efforts to secure a sponsorship that would launch the writers on the sea of fashion; but there was one that it was imperative he should receive that day and he did not receive it. It was from Mrs Fitzherbert. A warning of the cut.

He went off to his rooms, strolling carelessly as if merely sunning himself with his usual indolence. Many acquaintances passed and were acknowledged with the incomparable bow. He never took off his hat even to a lady, for this might disarrange the hair which was said to require three artists for its perfection, one each for the temples, the crown, and the back. But who missed it? The recognition was honour sufficient, especially if accompanied — for intimates — with a little flutter of the fingers in the air.

The Duke of Devonshire, meeting him, took his arm and strolled a little way, after his cold phlegmatic manner, scarcely speaking but enjoying his company. The Duke of Bedford succeeded when the other Duke turned into White's, and nothing could

be more cordial than his greeting and the invitation
to hunt at Woburn when the season should begin. It
was accepted, plans were made for meeting at Belvoir
— Fryatt should take down his horses; and the
Duke then asked casually whether the white tops
he had introduced would be worn next season instead
of brown. No question of that, Brummell said airily,
and so they parted; and yet at the moment two
thoughts and two only possessed him — one, that
ruin was hard at his heels and Dukes and other mag-
nificences shortly to be a memory; the other, vengeance on Mrs Fitzherbert and the Prince, to be
executed before the flight from England that began
to loom very near.

His rooms were like himself — the bed- and dressing-
room fitted with every device for the storing of a
magnificently complete wardrobe, and with glasses
sufficient to reflect a regiment of Beaux at every
imaginable angle. Money had been lavished here and
the result was such that not only the Prince of Wales
but every man who aspired to *ton* had asked permission to follow some of the conceptions evolved by
Brummell for the perfecting of the business of dressing. It was absolute. There was no questioning it.
It was even fitted with a bath-closet, supposed at that
time to be the only one in England. But the Beau
had a prejudice in favour of washing his whole person
daily — considered on the whole to be effeminate:
at all events this was not copied. The reception room
was naturally more a matter of taste. Men did not,
as a whole, feel compelled to imitate this, though it

was felt to be supremely elegant. His passion was for buhl and ormolu and there were splendid specimens of both, the buhl tables and a cabinet containing a set of Sèvres china, decorated with portraits of all the frail and famous French beauties of the courts of Louis Quatorze and Louis Quinze. These charming ladies were known as Brummell's seraglio, and he certainly derived much delight from their dumb company. The draperies were of the costliest velvet and damask, and any person viewing the rooms might well believe them the abode of a man of millions instead of one whose original fortune of £30,000 would not have done much more than furnish them as they stood.

At his rooms, in a gilded armchair of the French Regency period, was seated a visitor who seemed by no means at his ease in these luxurious surroundings, and sprang hurriedly to his feet as their owner entered.

"Mr Brummell, Sir, your most obedient!"

"Don't disarrange yourself, Grunbaum. Remain seated. Sorry to keep you waiting, but I was delayed by the Duke of Bedford. Now — if your information is complete, I am ready to hear you."

Mr Grunbaum shuffled nervously with a coloured pocket-handkerchief which Brummell beheld with unconcealed aversion.

"Why, you see, Mr Brummell, this has come into my hands in the way of business — and if it were to be suspected that it leaked through me, it would damage my trade to extinction."

"Can't quite see that, my good man. The world will go on wanting snuff to the end of time, and if yours is the best, which it sometimes is — "

"Always, Mr Brummell. Always, unless for accidents. But I have a grateful heart, whatever my trade may be, and the noble way in which you saved my credit when we got that consignment from Martinique six months ago left me your debtor to the end of my life."

"Why, you knew it was damned bad, Grunbaum, damned bad. I told you so directly you asked my opinion."

"So you did, Sir, like the best judge in England as you are, and God knows I saw the whole cargo left on my hands at an appalling loss, for what person would buy it if Mr Brummell's opinion against it got abroad? And we had a list of thousands of applicants. You observed my misery, Sir, for I could n't conceal it, and your compassionate heart was nobly moved. I saw the tear of sympathy in your eye, Sir, damme if I did n't! Good Gad, shall I ever forget my despair, and the relief when you allowed us to present you with three jars of the damned stuff and to say you thought well of it. I could laugh now, Sir, when I remember that in two days there was not a grain left to dust the bottom of a spoon!"

Brummell smiled superior. It was at moments like this he savoured his power to the full. For a moment he inhaled the incense, then returned to business.

"But now, Mr Grunbaum, now?"

"Now, Sir, I can be explicit. Have you seen Horne

Tooke's pamphlet? The person who shall be nameless between you and me brought it into my shop yesterday in manuscript. I declare to you, Sir, I sweat in recalling so much as the title, *The Reported Marriage of the Prince of Wales*, and it ends thus — I made a note."

He interrupted himself to fish from his pocket a piece of paper, so snuff-stained and otherwise so uninviting that Mr Brummell delicately waved it aside, and Mr Grunbaum read it aloud: —

It is not from the debates in either House of Parliament that the public will receive any solid or useful information on a point of so much importance to the Nation, to the Sovereign, and to a most amiable and justly valued Female Character, whom I conclude to be in all respects both legally, really, worthily, and happily for this country, her Royal Highness the Princess of Wales.

He stopped dramatically, looking at Brummell for the expected impression. Nothing could stir that colossal languor. It might have been a fly alighting on the hide of an elephant, so little did it move his serenity.

"Plain speaking!" he observed at length, opening his gold-and-enamel box with the left hand only — an elegant trick he had taught the Prince of Wales. "Well, Grunbaum, had it affected our friend?"

"Not our friend, Mr Brummell. It is not the principal whom I have seen. But this person declared to me that the principal is worked up into a fury, Mr Brummell, Sir. He declared that he would sooner lose his immortal soul than there should be silence in the House when the question of the Prince's debts was raised, and he would see that the truth was extracted as to whether a marriage had or had not taken place. There is no question but he thinks he has great Personages at his back in determining to discredit the Prince and the Papists, but who they be it is not for a humble individual like me to say, excepting only that I heard a mention that the country gentlemen are concerned to a man. A powerful interest, Sir!"

Brummell mused for an instant.

"Strange he should be so unguarded to you, Grunbaum!"

"Not strange, Sir, when the circumstances are considered, but those are confidential between him and me. And also you are aware he won't himself appear. He is not a member of Parliament, though his principal is. I understand it is already fixed who shall bring forward the motion."

"Then the enemy is in hopes the Prince's debts may be put forward in the House and relief demanded?"

"Absolutely, Sir. They reckon for certain that he will venture it, with Fox and Sheridan to speak for him."

"And they believe Mr Pitt has concerted with a Great Personage to take advantage of this false move, to put on the screw about the marriage?"

"Absolutely, Sir. And I, knowing you for a warm friend of his Royal Highness, wish to put it in your power to warn him, since all this is a dead secret.

The person who can do him that service should merit anything from his gratitude."

"His Royal Highness and I are so intimate, Grunbaum, as nothing can add to his regard."

"Very true, Mr Brummell, Sir. All the world is acquainted with that circumstance. Still, it must be a pleasure to a feeling heart to confer benefits. I rely on my name being sunk, Sir."

"Certainly, certainly. And I am considerably obliged to you, my worthy Grunbaum. It shall not be forgot in future dealings. And if — "

But at this moment, Robinson the valet entered the room with a message from the Countess of Upper Ossory, and Brummell continued serenely:—

"A moment, Robinson. Yes, Grunbaum, put my name on the list of subscribers for the next cargo of snuff from Martinique. But remember it must be prodigiously exquisite, for I can't otherwise be responsible with the Prince."

"Your own mixture, Sir. Your most chosen flavour. Permit me to retire, Sir, with grateful thanks for this condescending audience. Your most humble and obedient." Mr. Grunbaum bowed himself backwards out of the room and the Beau remained alone.

His brow was so anxious that he might have been meditating a choice between Bath coating and Superfine for his forthcoming garments. In a sense, that may be said to be the foundation of his reflections, for all future luxuries must hang on his decision, and therefore it was a crisis in his affairs, look at it how you will. He considered that Mrs Fitzherbert had

betrayed him in one direction or another. Either she
had betrayed the hint without mentioning to whom
she owed the service, or she had told it in such a
manner as aroused the Prince's anger and unbelief,
or she had sunk the whole matter rather than be
obliged to him. In any case she merited punishment.
As for the Prince, Brummell was not singular in his
contempt for him. Of his Royal Highness it may be
confidently said there was not a person who knew him
well enough to form a just opinion but disliked and
despised him — with the exception of his unfortunate
wife, who had sacrificed all for him and had nothing
else to trust to.

All now turned on the question, Should he or should
he not send the promised message to Mrs Fitzherbert.
If she did not receive it, she would allow matters
to take a course probably as fatal to herself as the
Prince. Well, what odds! She merited punishment if
ever a woman did, for she had had a week's grace
and at the end of it the Prince had publicly insulted
him. A dull smouldering anger, for he was not a
passionate man, burned in Brummell's heart, if
heart he had — say rather in his self-esteem, his only
vulnerable part and now most cruelly wounded.
That Mrs Fitzherbert did not and could not know the
real facts of the case — a rivalry between himself
and the Prince for the good graces of a very worthless
woman and his own infuriating success — counted for
nothing with him. She had failed, and that sufficed.

It would be tedious to record the various emotions
that guided him to a decision, but he had reached it

before returning to Watier's for dinner, and set out for that famous resort before going on to a ball at Lady Jersey's in what appeared to be the most equable spirits. One or two men chilled off a little in their manners to him. That was all that he could note. The news of the rupture had of course flown round the clubs, but most concluded it a lovers' quarrel, knowing how the Prince depended on Brummell's advice for much that made him the First Gentleman of Europe. It was felt that Lady Jersey's ball would throw more light on the narrow path of wisdom to be followed in future.

Carlton House itself could scarcely exceed the splendours of her Ladyship's mansion, though these were on a somewhat smaller scale. All his friends knew that the Prince must be entertained magnificently or not at all, and, as a somewhat vulgar profusion was his taste, all was profusion.

At this time the amour between his Royal Highness and Lady Jersey was in its earlier stages and though much discussed in the clubs and drawing-rooms, had not reached that degree of publicity which made it such a scandal at the time of his marriage to the unhappy Caroline of Brunswick. Still it placed her beauty and her influence at the very height of fashionable celebrity and inflicted all the agony on Mrs Fitzherbert that the most ardent rivalry could inspire.

"Where in the world is the Prince?" she said in a voice of alarm to the Duchess of Devonshire, as they stood together, twin stars of beauty, in the great outer drawing-room, all feathers and jewels and the perfection of the art of the milliner. Probably the two most fascinating women in Europe that night, and Mrs Fitzherbert was looking more than commonly beautiful with the white feathers softening the brightness of her hair and rivalling the hedge-rose tint of her delicately fair skin.

"Why, I believe Devonshire saw him in the boudoir with Lady Jersey. My dear, compose yourself. Don't look so agitated. He is and will be a flirt to his latest breath. 'T is nothing serious. We can't have our uncrowned Queen moping and dulling her lovely eyes for such a trifle."

The fair Duchess spoke to her so kindly that Mrs Fitzherbert struggled for a smile.

" 'Uncrowned' indeed! You never said a truer word, your Grace. Well — you are right. Do you dance to-night?"

"Yes of course. And you?"

"No. I'm chilly. I think I have a cold coming."

She drew the exquisite white cachemire about her shoulders and sank into a chair that commanded the incoming guests whose reception Lady Jersey had left for the moment to her lord while she amused herself with the Prince's attentions. Nearly all had arrived. Brummell was fashionably late. Almost the latest. He bowed and shook hands with Lord Jersey, looked about him for his hostess, noticed a few personal friends, and then, gazing serenely at Maria Fitzherbert, he cut her dead, and passed on to the upper end of the room.

The shock was so great to the poor lady that the prepared smile was frozen on her lips though they turned white as death for the moment. A quick shudder passed over her face. If a creature like Brummell dared such an insult, her day must be all but done. But she recovered herself gallantly, the hard discipline of her life standing her in good stead, and resumed her talk with her next neighbour, casting only an anxious glance after the Beau as he spoke to group after group of the most fashionable people in London on his semi-royal progress.

The boudoir was at the upper end of the two saloons, and Lady Jersey emerged, followed by the Prince. Never could she have looked more regal than in her glorious rose satin, a glitter of diamonds and rubies, with the rose and white plumes falling backward from her dark hair. Brummell bowed and smiled, and she returned his courtsey with a graceful word or two, and suddenly observing that the Prince took no notice of them and that Brummell recognised his presence as little as though he were a ghost, stood thunderstruck for a second, then moved hurriedly on, his Royal Highness following her.

Brummell turned, smiling coolly, to the Bedfords.

"I wonder you will have that animal here!" says the Prince, swelling with passion.

"But, Sir, what has he done? I thought he was a part of your society. He shall never enter these doors again."

"Nor any others, I hope, among my friends," cries the Prince. "I wish all the world to know that I consider the man a scoundrel, and that a friend of his is no friend of mine!"

"Then what shall I do now?" says the perturbed beauty. "Will you have him told to leave, Sir? A hint — "

"No, let him stay, but don't let him cross my path." It spoilt the ball for the hostess, the Prince, and Mrs Fitzherbert, but society itself was much interested and gratified by the quarrel and the delightful suspicions to which it gave rise. Brummell bore himself with a cool unconsciousness that in a better cause might well have won him admiration. And a further and fatal chance of insult came his way at the end of the ball.

The Duke of Bedford, who was behind him in the press waiting for his carriage, and who had seen nothing of what was going forward, called aloud: "Brummell, as you go down, call for Mrs Fitzherbert's carriage. She is waiting here."

It was his opportunity, and he took it. In his remarkably clear powerful voice, he shouted so that all the waiting society of London could hear: —

"*Mistress* Fitzherbert's carriage," and repeated it several times, then swinging lightly down the steps and out into the link-lit dark, he bowed and vanished.

She herself heard the title of by-gone days, now so long disused, revived to disgrace her, and sank back in her carriage weeping bitterly as soon as she was alone. The Prince remained behind.

She had done what she could with the Prince for Brummell, and only roused him to fury. Brummell

— that hound! If she cared for his affection she would never name the scoundrel again. He regretted that he had ever encouraged the man. He had behaved most dishonourably about a gaming debt, and so forth, with his usual torrent of words, until she was completely silenced. Unable to put forward her true reasons, she composed herself to wait as best she could for the chance of an explanation with Brummell. She ventured however, most timidly and quite apart from this, to question the wisdom of bringing the debts before the nation.

"My debts must come up in the House," he said angrily. "For the nation, if it wants the luxury of a Prince of Wales, — and I don't know where they can look for a better, — must needs pay the cost of upholding the position. As you know very well, Maria, I have applied to the King and he has refused me with scorn, chiefly I own, because of my connection with you."

"Then if the question of our marriage should be raised, what will you do!" asks she, trembling.

"Don't trouble your pretty head. I hate women that wrinkle their foreheads over men's matters, and don't know a woman that politics does n't make hideous, if it is n't the Duchess of Devonshire and Mrs Crewe. I like a soft yielding angel and — "

"But this is not politics — it is our marriage — "

"Leave it to me, I tell you. I have sure word that what you dread is not to be brought forward in the Commons. Fox knows it. And who would dare enquire into my private matters?"

She protested and protested until he was on the verge of one of his furies which had all the appearance of madness.

He charged her with interested motives that took no heed of his future — There was nothing he left unsaid; and when at last she perceived it was useless, and that if there were any help it would not be from him, she sank into a kind of wearied resignation to Fate. She had done her best. Possibly, since her cause was just, some unexpected accident would intervene. She could venture a word neither to Fox nor to Sheridan. They were wholly in the Prince's interest, and with terror she now perceived that might by no means coincide with hers.

Lady Jersey's ball overwhelmed her. She would have given her diamonds and more for an interview with Brummell, that matters might be explained. She ventured a note by the post, daring no other way, and whether it reached him or no she could not tell. She had no reply. She could only now count on his promise to warn her if the terrible need arose. Possibly his cutting her might be a matter of diplomacy, lest he should be suspected of giving information. She hoped so with all her terrified heart.

So the days went on.

There is no doubt the Prince was in extreme straits. The Whig leaders would have nothing to do with bringing his debts before the country, for they had no certainty but that the question of the marriage lay behind everything and not one was willing to risk the unpopularity of what must raise the question of

religion, if it came forward at all. Again and again
the Prince was warned that it would be better to
retrench, to endure any privations rather than raise
the question. It was pointed out to him that the
King would be compelled to come to his relief if he
showed an honest desire for amendment. But no —
all was of no avail. He persisted in believing that not
a living creature would have the courage to bring
the question of the marriage before the Commons.
Mrs Fitzherbert was helpless, and had at last come to
believe in her own secret heart that even if this did
take place the nation might possibly be eventually
reconciled to the contemplation of a decorous and
simple marriage with a woman of worthy character,
and that the dreadful uncertainties of her own position might be exchanged for peace. She coveted no
more, but it is possible that Lady Jersey's advent as
a danger did more than anything else to reconcile her
to the possible disclosure of her marriage. It is certain
she did not experience the same terror at the prospect
that she had done in Brummell's first communication.

Meanwhile cartoons and pasquinades raged about
the town in which no name was spared. Moore wrote
a pretended letter in verse from the Prince to Brummell, which was the rage everywhere, the very boys
yelling it in the streets: —

Neither have I resentments nor wish there should come ill
To mortal, except, now I think on 't, Beau Brummell,
Who threatened of late, in a superfine passion,
To cut me and bring the old King into fashion.

Brummell tasted this and other such triumphs to

the full. It was really believed by the multitude that it was he who had cut the Prince, and he acquired a momentary popularity among the No Popery and King's parties, which, could it have been translated into money terms, might have been of some service in his gradually increasing distresses.

And still he steadily withheld his hand. Not a word did he say to Mrs Fitzherbert. Grunbaum visited him again, with yet more detailed information about the plot in progress. Innocently, he put in Brummell's hand what would have saved the situation for Carlton House. He was glad to pay his debt with a service that cost himself nothing, and every word he could catch up he hastened with to Brummell's rooms, and there dropped it as into a well. It never reached the surface again. Brummell had never been happier. He even threw himself in the Prince's way that he might court his insults. It seemed that all thought of his own situation was drowned in the sullen lust of vengeance.

And so the great day came on.

It was the twentieth of April when an independent Member — for the Prince could find no other — rose in the House to ask Mr Pitt, the Chancellor of the Exchequer, whether "it was the design of Ministers to bring forward any proposition to rescue the Prince of Wales from his present very embarrassed condition — " A question which he supported by a very suitable speech.

Mr Pitt replied that, as such a subject could not be his duty to bring forward except by command of His Majesty, he could only say he had not been honoured with such a command.

Alderman Newnham, the member in question, then gave notice he should bring forward a motion in three weeks' time.

Great was the talking and whispering in Ministerial circles after this fluttering of the dovecotes. They could scarcely credit that the Prince would make such a move, and were inclined to think he had delivered himself into their hands. After a hurried consultation Mr Fox said that the circumstances were of the utmost delicacy, but as that delicacy would arise from the necessity of going into an investigation of causes, he hoped "something might be done in the interim to render it unnecessary for the honourable magistrate to prosecute his intention."

Mr Pitt at once intervened to say that the principal delicacy would certainly lie in the necessity for inquiring into causes.

There was a hush in the House, when a pin might have been heard to drop; for there was not a man present who did not understand the causes of Fox's fear and Pitt's threat, and Mrs Fitzherbert was present to every mind though not on a single lip. Members crowded out of the House, talking in excited whispers of what might and might not be the result, and Brummell watched in mingled hope and consternation for the emergence of the deus ex machina whom Mr Grunbaum had foretold.

On the twenty-seventh of April Alderman Newnham moved in a most excited House: "That a humble

address be presented to his Majesty, praying him to
take into his Royal consideration the present embarrassed state of affairs of the Prince of Wales, and to
grant him such relief as his Royal wisdom should
think fit, and the House would make good the same."

A stir of the profoundest interest ran through the
House and through the gallery where Brummell sat.

Then the Prince was showing fight, was persisting!
Whence had his courage come? What had he in
reserve? Was it all going to slip through without difficulty, and was Pitt's veiled threat of enquiry to go
for nothing? Disappointment, anger, were in many
a heart, though they flamed in none so fiercely as in
Brummell's.

He craned eagerly to look down upon the fray and
instantly perceived that Sheridan was on his legs.
If any man could get the Prince through he would —
but that it was possible to any man living was the
doubt, the fear, the hope that fluttered every heart
present in one direction or the other. That the
marriage must be owned, scarcely any doubted.

No, the Speaker would not see him; waved him
down; another member had the precedence; and then
arose a figure to fill the Prince and his supporters
with dismay, a stout Tory squire, John Rolle, mouth-
piece of the landed interest in the country, a tough
piece of unbendable English oak, a pig-headed, brave,
dogged man — a most alarming enemy.

The question in everyone's mind must be sifted, he
said, because it was one which immediately affected
the British Constitution in Church and State. In

no circumstances could it be let drop. And so forth.

With a movement of joy and relief inexpressible Brummell clasped his hands, as a long sigh of excitement went through the House. The gage was thrown down now, and battle must be joined. His information had not failed him.

Sheridan, representing the Prince, leaped to his feet again. His voice rang, his sparkling eyes glanced along the House. Every atom of his personal magnetism was flung in the faces of all who looked and listened. "Church and State!" he cried — What might that mean? Whatever was brought forward would meet with an unequivocal and complete reply from his Royal Highness.

And now all the heavy guns were being drawn into the debate, and Pitt rose slowly, and as it were unwillingly.

He was very much concerned, he said, that by such perseverance he should be driven, though with infinite reluctance, to the disclosure of circumstances which he should otherwise think it his duty to conceal. And when the proposed motion should be agitated, it was his determined and fixed resolution to give it his negative.

He sat down in a House seething with sensation, humming and buzzing like a hive of angry bees. No doubt there were many who were thrilling with the promised delight at revelations which might outpass all the country had guessed. As to Brummell, he clasped and unclasped his hands in a nervous agitation that made him quite unfit to expose himself to any chance meeting. It was dark now; he made his way into the streets and got back by the quietest way to his own rooms, where he shut himself in.

Sheridan did but delay until he could shake himself free of questions and comment and then almost ran to Carlton House, where the Prince was waiting in a fever of anxiety.

He sat, leaning forward in his chair, fiercely clutching at the arms of it, his full florid face purple with excitement.

"God bless you, Sheridan!" he cried with his insincere enthusiasm when the crisis was reached. "You did the best you could, but whoever would have supposed those dogs would dare raise the question as they have! The King—it's the King is behind it all—what am I to do? They have me in a cleft stick if it comes to investigation, damme if they have n't. My God, the fool I have been for a woman!"

"Why, I am afraid, Sir, it's a damned awkward business," said Sheridan, willing to say smooth things if possible, but quite unable to hide the truth. "If Fox had been there — "

"If he had, what then?" groaned the Prince. "Rolle represents public opinion against the Catholics and no power on earth can muzzle the English when they mean biting, and they mean it now. What on God's earth shall I do? I am a ruined man. No, Sheridan, the game's up! I shall never be King of England. You may fool with anything but Popery in this damned country, but a hint of that is fatal."

Then gathering his courage, Sheridan spoke out.

"That is true, Sir. Your Royal Highness never spoke a truer word. And things have now come to that pass that the marriage must be either avowed or disavowed. The question of the debts should never have come before the House lest the other terrible business should be raked up. I believe I said that when we met to discuss it at Mrs Fitzherbert's house, but your Royal Highness thought otherwise. But that being done — "

"She begged me — she entreated me on her knees not to do it," said the Prince. "Oh that I had listened to her! She has more sense in her little finger than all of you in your whole bodies."

This was unjust, as Sheridan knew. Rivers of advice had been flowing for months past, but who could persuade a fool where his inclinations were involved? He lost patience at last with the almost weeping Prince. His indecisions maddened him, his innate falseness to himself and his friends inspired nothing but an almost loathing contempt.

"If your Royal Highness will indicate the course you mean to take, your friends in the House will do their best to follow it, Sir," said Sheridan with scarcely concealed impatience. "But until we know whether you propose to avow or disavow a marriage ceremony, nothing can be done. Perhaps I had better retire and consult Fox."

He rose, and the Prince caught wildly at his sleeve.

"My dear Sheridan, you sha n't, you can't leave me," he cried, the tears brimming in his eyes as they always did in moments of emotion. "I have decided,

I swear I have. What man could give up the crown
of England for a woman? It would be forsaking my
duty to my country. Every patriot must consider
that, must he not, Sheridan? You agree with me, my
dear friend? I know you do! When I am King I shall
know how to reward such priceless fidelity as yours.
If I am ruined otherwise, at least I am rich in such
friends as you and Fox."

"What's this the prelude to?" thought Sheridan.
"What dirty work is he going to shoulder off on me
now?" He found it hard to endure the man at all.
Certainly it was not desirable from the party point
of view that the marriage should be avowed, yet
Sheridan was half frightened at the strong distaste he
felt arise within him, if some sort of justice were not
done to a woman who had trusted all to the man half
blubbering before him.

"My dear Sheridan, you are the one person whose
tact and perfect refinement I can trust on an occasion
like the present. Will you take a carriage here, and
drive across· to Mrs Fitzherbert's and prepare her
for what's coming? I have always said there is no
one who is such a gentleman as yourself, and this is
eminently a gentleman's work. She abhors Fox, as
you know, and, much as I love Fox, I own the licence
that appears nothing to men of the world repels an
elegant woman. You carry your gaieties more
lightly, my dear man. Go you now and prepare my
beloved Mrs Fitz."

Not one word would Sheridan spare him. Besides,
he knew the Prince too well to risk being thrown over

afterwards — a common danger with him. He was
therefore precise.

"Am I to tell Mrs Fitzherbert, Sir, that the marriage is to be disowned in the House? I must have
clear instructions, if you please."

"My God, no!" cried the Prince, as if genuinely
shocked. "No. Prepare her for the necessity of the
deepest secrecy and ambiguity. Tell her — but she
knows it — that it is ruin for her as well as me if it
leaks out now, when I am at enmity both with the
King and the people, and *comblé* with debt. Say all
the most feeling heart can dictate, and implore her
not to speak to me on the subject until the debate is
over. Tell her I shall have one of my attacks if I am
exposed to any more agitation than is absolutely
needful. She knows how I suffer."

Even Sheridan's acuteness could not decipher the
Prince's intentions exactly. He knew the marriage
would not be acknowledged, but for the life of him
could not see exactly how the situation must be met.
All must depend on what move the enemy might
make, and that no one could foresee.

"Thank God, that's Fox's affair!" he thought as he
devoted himself to getting a note of these instructions.
It was difficult without expressing the complete
distrust he felt, but he achieved it at last and drove
off to St James's Square, knowing that, late as it was,
he would find her waiting for her husband.

He sent up his name and found her in the drawing-
room, pale as the white rose the Prince sometimes
called her. Her bright hair in its intricate waves and

curls was more beautiful than any crown, and there was a royal grace and ease in the lines of her figure with its heavy drapery of violet velvet. She wore about her neck a locket in diamonds with the Prince's miniature.

"Mr Sheridan — Oh I have been so profoundly anxious for news from the House. You know — you must know, how averse I have been from dragging the Prince's debts there. I knew that this must happen. And now — see what we are faced with!"

"Indeed, Madam, your prescience is justified but too clearly," he answered, bowing as he drew a chair beside her. Drink, dissipation, and cruel late hours had told upon Sheridan by this time, as they did on most men of the world. The beautiful clear outline of his face was lost in a fullness of the jaw and chin that gave him ten years more than he had lived. The hair at his temples was grizzled; there were puffy swellings beneath his eyes, but their beauty survived and illumined his face with a light, sometimes melancholy, sometimes reckless, always arresting and winning beyond description. They gave, as it were, the last promise of survival of something ethereal and spiritual, when all else should be sunk in the mire of the Pit.

He told her, as he could, a part of what had taken place, said that he had seen the Prince — and paused.

"I know — I knew it could not be avowed!" she cried, but there was a piercing note that made the assertion a question. Sheridan slowly shook his head, looking at the ground.

"It would ruin him — ruin him!" she repeated, and again the words were a question.

"He would never ascend the Throne, Madam. The Duke of York would take his place."

She went so pale that he instinctively glanced at the bell. She put out her hand.

"No, no — it is all right. Mr Sheridan, I know what you say is true. This has been a carefully concerted attack. I had word of it some time ago."

"From whom? You should have told us."

"I could not tell you from whom. I never knew. But Brummell warned me."

"Brummell. Good God!"

The amazement in his voice spoke for itself. That a contemptible butterfly — for so Sheridan must hold him — should have meddled in such a matter! But there was more: had this anything to do with the quarrel that half the world had laughed at?

"How could he know, Madam?"

"I can't tell you. He warned me. He told me not to trust the Prince with the information, but to use all my influence to keep the debts from the House — to make the Prince try the King, anything rather than that. He told me if I heard no more from him it would mean they would not dare to raise the marriage question, and I might be at rest. If he warned me again, I was to tell the Prince at once. I never heard. Probably the Prince had wounded him too deeply. I see that now."

"And his price? I have almost ceased to believe in disinterestedness."

"Only the continuance of the Prince's countenance. He said it was valuable to him."

"To his despicable life it is undoubtedly. And what did you do, may I ask?"

"Worked on the Prince by every means in my power — and failed. He cut Brummell publicly a few days later. And Brummell cut me since. Whatever he knew is beyond our reach now. It may all have been idle boasting. Just to frighten me into countenancing him."

"I'll try to see him," Sheridan said. Then passing to the graver issue: "Madam, can we count on your inviolable secrecy during this matter? It is not only for the Prince's sake but your own. The Protestants are capable of raising a riot that may end in your death if this opens out."

"Sir, you need not attempt to frighten me. It is unworthy of us both. That is not the way in which to approach me."

He bowed and apologised with sincerity. The pale flush on her cheek and the light in her eyes were beautiful, almost inspired, he thought. She continued.

"I have been silent through bitter misrepresentations. You can trust me. The question is rather: Can I trust you gentlemen? You know I am like a dog with a log tied about its neck ready for drowning, if that be your will. But I think better of you than to believe you will doom a guiltless woman to worse than death."

His eyes caught fire from hers.

"Only for myself can I answer!" he said, "but,

Madam, you know your royal husband. Things will be no worse for you than heretofore. Secret the matter has been, secret it must remain until the Prince attains power. And then, if he thought as this very humble individual thinks, there should be a full reward for such a noble fidelity."

She looked at him with speechless gratitude. No need to detail the rest of the conversation. It was all reassurance on his side, all trust on hers. She liked the man; in common with most others she recognised the ethereal spark in him. He served the Prince's purpose well that night. Had Fox resembled him, had the two together dominated the Prince's sensual weakness and fear, it is possible that history might have taken a different turn. But Fox thought otherwise.

On the thirtieth of April the House of Commons was tense with apprehension and excitement, for it was known that Fox would make a statement.

With the utmost difficulty and only by a strenuous use of his waning influence Brummell had got himself into the gallery to enjoy this triumph to the full: the Prince's ruin combined with that of Mrs Fitzherbert. It was a strange consideration for any observer that this great gathering of men, eminent and otherwise, was assembled in reality for the dissection of a woman's heart and life, that her fair fame hung on their verdict, that through her the destiny of a mighty Empire was to be decided. For this question involved so many other problems of Church and State that not the wisest could foresee where it would end.

To Brummell it was merely the personal question of an individual triumph. He was dressed with even more than his usual care, and had an air of hidden exultation, which more than one noticed.

Newnham rose, the sum of his speech being to the effect that Mr Pitt was bound to explain his allusion of the previous sitting. *What* were the circumstances relating to a Royal Personage which he "should otherwise think it his duty to conceal?"

Fox rose instantly on the other's resuming his seat. His coarse face and beetling brows, the black stubble about his ill-shaven chin, all had a strangely impressive effect, as of a man so swallowed up in the business on hand as to have no time to consider his appearance or himself. His uncared-for linen, clumsy coat, and bagging stockings heightened this Jacobin touch as much as if they had been carefully studied. His voice was not so much calm as iron in its monotony. Not a trace of feeling.

He desired it to be understood, he said, that what he was about to say was by the direct authority of the Prince of Wales. There was no part of his conduct that the Prince feared to have investigated. With regard to his debt, he would give an account in writing of every branch of it.

A strained pause. Not a man stirred. All were fixed like breathing statues, listening — listening! He resumed, consulting a note in his hand. This was the other — the true issue. They waited that, straining.

"When I consider that his Royal Highness is the

first subject in the Kingdom, I am at a loss to imagine what party can have fabricated so base and scandalous a calumny, a tale in every particular so unfounded, and for which there was not the shadow of anything like reality." The whole of his debts the Prince was ready to submit to the House, and he was equally ready to submit the other circumstance. He was ready, as a Peer of Parliament in the other House, to submit to the most pointed questions which could be put to him concerning it and to afford the fullest assurances of the utter falsehood of the facts in question. What was asserted was a thing impossible to have happened.

A shiver of interest passed over the House. Could it be possible?

"No, no!" said Brummell, half aloud, leaning his chin on his arms. "They won't take it from him. They know him for the liar he is. It's a quibble. They'll see through it. Now, Rolle, on, on!"

Mr Rolle rose with cool scepticism.

"The right honourable gentleman says it is impossible this should have happened. We all know there are certain laws and Acts of Parliament which forbade it, but though it could not be done under the formal sanction of the law, there were ways in which it might have taken place, and these laws have been evaded, and yet the fact might be productive of the most alarming consequences. It ought therefore to be cleared up."

There was a sensible pause. The blood beat so fast in Brummell's eyes, with his pulses, that he literally could scarcely see Fox's figure as he rose to speak.

"Now," he thought, "it comes. The man is ruined. Fox won't dare! They've got him! I have him at last!"

Fox's voice was iron still. He drew himself up with a solemn dignity as he faced the House.

"Mr Speaker, I do not deny the calumny in question merely with regard to the effect of existing laws. I deny it in toto, in point of fact as well as law. The fact not only could never have happened legally, but never did happen in any way whatsoever, and is a base and malicious falsehood."

Mr Rolle asked whether the right honourable gentleman spoke by direct authority?

"I speak by direct authority," was the reply.

Brummell turned so sick and white that a man near him pushed a brandy flask into his hand.

He thrust it aside and concentrated fiercely on the House again.

Why tell what followed? The Prince's word, not good enough now to back a bill, was not good enough to induce many in the House to accept the denial of a fact so widely known. But it confused the issue, and it was the part of enemy as well as friend to realise what a danger was escaped, since the Prince had had the evil courage to make the denial. What party, what malice could dare to brand him publicly as a liar, even for reasons of policy?

And also those who most distrusted him knew that if Mrs Fitzherbert chose to be silent, proof of his falsehood would be almost impossible to attain.

"Audacity alone will save you!" Fox had said to him, and he was right.

Mr Rolle's manner and that of others were an insult to H. R. H. in the tumult that arose. Pitt threw oil on the troubled waters. Sheridan rose to ask haughtily if it was fair or candid that Mr Rolle should not announce himself satisfied. Rolle replied coldly that he had not announced that he was *not* satisfied. That was all they could get from him, and so the House adjourned. Brummell crept out, a stunned man.

Next must the Prince consider dealing with the woman he had thrown to the wolves and who, in his base belief, might retaliate in kind. He sent for Sheridan. Sheridan pleaded illness, and was ill in truth, so did his manhood sicken at the part he had been made to play. Fox might and did take it more lightly. What was a woman's honour compared with reasons of State? The Prince might make her a Duchess when he succeeded. Kings had always done that, and women had never refused the distinction.

Yet even Fox quailed when that night, at Brooks's, a man named Orlando Bridgman walked up to him.

"Mr Fox, I hear you denied in the House the Prince's marriage to Mrs Fitzherbert. I was present at it."

Fox shuffled off speechless, damning the Prince to all eternity in his heart. He avoided Carlton House like the pest, and presently went abroad. How meet the man who had put him in such a position! And he would have sooner faced the House again than

Mrs Fitzherbert. So the Prince was left to deal with his wife as best he might. He did it characteristically.

He called next morning, and met her with more than usual tenderness. He put his arm about her and drew her head to his breast, kissing the bright curls tenderly. He caught both her hands in his, and kissed each of them before he spoke — lightly enough to outward seeming.

"Only think, Maria, what Fox did yesterday! He went down to the House and denied that you and I are man and wife. Did you ever hear such a thing?"

Silence. He felt a quiver in the bosom his arm encircled, but not a word was said. Pale as ashes she disengaged herself and stood looking at him. He did not lack for words. There was never a crisis in life when he did not believe that words, words, would mend it and he had no more conception, could have no more conception of what a proud and pure woman might feel in such a case, than as if they had been beings of different worlds.

The marriage had been denied. Yes — he must admit that. "But then, you know, my Maria, it was not legal. We could not have asserted it was. It was canonical, but the House could never be made to see the difference. It was always a secret. It remains so. That is all we can say."

If it were so — But who could trust him? Not she, who knew him better than any living soul. There was a lie in his eyes and laugh.

Was there more? Was anything hidden?

She got rid of him and his fluency as soon as she

could, in frightful anxiety as to the real event. "I am ill. I must rest. Leave me, I entreat you," she said, and when the door was closed on his protestations, sent a message to her uncle, Mr Errington.

He came, almost as pale as herself, unspeakably dreading the interview.

"You must brace yourself, my dear niece, to bear the worst," he said. "I won't waste a word of detailing this piece of scoundrelism. Fox denied in the House, not only the marriage from a legal point of view, but in toto. There had been no ceremony. Nothing. You are the man's mistress, no more — And I was present at the ceremony. Good God! was ever such infamy!"

They stood confronting each other, and still she clutched at composure.

"But it was Fox denied it," she said in a low voice more dreadful than cries. "Men would know him unscrupulous. They would not believe it. The Prince would — "

"He denied it on your husband's direct authority. Your husband stamped you a — No, my tongue refuses it. My beloved niece, leave him. Such company defiles you and is the sole thing that can."

But she heard no more. Her knees trembled beneath her, and but that Errington caught her in his arms, she would have fallen across the table. He lifted her to the sofa, and waited till the eyelids fluttered; then he went out.

He too could not face her.

That wrong was never righted till she was dust, for

she kept silence. Whatever failed her, her truth should stand, and it stood unshaken.

Sheridan, fuming, foaming, unable to endure her public degradation, went down to the House a few days later, having assured the Prince that something must be said or done to rescue him from the character of an utter poltroon. Some word of chivalry. "No, not chivalry," he added bitterly, "for what have we to do with that? — but some phrase to rescue ourselves from such a situation." Fettered as he was, he could not speak more plainly, but now the Prince was compelled to understand a possible loss of popularity through the phrases in which Sheridan evaded the hateful truth. So he went.

Newnham withdrew his motion on the strength of Fox's assurance, and then Sheridan got up, strained and white, though he had fortified himself with spirits — the Prince's famous brandy which he called Diabolino. And even then the Sheridan brilliance had disappeared. He stammered and halted like a beginner through the dryness of his throat. The House wondered, yet possibly understood in part.

"While his Royal Highness's feelings have doubtless been considered, I must take the liberty of saying there is another person entitled in every honourable and delicate mind to the same attention, whom I will not describe or allude to except to say that ignorance or vulgar malice alone can have attempted to injure one on whose conduct truth can fix no reproach, and whose character claims and is entitled to the truest, most general respect."

It was the best he could do, but naturally men smiled at the position Fox had left her in, followed by Sheridan's lame and contradictory attempt at softening. She must be either the Prince's wife or a light woman. There was no evading facts. The game was won — and lost.

Coming out of the House, Sheridan saw Brummell walking moodily up Whitehall, evidently lost in thought. He darted across the road and after him.

"A word with you, Sir. Mrs Fitzherbert has confided in me. Why was your warning not sent? If you had in your power what you gave her to understand, let me tell you you have exposed one of the best of women to the most cruel and unmerited suffering. You are no gentleman."

"I scarcely consider Mr Sheridan a judge," said the Beau, serenely pursuing his way in the moonlight. "A man who can wear a coat cut as yours is at this moment, whose linen has quite obviously not been changed since the morning, cannot be seriously considered as a judge on that point."

Was it worth while to raise any question with a fool? That was Sheridan's thought. He must have been mistaken. Who would trust such a barber's block with a word of consequence?

"Then you assert the lady misunderstood you, Sir? Otherwise it will be my duty to call you to account very seriously."

"No person shall call me to account whose appearance precludes his accompanying me through the street," says Brummell. "But of course the lady misunderstood me. They always do. Politics is no trade for a gentleman — never was nor will be; and I will see the Prince damned before I meddle in his politics or his love affairs or anything outside the cut of his coat."

It was vain to say more. His reputation served his turn and shielded him effectually. Sheridan sheered off angrily to the other side of the street, as thoroughly baffled as by the most consummate diplomacy. A man could but make his cause absurd by brawling with such a creature as the Beau.

Brummell strolled on, a broken man. He knew the end at hand. The Prince carried the heavier guns. Man after man dropped him, his creditors gathered to the carnage, there was talk of some card scandal. He fled to Calais and to the hideous and squalid old age that those who had known him in his days of brilliance must shudder to contemplate.

The Prince belongs to History, though it should be beneath the dignity of that Muse to record his shameless marriage with the Princess Caroline of Brunswick, his scarcely more shameless amours. Best forgot, one and all. Yet let one touch of human feeling survive — a faintly flickering gleam in a very great blackness.

When he died at the age of sixty-eight, Maria Fitzherbert was a beautiful old woman. She had lived apart from him for many long years. She had refused a Duchess-ship saying calmly that she had no ambition to resemble such Duchesses. She could look back with serene detachment, the flower of a deep spiritual peace and much self-forgetfulness and care for others. No woman received more respect, from the Royal family — who knew her strange history — down to the poorest, who — only guessing it in part — knew her as an angel of charity in their need. Childless herself, she had had a child's love about her, for she adopted the granddaughter of that hapless Walpole beauty who had, like herself, married a Prince, and had had only less reason to regret it.

When George IV died, his brother, King William, returned to her in all affection the various gifts she had long ago given the dead King. One of these, a small miniature of herself set in gold and covered with a diamond, was missing. She wrote to the King, asking that enquiry might be made. The answer came: According to his directions, it had been buried with him.

There, sitting alone, crowned with white hair instead of the bright curls which had won him, she unlocked a box and spread out before her the will he had made long since and had given her to keep, in expiation of the cruel wrong done to her fidelity. She read these words: —

And I direct that the picture of my beloved wife, my Maria Fitzherbert, may be interred with me, suspended round my neck with a ribbon as I used to wear it when I lived, and placed upon my heart. To her, my Maria, my wife, my life, my soul, do I bid my last adieu.

It had been done. The great Duke of Wellington, standing beside the dead man, had seen it lying there, and with his own hand had drawn the shroud over the fair and true face that through all the black and sordid infidelities of his life had lain upon the dead man's heart. And as she read these words, the hot tears, the last he would ever wring from her, ran down her cheeks, bearing away with them all memories of pain and anger and even of those women who had dispossessed her, leaving her face to face once more and for ever with the Prince of her dreams, the lover of her youth.

Love cannot lose the reward of its own lovingness, for the things that divide are earthly and perishable, but the things that unite are eternal and can await the processes of eternity.

THE WOOING OF SIR PETER TEAZLE

SIR PETER TEAZLE

(The School for Scandal)

"FINISHED, at last, thank God!" wrote Sheridan on the last page of his play. And "Amen!" added the prompter. For the company was all assembled, and, no doubt, had learned the rest of the comedy before the author could be made to complete it.

But in spite of delays and vexatious rehearsals, the first performance, on May 8, 1777, was a tremendous success. The cast was notable, Mrs Abingdon playing Lady Teazle, and John Palmer portraying Joseph Surface "as by all accounts he has never been since and is unlikely to be again." When the screen fell, a journalist who happened to be passing the theatre ran for his life, expecting the collapse of the building from the thunderous applause.

Walter Sichel, Sheridan's biographer, says that Sir Peter "ceased to be an antique laughingstock and became a middle-aged human being" for the first time when, in Beerbohm Tree's production of the play in 1909, Miss Marie Löhr restored, more successfully than her famous but maturer predecessors, the author's conception of Lady Teazle—the country girl aspiring to be the lady of fashion. A middle-aged, and lonely, and over-credulous human being Sir Peter must have been in the period of his wooing. And the story tells how it all came about.

William Farren (1786–1861), who represents Sir Peter in our portrait gallery, was one of a famous theatrical family. He made his first London appearance in this rôle, and his name is always associated with the part.

Claton, pinxt.   Kennerley Sculpt.

Mr. W. Farren as Sir Peter Teazle

VII

THE WOOING OF SIR PETER TEAZLE

LADY TEAZLE. Did n't I refuse Sir Tivy Terrier, who everybody said
would have been a better match? For his estate is just as good as yours,
and he has broke his neck since we have been married!
SIR PETER. I have done with you, Madam!
—The School for Scandal

HARDACRE HALL, the seat of Sir Tivy Terrier in the
south of the county of Kent, was indeed as agreeable
a sight to an English eye as could be desired, so much
did it express in all its aspects what most conciliates
national character. It was a handsome mansion of
red brick with white stone facings, built in the time
of their Majesties, King William (of Orange) and his
Consort Queen Mary, of happy memory, A. D. 1692.
It offered as cheerful, homely, and sunny an air of
solid comfort as shall be met with in six months'
travel over the beauties of the Southern counties,
and at the time this veracious history opens the brick
was mellowed to a pleasingly warm tint by near
eighty years' summer suns and winter rains, and the
ivy had found foothold in the mortar and encircled
the lower windows with its garlands of polished green,
elegantly intermingled here and there with the blooms
of the China rose which supported itself on the background of the stronger creeper. The garden, which
my Lady's parlour window commanded, was laid out
in the Dutch taste with formal trimmed hedges of
yew and juniper and such old-fashioned country
flowers as did not demand the services of a new-

fangled skilled gardener and his underlings — which would have been beyond Sir Tivy's means and wishes alike, the house being, as it was, as much as he could well support on the incoming of the estate. Indeed, but for my Lady's close supervision, it could scarce have presented the neat aspect it did, and the same guardian care extended over the kitchen and herb gardens and was even more needful in those regions, as his table was a point where Sir Tivy would bear no economies; and not only the manor house itself but not a few of the poorer abodes in the village of Hardacre depended on the high-walled garden for its succulent produce. There were two days in every week when 't was ask and have, and 't was an agreeable sight to behold her Ladyship, a comely woman of fifty, with Job Morris the head gardener beside her, ordering the distribution of carrots and cabbages and such garden stuff to the rosy-cheeked boys and girls standing a-row with their baskets.

"Why should I or they be stinted?" cries Sir Tivy, his own cheeks a fair match for his hunting pink. "Don't my horses produce me a plenty of manure, and don't the Rede running by the garden give me a plenty of water, and 'baint those the two stout legs a garden stands on? No — old Aaron and Jess and their like shall never want a cabbage while Rede runs and horses breed, and I won't say but what a joint of salted pork shall go to boil with it now and again."

"Why indeed, Sir Tivy, your wish is my law," responded my Lady, standing beside him in her bunched-up gown and clogs, a big bunch of keys at her side. "All the same I'd have you to know that old Aaron is a drunken sot and Jess no better than she should be."

"Zounds, Madam, don't their poor innards want cabbage for all that? And 't is hard to blame a fellow that's lived all his life amid the finest hop fields in the world for standing to his can like a man. And as for Jess — "

My Lady interrupted here. "Have you a mind, Sir Tivy, to walk down to the farm with me? I have my clogs on, and we'll choose a good pig for killing, for you tell me Sir Peter always loved pig soused, and 't is a good dish for the sideboard if the frost should lift and the hunting come on again."

"Dash and drabbit the frost!" says Sir Tivy, who counted on the hunting for a sport for his old friend. "And yet, I know not, my Lady. Sir Peter was never a hard rider to hounds and he don't get younger with the years. He fills his saddle a bit too well now, and don't dislike the warm chimney-corner as much as he did when first I remember him."

"Well, Sir Tivy, as I have n't the honor to know the gentleman, 't is not for me to offer an opinion. But the frost is come to stay or I'm much mistook. See how hard the sky looks over Fox Brush coppice, and for all the snow's not deep, it's as crisp as salt. But will you come see the pigs?"

They trudged down through the park to the Home Farm.

"He was better with a gun," says Sir Tivy, the snow crunching under his big boots. "I don't know

as I ever saw a sweeter shot with a rocketer, and no
bad angler neither. If 't was the weather, he'd fetch
you a trout out of Rede while you'd say Jack Robinson. He was a rare one too for tickling a trout! But
I dare swear he's not what he was. A London life —
sure it makes a mollycoddle of a man, good for
nothing but to hang about in ladies' parlours and talk
whipped cream to 'em and lucky if no worse."

"Is he a personable figure of a man, Sir Tivy?"

"Why, that's all in the eye that sees, and I reckon
I'm no judge of what pleases a woman. I have n't
clapped an eye on him for eight year. But he was
well enough last time I saw him. May be a bit too
fleshy, but nothing amiss so far as I recall."

"What time to-morrow does he arrive? Janet and
Sally have his sheets airing now. We took them out
of lavender this morning. He is to lie in the brown
chamber."

"Why, the coach passes Tipton Hill at three o'clock,
and there Martin and I will meet him with the
horses, and then 't is but a flea-bite of eight miles to
ride. The roads ain't slippery, thanks to the snow.
Come along, dame; you get no lighter neither.
Well, don't pull a wry face for that. It compliments
your own providing, and you're a rare fine woman
of your years."

It was so unusual a thing to have a guest from
London at Hardacre that my Lady could scarce get
her preparations out of her head. There was abun-
dance of people coming and going from the countryside, neighboring and far-away squires with their

wives and daughters and such-like, but a London gentleman was a novelty, and she went twice over his bedchamber next day from the lavendered sheets to the pincushion stuck with *Welcome* in new pins, before she could be satisfied. But indeed there was nothing to complain of if the gentleman did not ask fashion to supplement his comforts. All was clean as country air and hands could make it, the bed billowed, stuffed with the best goose-down from the Home Farm, the fire roared up the wide chimney fed with logs cut from the heart of the best oaks the last winter's storms had felled, and sitting on the deep window-seat, the guest might command as pretty a prospect of gentle slopes, nobly wooded coppices and spinneys as heart could wish, until the eye out-passed the park and lost itself in the woodlands beyond.

"But, Lord! I mustn't stand here wool-gathering," says my Lady. "There's the dinner to be thought on, and not only Mrs Sparks but the maids need me at their shoulders. I don't know what's coming to the maids nowadays — they're such idle hussies!"

It will be seen Sir Peter's comforts were assured. And indeed he heaved a sigh of something resembling envy as, riding on a stout cob beside Sir Tivy's stouter, they came in sight of the long glade up which the house might be perceived seated on its gentle eminence.

You are now to imagine Hardacre Hall set in trees and fields all powdered with snow, the lake frozen hard, the swans wandering disconsolate in the sedges, the woods silent as death but for the startling cry of a pheasant, the tracks of Reynard, clear in the white waste, pointing to the poultry yard.

"Dash and drabbit the little red rascal!" cries Sir Tivy. "If he gets his teeth among my Christmas geese and turkeys I'll — And yet I don't know — If he was n't there the countryside would be the duller, and the rogue must live as well as the rest of us. Eh, Sir Peter?"

"Why so he must, my good Sir Tivy, and you that have so many comforts about you may spare him one once in a while to take to his vixen and cubs. Ah, that house warms a man's heart! It seems to send a glow out and round about it from those tall chimneys belching their hospitable smoke. I hear Lady Terrier is a notable woman, Sir Tivy."

"Why, not so bad! Her still-room is a sight with all the jams and jellies and cordials put away. Her sloe brandy — Ah well, you'll sample it presently. But there's more to it than that. When a man comes in tired from a long day's hunting he likes to know there's better than a hireling to warm his slippers. And when you've the gout on you — Drabbit the gout! — 't is an agreeable thing to have someone to make you a posset and put on the flannel and tuck you up snug."

Sir Peter sighed again. His house in London was cold and empty in spite of warm means. The great mahogany sideboard in the dining-room was the very tomb of all the light the wax candles could give and he had never the heart to enter the vast drawing-room upstairs. When he had a touch of the gout —

as yet 't was no worse — his housekeeper brought
the posset on a silver salver and setting it down,
respectfully retired, and there he might remain till
he grew better or died, his only diversion the visits
of his two wards, Mr Joseph Surface and Mr Charles
Surface, and the latter more of a care than a pleasure,
so spendthrift and extravagant a young fellow was
he. Reckoning up his solid comforts, Sir Peter could
not set much more to his own account than his money
and the necessaries it produced him, his sound health
(for what is a touch of the enemy?), and the moral
support of his nephew Joseph, an excellent young
man indeed.

The comforts surrounding Sir Tivy, his open,
cheerful content and the eye of mastership he cast
over his broad acres and fine house made Sir Peter
all but melancholy as he thought of that vast vault
of a house in London. Lord help us, how came his
father to buy it and saddle it on the shoulders of an
old bachelor of a son, and permit Teazleton House in
Sussex to be neglected and so out of repair? Why
here, a man could find something to amuse him all
day long in park and garden, and if — But they had
entered on the long drive and now saw every window
a-glitter with hospitable fires.

"We'll rouse my Lady and let her know we're in
sight," cries Sir Tivy, and dropping the reins, he put
his hands to his mouth and roared out such an hal-
loo that the very rooks rose in a cloud out of the elms
and went off in a black whirlwind down the woods.

At this the horses started off in a brisk canter, and

in less than ten minutes they were dismounting at the wide steps with a glow and a hunger on them that did the Kentish air infinite credit.

"That's a right welcome!" thinks Sir Peter, as Sir Tivy, taking his hand, presented him to the smiling hostess.

"Sir Peter Teazle, my Lady, and before another word be said, have out the sloe brandy and a bisket to stay his stomach till dinner be ready. Come, Molly! Susan!—Help your lady. Bestir!—The gentleman is half frozen."

'T was his heart was colder than his feet as he looked about the vast firelit hall with the reflections dancing in the polished oak until it winked again. But far more feelingly did his eye rest on her Ladyship's cheerful smile and buxom comeliness in her brown-and-gold sacque and looped petticoat and hair drawn up over a cushion and powdered, with a fly-cap of lace perched a-top. For be the hall what it would, he knew very well that beaming Madam was the soul of it all. Could he not remember it eight years since, in Sir Tivy's bachelor days, all stinking of dogs and horses and dead tobacco-smoke and dust on everything a man sat down on, and whips and fishing rods stuck all anyhow about the walls, and every odd-come-short in the world tumbling where you had no use for it? And now, all was orderly and handsome. The walls were ornamented with elegant portraits of bygone Terriers, male and female, and about them were bound the Christmas garlands of gleaming holly and laurels, and in the midst a smiling bunch of mistletoe as large as a bush, and at the far end a glorious holly-tree in a tub with such a sheen of red berries in the rich foliage as dazzled the eyes.

"Why, Madam, the pleasure's so great to visit you in your own mansion, that as the wife of my old friend I trust you'll permit me the privilege — " says Sir Peter; and taking the lady gallantly by the hand, he led her under the mistletoe and saluted her with respectful cordiality, calling up such a comely flush in her round cheek as charmed him the more. She filled the sloe brandy to the gentlemen and drank Sir Peter's health and welcome, and then departed to her household cares and left them to their long pipes and feet upon the comfortable hearth, each in his leather armchair.

Sir Peter was silent for a moment, and then it broke forth.

"You dog, you! You don't half guess your own good fortune. Why, my Lady's face is better than the fire, than the park, than your pipe and glass. If a man had *that* about him — "

"But, God bless me, Sir, what prevents you? A woman can't come up and capture your hand by force. If a thing's worth having, it's worth asking for. My Lady Terrier would n't be here if I had n't spoke the word. Gad's life, Sir, a man has himself to thank if he sits alone like a toothless mastiff snarling at all the world from his kennel. I made up my mind to marry after you was here last, and after a miss I made a fair bull's-eye, and there she goes! 'T was a Miss, by the same token!"

My Lady passed the upper end of the hall, hastening along with the housekeeper after her, and waved her hand.

"Ay, ay, that's well enough; but how about the Miss, Sir Tivy? Suppose you'd married the wrong woman after all — that would have been amiss, eh?"

"A miss is as good as a mile — and there's a joke for yours! But you're in the right. She was as pretty a little chestnut filly as ever ran for the stakes of a man's heart. But young — young! And what the devil would an old man like me do with a girl that all the beaux will be ogling? I'd have been chained in Bedlam in a year. 'T was the happiest escape ever befell me that she refused me for an old zany. But setting aside such follies, any sensible married man knows that when you're a year married, one woman's as good as another. So far as looks go. 'T is all in the way you handle 'em. Ride 'em on the curb, and they'll follow you like my Nancy mare snuffing for a lump o' sugar. Give 'em their head and you're a lost man. That's the secret!"

"What's the secret?"

"Why, let 'em know from the start you're master and more. Ah, Sir Peter, there's a woman near here, — Squire Parsons's sister, Mrs Deborah Parsons, — a clever notable woman with an eye like a razor over the maids and men, a good stockingful of savings too — if you could take a liking to her, you need never envy a man in England after!"

"The savings don't trouble me! I've enough and to spare. But would she take a liking to me, Sir, I ask you? I'm fifty to-morrow and don't care who knows it. Why should a woman engage to look after a crusty old bachelor?"

"Why, Sir Peter, they have their reasons, and some we may guess and some we may n't. But come now, putting modesty aside, ain't you a fine personable man of your years? Six feet high, and if a bit broad in the girth, she can look at your shoulders instead. If your hair's grey, who's to tell that under your wig? And you bain't no more wrinkled than an autumn pippin. And a fine house in London and a fine purse to keep it going. And to be My Lady is like sugar and honey to the women. Why there is n't a young fellow can touch you in the baits you have for 'em. I don't say but what the Miss herself — she turned up her pretty nose at me, but you're another guess sort. Heaven protect you if she took you!"

"Who is the lady you allude to, Sir?"

Sir Tivy drove the topmost log home on the fire with a dextrous dig of his heel, and it fell into the cavern beneath, scattering showers of sparks and cinders.

"Why, as dainty a little bit of Eve's flesh as ever you saw, Sir Peter. Little Melissa Parsons, the Squire's daughter. I asked her when she was sixteen, for I thought she might be glad to get away from Mrs Deborah's tutelage. That's but human nature, you know. And I offered her Hardacre and the hand of a man of forty-eight, sound in wind and limb, hale and hearty. And the little vixen would n't — She would n't, by Gad. Said she was n't worthy, was n't experienced. In short, would n't spend a look on me. So I made my bow and left her for Mrs Lucy Hawtry, the present Lady Terrier. And thank God daily for a good deliverance."

"Melissa — 't is a sweet name," says Sir Peter looking into the fire. "It has a dulcet sound like honey. Stay — did n't we learn at Oxford 'Melissa' was the Greek for a bee? The busy bee."

"The lady is as busy as any bee, Sir Peter; but you'll have the opportunity to judge to-night, for they always dine with us before Christmas Eve. A fair beauty with auburn hair, and eyes — well, they did my business, though I recovered as a healthy man will. But a perfect mistress of accompts and the spinet. The parlor at Dunton Everard is all hung with her needleworks — elegant fruit and flower pieces in wools. And sings like a linnet!"

"Why the girl's a paragon, Sir Tivy!"

"She's a very pretty blossom of a Kentish maid. But she's not for you, Sir Peter. No, no. When I made love to her father for her 't was two years ago, and you and me — we're two years older now. And 't was fool's folly then. Janiwary and May, Sir."

"So is the lady older. What age is she?"

"Nineteen next grass. No, no, Sir Peter! 'Twon't do noways. Her aunt that brought her up, Mrs Deborah Parsons, she's your mark, and lucky if you get her. 'T was all a flam about the other. Mrs Deborah's your match."

"How old is she?"

"Fifty next grass. And a comely-looking woman

in her paduasoy and mob. Seems like as if Providence brought you together along of me. She's your match."

"She may be more than my match, Sir Tivy. Could you break in that lady, do you think?"

"Why, Sir, the woman does n't breathe that I could n't break into the amble, the trot, the canter, in a month. But say no more now. Look over her paces to-morrow and form your own judgment. I declare it goes through my heart like a gimlet to think of you returning to that vast lonely barracks in London. You couple up with Mrs Deborah and settle down here. There's that neat little estate of old Dawson's going a-begging, he asks so little for it, and as good a house as this, and the cover shooting there first-rate, with his own breed of setters to shoot over. You don't want an heir, Sir Peter, you've a ready-made heir in your ward. You've only yourself to consider."

His wards the gentlemen had forgot for the moment, but this recalled them.

"Why, certainly such a marriage would please my ward, Joseph Surface. That is as worthy a young man, Sir Tivy, as you would see in a day's march. Grave, sober, considerate. 'T was only t'other day he says, 'Why, Sir Peter, do you not find a spouse that would be a valuable woman and comfort your declining years? All who love you must wish to see you settled with a staid reliable woman to consult your comforts. Let her not be young, I beseech you, for the young women of the present day would bring down your grey hairs with sorrow to the grave.

Expensive, extravagant, luxurious dolls, with never a household thought in their empty noddles, and mere butterflies of fashion and folly. O Sir Peter,' says he, throwing up his eyes, 'I could not bear to see my worthy protector the prey of such vultures. The man who could endure such a sight with composure would be but a villain and a coward, that had not the courage to speak his mind in time and save his honored relative from such a fate.' "

"Ay, no doubt he was in the right. 'T is not often you find young men so considerate. What said the other?"

"Charles? Why, Charles never gave the matter a thought till Joseph broached the matter, and then says he, laughing: 'Don't you heed him, Sir Peter, with his sanctimonious long face! Don't you run in harness with a woman of fifty, the milk of human kindness all soured to lemon juice. Did n't King David pick up a pretty little Jewess to keep him warm when his first bloom was long gone off — and if he was n't Solomon, he was his father and passed for a wise man. You had best secure something you like to look at first thing in the morning and last thing at night. They 're as good as the sour old maids when 's all said, and a sight pleasanter about a man. "Here's to the maiden of bashful fifteen!" says I.' That was Charles's verdict."

"Ah — young and foolish!" says Sir Tivy, wagging his head. "Joseph for me! He has n't his name for nothing. I warrant him. He knows the sex. But come, Sir Peter. I 'll squire you to your room, for the bell will sound for dinner by the time you're in trim for it."

Later, in the hall outside sat Sir Tivy in his elbow chair, watch like a gold warming-pan in hand, for the guests were ten minutes late, — a serious default, — and my Lady was tripping anxiously between the door and fire, Sir Peter doing his best to cheer the interval with talk and jest.

Lord! the relief when the crunching of wheels was heard, the hoofs deadened on the snow, and then the hospitable door flung open and the ruddy firelight streaming out over the black-and-white without, and the stream of fresh frosty air that accompanied the ladies all hooded and rolled in furs, their little breaths steaming as they entered!

What need to tell of the hand-wringing, the congratulations, the curtseys and kisses to my Lady, and the hearty welcome to Squire Parsons, and the account of how the off-wheeler shyed at the gallows on Deadman's Moor and delayed them the ten minutes with the flurry of it.

The dinner, it must be owned, confirmed Sir Peter's longing for the comfort of the presiding genius of a home.

The paneled oak of the dining-room, supporting branches of sconces for candles, was also garlanded with holly, and even the casque of the Sir Alured Terrier that fought in the Low Country wars had sprigs stuck in the vizor. The huge fire was dancing in the polish of the great cabinets and the backs of the oak chairs, and the red velvet curtains were drawn close against the cold. What shall match old English Christmas hospitality and plenty?

Sir Peter bethought him again of his melancholy London house, as with loud laughter and jest Sir Tivy led the way, squiring Mrs Deborah by the hand, and he himself followed with the pretty slip of a girl, and Squire Parsons brought up the rear with my Lady.

'T was not till they were at table he had leisure to survey the newcomers, but especially the elder madam.

Sir Tivy had not over-rated her mature charms. She was a grave discreet woman of fifty, of comfortable proportions yet not obese. Her features were not amiss, and neither faulty nor handsome enough to vex the hearts of her neighbours. Her grey hair was drawn over a cushion with rolled cannon curls at each side, a chain with a cameo decorating it in front below the mob. She was dressed in a quilted satin gown of sober purple with stiff pointed stomacher and bodice, an underdress of lutestring over the wide hip-hoops of the last reign. A fresh country color bespeaking health, and a glance of the eye bespeaking authority, from being so long Prime Minister of all her brother's concerns, completed the portrait of the lady. He was a cheerful-complexioned gentleman of florid habit, but no especial note save for a fine breed of Berkshire pigs introduced in the best porcine society of the Weald.

But Miss! Miss was as silent and shy as one of the flowers in the park, could such be introduced

into company. Her muslin gown with blue ribbons —
't was too simple to be either old- or new-fashioned,
and all Sir Peter could judge was that white became
very well the fine healthy flush she brought in from
the frost. Her hair was a lovely chestnut, resembling
that of the pictures he recalled in Italy on making
the Grand Tour, and was rolled up like her aunt's
over a cushion, but the curls tumbling loose at the
sides from the blue riband that attempted to control
their luxuriance. Add to this a pair of cherry lips set
in with a dimple at each corner, and a little nose over
which Venus had concerned herself personally before
she turned her attention to the eyes for her master-
piece; and there it must be owned the goddess took
her own for pattern, so blue they were, under gold-
tipped lashes, with such melting profundities of azure
and demure sparkles concealing the dangerous deeps
beneath!

Not indeed that Sir Peter saw all this at a glance.
'T is to be owned his first thought was that the young
lady's arms and hands were somewhat sunburnt and
freckled, and he merely concluded her a pretty
hoyden, if better dressed out. The dinner was of
more moment, for his ride had brought him a lusty
appetite.

And here my Lady Terrier had as far excelled
herself as Madam Venus with Miss Melissa's countenance. The oaken board, solid as it was, groaned
beneath the noble first course.

Boiled fowls, bacon and greens before Sir Tivy, a
sir-loin of beef roast before my Lady, and she so

busy in carving she had scarce a word for the Squire.
In the midst, a glorious plum pottage, with removes
of minced pies and a chine and turkey on either side.
It might not be the mode. Indeed, in fashionable
circles in town the taste veered to kickshaws in the
French style; but here in this oaken dining-room, and
the winter sky low over Hardacre Hall, Sir Peter's
appetite admitted it a fine old English dinner; and
when the second course followed with a goose roast,
a great dish of woodcocks and snipes, with patties of
lobsters from Folkestone at one side and broiled
sweetbreads to match, and a gallant pear-pie creamed
in the midst, he could but compliment my Lady from
his heart on her cook and her invention. She received
the general applause most graciously, scarce pausing
to eat herself for her assiduity in serving her guests.

"Alas, the generous old roast and boiled!" says Sir
Peter. "They are vanishing with all the cheerful
venerable customs of the past. 'T is much if I can
persuade my housekeeper that I would have good
English meat simply cooked, in preference to all the
French ragouts and fricassees. But I'm forced to
endure it, for if I leave my own table I meet the same
foreigners at the houses of all my friends."

"Why, Squire, I spent my time before dinner
persuading Sir Peter that until he bespoke a notable
English wife he would have neither English dinners
nor English comforts," cries Sir Tivy, with a side
glance at Mrs Deborah.

"The dull old fogeys!" thinks Miss to herself,
fastidiously picking the bones of her snipe. "Caring

for nothing but eating and drinking! And who would marry that old gentleman in his plum-color velvet and old-fashioned brush-wig! I dare be sworn he has some glum country grange down Sussex way and lives there year in and year out like a moth in a blanket. 'T will be scarce less dull in the family vault. If he would but carry my Aunt Deborah to share it with him! But 't is too much to hope."

"When I came from town," began Sir Peter, and oh how the blue eyes flashed up at him in hearing that enchanting word. Town! 'T was what the fair Melissa dreamed of night and day. Whenever an old news-print strayed its way to Dunton Everard, it was there her eye fell and fastened. The shops, the lace-women that sell fine ribands and head-dresses, the routs, the masquerades and ridottos and what not, in these was all her recreation. But not a word escaped her; 't was as much as her place was worth, for Mrs Deborah was a starched Churchwoman and firmly believed the great Devil walked unabashed through London streets. The country for virtue, if a woman can but close her eyes to the truth!

But as Sir Peter spoke of the charming town, he had the eagerest listener by his side and knew it not. The downy lashes were sealed on her cheek, her eyes on her plate, silent as became so young a woman in the presence of her elders, but through that golden screen she peeped more than once at the gentleman who had the good fortune to attend the King's levees, to see the Queen's coach go by, and all the brave ladies attending a Birthnight celebration. Indeed she could have listened for ever to such music, and under all her sweet smile was not best pleased when Sir Tivy summoned in the waits from their plum pottage in the kitchen to regale the company with carols, and this done, called on them to bear the chorus and prepared to indulge the company with a song — none of your puling modern sentimentalities, but a good old Tudor English ballad with a chorus to cut and come again.

" 'T is the song of the man that went a wooing in Kent," says he, with an eye on Sir Peter, and broke forth in a good windy bass: —

> 'I have a house and land in Kent,
> And if you'll love me, love me now.
> Two pence half-penny is my rent,
> I cannot come every day to woo.'
> (*Chorus*) Two pence half-penny is his rent,
> And he cannot come every day to woo.

> 'I will put on my best white slops
> And I will wear my yellow hose,
> And on my head my good grey hat
> And in 't I'll stick a lovely rose!'
> (*Chorus*) And on his head a good grey hat,
> And in 't he'll stick a lovely rose.

> 'Wherefore cease off, make no delay,
> And if you'll love me, love me now!
> Or else I'll seek some other where,
> For I cannot come every day to woo.'
> (*Chorus*) Or else he'll seek some other where,
> For he cannot come every day to woo.

"That song was sung when the Eighth Harry was on the throne," says Sir Tivy, "and the lesson is as

good now as then. Let every fair lady know her
own mind, and catch Time by the forelock, for he's
bald behind. And that's poetry, though I did n't
mean it so!"

"Ah, neighbor, that's not the way to tempt the
young women now," cries Squire Parsons. "What do
they care for a mouldy old grange in Kent? I dare
swear my young Miss here would turn the honest
gentleman off with a flat No if he offered her no better
than that. Here, daughter, sing the company the
song you got from the chapman last time he came our
way. 'T is a very different guess sort from Sir Tivy's.''

Miss parleyed and pleaded she loved only country
songs and had no taste for town grandeurs. She
swore her pretty oath of yea and nay that she could
not, would not sing, and then was forced to by her
father and a stern look from Mrs Deborah, and piped
up in a small flute-like voice that assorted with the
innocent blue of her eyes: —

> When his Grace of Leeds shall married be
> To a fine young lady of high quality,
> How happy will that gentlewoman be
> In his Grace of Leeds' good company!
>
> She shall have all that's fine and fair,
> And the best of silk and satin to wear,
> And ride in a coach to take the air,
> And have a house in St. James's Square —

"No! my papa, indeed I can't!" says Miss, breaking off. "I can't sing before fine London company —
it frights me so!"

Sir Peter did his best to reassure the tender thing,

but to no purpose, and the rest of the evening past in Pope Joan and backgammon, the young lady taking her part with so much good-humor that Sir Peter concluded her the sweetest simple country lass, the very queen of curds and cream. Indeed, as he talked with Mrs Deborah, his eye travelled frequently to the young head, so fresh against the ancient pictures.

The Parsons family lay there that night on account of the snow, and when they met next morning, even the white pall outside could not shame Miss Melissa's glowing cheeks and ivory neck. She past the morning over my Lady's tambour-frame showing her a stitch in woolworks learned from old Madam Bumbleby of Snoreton House, and drew her two patterns for ruffles, rejoining, on her thanks, that she had no lace or cambric of her own to make them up and could wish to see how the device became my Lady.

"We have nothing gay nor pretty down here," she added, with a melancholy which obliged Sir Peter to say with a flourish that on looking on the three Graces before him, he could not subscribe to that opinion.

'T was when Sir Peter joined the other two gentlemen to consider the pigs at the Home Farm and the hounds later, — no scent lying for hunting, — that the conversation took a turn of more interest to Miss.

"What think you of Sir Peter Teazle, Mrs Parsons?" asks my Lady, stitching at Susannah's nose in her tambour-work of Susannah and the Elders.

"Why — that he is a very genteel-looking man of his age; and he hath an agreeable flow of talk. A widower, I conclude?"

"No, Madam, an old bachelor, and wearies of the single state," answers my Lady, under instructions from Sir Tivy. "He has a fine house in London and good means to match it. A warm comfortable man, and no heir but two young gentlemen wards. Luckily his affections are much engaged with them both, so that's no care to him. But his little comforts! My heart bleeds to think of a housekeeper lining her pockets with his ignorance, for all passes through her hands. Lord! what's a man but a sheep for fleecing to such gentry!"

"And nothing to show for it. You say true, Madam. But, your Ladyship, hath Sir Peter no sister, no female cousin to oversee matters?"

"Not a female relation in the world, Madam. He knows his solitude most feelingly, says Sir Tivy. As for his wards, they are brothers, but differ astonishingly. Joseph Surface, the elder, is all solid worth, and thinks not of himself, urging Sir Peter to take a wife to comfort his declining years, if so be as he chooses wisely, rightly urging that what he needs is a staid kindly woman notable in housekeeping and management to look after his affairs."

" 'T is a generous motion, since a jointure would stand in his own light."

"Why, as to that, we may consider that he might dread Sir Peter taking a young wife to bring him an heir, and we all know the saying of half a loaf being better than no bread. Still, I own the good sense. Mr Charles Surface, the younger brother, a ranting roaring extravagant young man, exhorts his uncle to please himself and consider beauty as well as worth, but nobody marks him."

"Is he a well-looking man, your La'ship?" puts in Miss Melissa.

"Sir Tivy declares him as handsome a beau as any in London, but sadly in debt. O, child, if ever you wed, choose good sense in preference to good looks. Not but what Mr Joseph Surface is a well-looking man, they say, in a sober way of shining."

"I wish they were down here also," sighs Miss Melissa. "I weary for a dance. I have not shaken a foot since the last race ball, and you know, Madam, when that was!"

My Lady kindly checked the frown on Mrs Deborah's brow. "Oh, Madam, girls will be girls. Don't I remember when you loved a country dance as well as any, and made a most elegant figure in it! I don't decry Miss's good looks when I say she has still to pass what her aunt was at eighteen."

This compliment being graciously received, and Miss leaving the room, her aunt took occasion to satisfy herself still further concerning Sir Peter's means.

"Why, indeed they are excellent, Madam, and the poor man himself's alive to his solitary state. I understand, though not plainly said, that he's down here to look for a wife, knowing too much of the London ladies to trust himself in such hands."

It may be supposed Sir Peter was kindly received when he returned from the farm with the gentlemen and found waiting each a tankard, mulled, of the best

October ale, five quarters of malt to the eighteen
pounds of hops, and three or four over for luck.
A warming and comfortable beverage, of a chill
December day.

And when the Parsons family left 't was not without cordial invitations to their kind hosts and guest
for a return visit at Dunton Everard.

Sir Peter returned to London when the Christmas
and all its rejoicings were over, but not the man he
came, for he carried a dart in his breast, not of Love's
choosing, though the heart of fifty be no more exempt
from the bow of that universal archer than from that
of his brother with the skull and cross-bones; 'T was
the dart of discontent, and his great house never
appeared so dull to him. His foot sent an echo flying
up the stairs, and when he sneezed after his rappee,
a ghostly regiment, sneezing, answered him from the
top landing. He smelt strong waters moreover on
Mrs. Housekeeper's person when she came for orders
and had reason to suppose from a neighbour's complaint that there had been unseemly noise and riot
to spare in keeping the Christmas during his absence.
As he sat, looking at the ruby reflection of his glass
of port in the mahogany, he imagined Mrs. Deborah,
staid and agreeable, smiling in vision beside it. He
saw the fair Melissa duteously attending her aunt
and receiving her admonishments soberly.

"If I married the aunt, I could condition to have
the niece about us," he thinks to himself, filling again.
"Miss would bring a little life into the house, for all
she's such a quiet sensible young thing. And who

knows but she might n't take a liking to my worthy
Joseph or even to Charles and raise up a posy of
young ones about us. 'T is certain when old Parsons
goes, she 'll have what he can 't take with him. I 'll
sound Joseph, as sure as I live."

It was pursuant to this resolve that Mr. Joseph
Surface and Charles Surface dined the next day with
Sir Peter and heard his account of his Odyssey to
the country — for 't was little less, with the miry
roads and no-roads. It might perhaps add zest to
his feelings that the fine umble pie he counted on
from the umbles of the venison he brought up from
Hardacre was spoilt in the dressing by Mrs. Housekeeper's drunkenness, and the salpicon so full of
pepper as it brought tears to his eyes and was forced
to be sent from table.

"I swear by Heaven," cries Sir Peter, "that it
makes a man sick of his life to be paying wages to
these rascally women and men that batten on a
man like mites in cheese and do as little for it."

"You should marry, Sir Peter. Did n't I always
say so?" says Charles, gay and handsome in his
laced coat of lavender velvet with ruffles and flowered waistcoat. He wore the fashionable black ribbon
about his neck to set off his fair complexion and
appeared as handsome and dashing a young fellow as
heart could wish. Indeed, his silk stockings showed
the handsomest leg in London, so adjudged even by
the Macaroni ladies. Joseph, older and graver, was
in a handsome black suit embroidered in steel, with
much lace about the throat and wrists, a personable

man too, his bag-wig and powder setting off good features and address.

"Marry!" says Sir Peter, willing to test them. "I hope I'm no coward, and have given my proofs as well as another, but marriage —"

Charles winked upon his brother.

"Why, Sir Peter, what's to fear in a little downy nestling beauty, all softness, smiles, and kisses, that will weep if you raise your finger and smile if you do but pronounce her name kindly. Does not Miss Maria Goodchild, your old friend's daughter, raise your opinion of the sex? Sure you never feared her?"

"Maria is not my wife but my god-daughter, Sir, and as long as she consults her father with regard to her choice her doings in marriage concern me not. But a pretty object should I be with a gay young wife tagging after my rheumatic bones."

"Indeed, Sir Peter, you speak with your wonted wisdom," says Mr Joseph, pushing aside his nuts, and refilling his glass, "A young wife is the very devil, as many worthy men here know to their cost. Since the Macaroni Club was founded, there's more elderly husbands have lost their peace of mind through young wives than would people the Colony of Massachusetts with loyalists for rebels. Look at poor Lord Buffalo! and as for Sir Thomas Splint — I declare, the man who could not feel for such sufferings is worthy to be turned into a pillar of salt like Lot's wife for his insensibility."

Mr Charles, however, laughed till he was obliged to dry his eyes with his fine laced handkerchief.

"Why, as to Lord Buffalo, Sir Peter — that's a precious circumstance if you heard the rights of it! He had himself an assignation at the house where he met his lady likewise engaged, and 't is suspected the happy lover is no other than — "

"Charles, Charles, for Heaven's sake — you're spilling your wine over your ruffles!" cries Mr Joseph in a violent hurry, interrupting the information, and Mr Charles laughing more heartily than ever, Joseph takes the chance to cut in.

"Why, Sir Peter, it must be perhaps owned that Lord Buffalo has not much to reproach my Lady with; and to be sure your own worthy heart would never give your lady cause to retaliate. Yet consider Sir Thomas Splint! I don't imagine even Charles can excuse Lady Splint's conduct to so valuable a man."

"Why as to that, Sir Peter, her Ladyship is as arrant a little jilt as ever flirted a fan, and if a worthy man is a fool he as surely runs up a score that Fate will pay as the knave. Indeed surer, for the knave may find a way out, but the fool never. Is n't Sir Thomas Splint a fool, Sir Peter? Have n't I often heard yourself lament the circumstance? and a man like that to choose a young, pretty woman! Why, Minerva herself, if he had married her, couldn't have kept him from misfortune. His prosing dullness would have driven her to keep company with Mars — and poor Lady Splint did no worse."

"Well, Charles, you're very ready to laugh at your neighbours' misfortunes, but might like your

own none the better. Would you have any pity on
me if I went the way of all flesh? for so it may be
called nowadays?"

"Indeed, Sir Peter, you'd find me decorum itself
where a Lady Teazle kicked over the traces, but I
vow I see no more chance of it than of my paying my
tailor. A man with your looks, with your means,
and your easy agreeable temper — why, what's to
fear? I swear I'll be the lady's cicerone myself and
keep every pretender off with my cane!"

"Charles is ever heedless, Sir Peter," says Mr
Joseph very seriously, "and we are not to take his
jests for earnest. His heart is better than his words.
But if you should consider the matter gravely, —
and Heaven knows I have often pressed it on your
consideration, — I entreat you by all that's honest
to go warily, for in this town the state of morals is
deplorable. The man who could view it without
alarm must have a soul insensible to the degradation
of his country and the sufferings of his friends. Look
at Lady Betty Curricle — what man of spirit would
have his lady driving all the day in Hyde Park with
Sir Benjamin Backbite and sitting up all night with
scandals and cards, and well she's no worse occupied.
Lord, what would be my grief if I saw you so used!
A creature of your sensibility and goodness so treated,
I declare the very thought overcomes me."

"Don't cry, Joseph — Hold up!" says Mr Charles,
clapping him on the back. "Sir Peter isn't damned
in a fair wife yet. Every woman isn't a Lady Betty,
and sure you may credit him with a grain of common

sense. Don't let him fright you, Sir Peter. And here's poor Maria, your god-daughter, mewed up with a gouty old father. If you provided a playmate for her of her own age, eighteen or thereabouts, you could take the poor thing into your own home and make much of her instead of leaving her with a crusty old invalid that makes her miserable."

"So then I am to marry to make a home for my god-daughter," says Sir Peter. "Little would I have accepted the trust had I thought it involved the immolation of my own peace of mind. Still — "

"Well, Sir Peter, if doubtful, why not take Joseph wife-hunting with you? You'll never be utterly undone with any lady he approves, for his sentiment is only equalled by his prudence."

"Your jeer is truer than you allow, Charles," says Sir Peter gravely. "And I only wish your feather-head had but a little of the same ballast as your brother's. Could you but pretend to his judgment — "

"Why then, you'd entrust me to choose a Lady Teazle. No, Sir Peter, drunk or sober, I have at least too much judgment for that undertaking; but I'll wish you, with the Prayer-book, a happy issue out of all your afflictions."

There is no doubt but this conversation helped to form Sir Peter's resolution, or to use Mr Charles Surface's idiom, greased his wheels. Yet he took time to consider further, and in the budding Spring, when all things go a-wooing, he posted down to Dunton

Everard, having recalled himself to the agreeable recollections of Mrs Deborah Parsons and the Squire, and pleading a wish to enjoy their good company.

O how smiling lay the prospect before him! The trees in all their vernal leafage, the birds singing on every spray, and all the meads enamelled with flowers. The garden a mass of daffadillies dancing in the sunshine. Cold and dull would be the heart that did not expand in such charming circumstances, and Sir Peter's was neither.

He leaned out of his post-chaise to inhale the perfumed air, and so caught a glimpse of the prettiest dairy-maid ever beheld, tripping across the avenue, with her figured linen gown pulled up through the pockets and disclosing a flowered chintz petticoat and slender ankles and feet. They caught his eye first, and then the chestnut hair shining in the sunshine playing through the young leaves. 'T was the work of a moment to pull the check-string and descend, ordering the chaise to proceed to the house.

"Why, my child — why, Miss Melissa, how do you? But need I ask? I thought 't was the very Spring herself tripping along under the trees. Your eyes are bluer, your cheeks rosier than ever!"

Greatly fluttered, the young lady dropt her pretty curtsey.

"Sir Peter, I'm just ashamed to see you thus. Hetty the milk-maid has sprained her ankle and I've been a-milking Daisy myself. Had I known you would be so early, I'd have put on my company gown. Mercy on me — look at my hair!"

Indeed 't was worth the pains: every curly thread fluttering a red-gold mist about her head. The daffadillies themselves were not so fresh and gay. Her lips — are rosebuds warm and vocal? For if not, how dare they be compared to those speaking flowers? Her eyes — the sky may be clouded, but nought can dim that Summer azure. Indeed all natural comparisons fall short of a lovely young woman bent on making herself agreeable.

Sir Peter relieved her of the pail, and they lingered under the elms.

"Are you sorry to see me, young Madam?" says he in a jest. She clasped her hands.

"O if you could but know how glad! The winter — I thought 't would never end! My Aunt Deborah — her rheumatics have made her temper — Lord! what do I say! 'T is most undutiful in me, but indeed — "

"Rheumatics? — Mrs Deborah suffers from rheumatics?"

"I think Dr Slop calls it gout, but sure 't is the same thing, is n't it?" says Miss innocently. "Indeed, my poor aunt has been a martyr all the winter, though she would keep about. But don't speak of it, dear Sir Peter, for she would not have it known."

'T was damping for so thriving a wooer, but he promised. The gout! That should be a monopoly of the men.

"And yourself, my child — how has the winter used you?"

"Very busily, Sir Peter. Superintending the poultry. You shall see the results. I have six broods of the finest pullets ever you saw, and as for my turkeys — If you won't think it beneath you, I'll show you my little families!"

"Beneath me! Could there be a more charming sight in all England than a young lady so usefully employed and with all her feathered favourites about her?"

"Yes, Sir Peter, indeed 't is my aim to be useful, as my Aunt Deborah ages. Who shall take her place if not I? And indeed we have a turkey poult for dinner to-day, with Folkestone oysters after the Dutch fashion and a quaking pudding after it, made with my own hands, and a maiden cream from the dairy. But Lord, look how I talk as if I had known you all my days! Why are you so kind that you will bring it on yourself?"

Sir Peter was charmed. Such housewifely good sense in such a fair young creature! Perfection added to perfection. He told her so, and she listened seriously, with the modestest smile.

"O, but Sir, 't is time I took thought. I grow old. Do you know — I shall quit my teens and be twenty next year? I hope I have profited by my Aunt Deborah's sermons. She preaches all day long, and if I found it wearisome when I was young, I see and acknowledge my obligation now."

"Then, my child, you have passed all your life with elderly persons. Don't you crave for the society of the young?"

"We can't crave for what we don't know, Sir

Peter. I see my cousin Sophy occasionally, but don't love to talk with her; she's a giddy gipsy."

"And you see no young men, Madam?"

"Lud, Sir Peter, no! Sure all are gone to the wars, or for ever frequenting the fairs, and for my part, I don't miss them."

"And no bees to hover round this charming flower?"

Miss simpered prettily. "Well, Sir Peter, if Sir Tivy may be called a bee — But sure you would only compliment me."

"My dear, I am aware of that attachment," says Sir Peter seriously. "May I presume to enquire your reason for refusing so eligible a match? Your modesty and charming looks interest me in all that concerns you. Was it his age repelled you?"

The milkmaid hung her head with the coyest grace. "His age? O no, no, Sir Peter! You may see the course of my life made that no objection whatever. I could have respected as well as preferred him, and is not that best for a wife?"

"Indeed it is, my dear. Every word you speak is a pearl of good sense. The husband must be looked up to. Then 't is probable that, weary of the country, you pine for the delights of the town?"

"You know me little, Sir, if you judge thus," says Chloe, her sweet eyes beaming fond assurance at her elderly Strephon. "No, my little round of duties leaves me no time to be tedious. I will tell you the truth, with your kind promise not to reveal it to my papa, who was eager at one time for the match.

'T was that Sir Tivy is such a hard rider to hounds that I dared not run the daily risk of losing one I should grow to esteem. 'T is me for a feeling heart, Sir Peter, and were my husband to go before me, I could but break it and die."

The voices of the doves in the great pigeon-cote hard by were not more tender, and the corner of her little lip trembled. He was obliged to take her hand for comfort.

"Why, my dear, your consideration is far beyond your years. And could you indeed have become so far attached to a man of Sir Tivy's age as to regret him thus, had you been his wife? O, a country breeding for virtue and sensibility! Why, child, you will hardly believe it, but the aspiration of every fashionable young woman is to be a widow?"

"To lose all her earthly comfort, Sir? And for what? Surely you mistake?"

"No, child. 'T is too true. That they may be their own mistress and worse. O, the iniquity — But who's this I see come from the house?"

"My Aunt Deborah!" cries Miss, seizing the milk-pail. "O, she will so rebuke me for delay! Come, Sir Peter. She must not walk far. You will observe she goes lame of one leg. And I would not rouse her temper for worlds!"

Mrs Deborah was advancing briskly, and if she went lame 't was so little as to be imperceptible to Sir Peter unless he had been informed. He advanced to meet her, bowing.

"Madam, your most obedient. I trust I see you in

charming health, but need not ask, you look so becoming."

Mrs Deborah's countenance was all smiles, and her welcome of the warmest, and she and the guest walked together to the house, Miss hurrying before them.

"That naughty chit is unpardonable to delay you, Sir Peter, and you fatigued from your journey. The most heedless little feather-brain, and keeps me running after her all day long. She reads and thinks of nothing but romances and the modes, and her head's stuffed so full of nonsense that there's no room for a grain of sense."

Indeed to hear Mrs Deborah talk one should suppose there was as much trouble to keep Miss to her sampler and her duties as to take a pig to market, a difficulty that needs no description. And as they reached the house she concluded thus: —

"As I always tell my brother, her best hope is marriage. These giddy girls never settle down till they are wives and must face the realities of life."

"Is it not true, Madam, that our friend, Sir Tivy, was a suitor for Miss's hand?"

"It is true, Sir, and I own to but a poor opinion of Sir Tivy's judgment in consequence. A man of his age, to consider allying himself with a mere chit of a girl that's thinking of nought but pleasures and how to avoid her duties —what sensible man of his years could form such a notion? Sure he could but be universally ridiculed if it had been brought to bear. My Lady Terrier was a suitable helpmeet, and so he now owns. Disparity of age in marriage is moonstruck madness."

Sir Peter agreed with his voice and his reason, but some little unnamed traitor within would hear neither, but persisted in depicting Miss's nets of shining hair, and the smiling eyes beneath it. Her skin, fine and fair as a privet flower, could bear the sunshine on it without painful disclosures, and so much could not be said for Mrs Deborah's respectable countenance. Youth triumphant attended by Venus and the Graces — sure it must be a losing battle against it unless the heart is panoplied in steel. And Sir Peter had been a gallant man in his youth, known in the green-rooms as well as the withdrawing rooms of London. There were memories to contend with as well as hopes in his case.

Squire Parsons, with a gouty leg well swaddled on a rest, bestowed a hearty welcome on the guest and was well pleased to secure company and talk for a fortnight.

"For look you, Sir Peter," says he, " 'T is all very well down here while a man can keep about his estate, what with the beasts, the arable, and the dairy, and market days, fairs, and so forth, but what's to do when he's laid by? If it was n't for a cheerful glass and good company I should be in a glouting humor indeed. Still, I would not have you confine yourself, Sir, with a poor invalid. Miss can give you a lead 'cross country as well as her dad. She is a fine seat on a horse, though her father says it."

It fell into that, for Sir Peter was eager for horse

exercise for his figure's sake, the good country fare, the cream, and pea-fed bacon putting on him two pounds in the first week, and Miss was but too willing to quit her tasks and become a Dian for his sake. There Mrs Deborah could not supervise them as at home, and would stand on the steps of the Hall, shading her eyes to see them go, with a smile intended to be pleasant but flavored with green gooseberries and verjuice.

Who but Miss in her glory, flying over hedge and ditch with bright hair streaming and bright cheeks flushed to set off yet brighter eyes! But no Miss Hoyden for all. The quiet good sense of their first meeting pervaded all her words. She lamented feelingly to Sir Peter, when they drew bridle on Harkaway Hill, that Mrs Deborah should be as short in her temper as long in body.

"For," says she earnestly, "I would have you know that I do all my possible to conciliate her, as I am in duty bound, and still to no purpose. O, Sir Peter, you are a man and full of bravery and resolution, yet if you had to read sermons to my aunt daily, I think you would weary of it."

"I think so too," says Sir Peter edging his horse nearer, that he might take the fair hand lying on the saddle-bow, "yet I think moreover that the sermons and Mrs Deborah between them have turned you into a little angel before your time. My child, I know the world well and can tell you 't is seldom indeed beauty is to be found in company with right notions!"

"Beauty! I'm no beauty!" Her smile was quite delightful in its pretty contempt of her looks.

"Ask your looking-glass else! But my experiences with your sex — alas, many — tell me how rare a jewel shines at Dunton Everard."

"Lord, Sir Peter, you mistake sadly. But tell me — have you ever been in love?"

"Have you, my pretty maid?" says he, parrying.

"Mercy on me, never! Who should I be in love with? I don't even guess what it means. That's why I ask. What are the signs?"

To instruct a fair vestal in the symptoms of the ailment were a fine occupation for a lovely day in Spring, with all the copses and hedgerows set with primroses and violets and the frail windflower, and the cuckoos calling softly from immeasurable distances over Harkaway Hill. But before he could reply, the lady had flashed away from the subject and was pointing out a silver gleam of the sea far away, and when he would recur to it, she had the old windmill on the height to show him, and again the ruins of Tilton, and so forth. And the more she sidled and shyed at it, the more eager became Sir Peter to instruct her.

Poor Mrs Deborah, at home, stitching at her pinners, stood but a poor chance with Sir Peter exposed to the assault and battery of Miss Melissa's youthful airs and graces, combined with the charms of a sweet companionship on such a day and in such a place as Harkaway Hill.

He coaxed the charmer back to the subject as the horses stood side by side on the height, and recalling old memories, depicted the anxieties of the tender passion in a manner the most pleasing.

"It is to long for the company of one, to feel the soul expand in that dear society as in no other, so that either in silence or in speech there is still a perfect understanding and sweet companionship. It is — "

"O, but no, Sir Peter, sure it can't be that," says Miss, very seriously, "for why I think not — You see, that is what I feel for you; for indeed you are the only person I ever cared to talk with in all my life. So that can't be love. No — tell me what you felt in your first passion."

'T is to be judged that Sir Peter was flattered by this innocent avowal. Indeed, whatever his power of describing the symptoms verbally, he experienced them, for his heart fluttered like a boy's. But he would not be hasty. And perhaps a little willingness to have the lady suppose him desirable and not too easily conquered might be a motive.

"My dear," he replied gravely, "this is certainly a symptom in combination with others. But my first passion — alas, you recall painful memories. I was a young man then and judged not unprepossessing, and a lady fixed her heart on me — But no! A man of my age must appear ridiculous in young eyes. Take it, my child, that I never was loved nor loved, and let the past be past."

But she entreated so movingly and in such sweet melting accents to hear those tales of love (" 'T is like reading a wonderful romance!") that he yielded and recalled such scenes as showed the fair Melissa very plainly that Sir Peter had moved in circles of the first fashion, and that even great ladies had not disdained to cast a compassionate eye on his pangs. Even while she sighed to hear the amorous tale, she noted these matters for reflection, and, had he but known it, was as complete and finished a little coquette as any he described flaunting their silks and satins along the Mall.

But though he never suspected this fact, there was a lady at Dunton Everard who did, and as the rides and the strolls under the elm trees — when, to be sure, the stories of ancient gallantries were resumed — grew more frequent, this lady grew more uneasy. Two powerful motives were at work in her heart. The one to see the charming Melissa safely wooed and wedded, that she herself might remain sole mistress at Dunton Everard, the other to be wedded herself and mistress of a handsome household of her own, and as this was the more powerful of the two, so she concerted means to that end.

With the concurrence of the Squire she therefore sat down one day and penned a billet to Mr Joseph Surface in London, bidding him come spend a week in the country in his guardian's delightful society. For indeed it appeared to Mrs Deborah that a gay young London spark might divert Miss's mind from the nobler quarry, and that Sir Peter, noting this, might realise the instability of youth and the superior value of mellowed constancy. She informed him, with many smiling nods and winks, that a pleasant surprise was in store, and there the matter stayed.

She might undervalue the power of the passion at

fifty, when perhaps it is the hotter, as the afternoon
rays of the summer sun are more torrid than those of
the morning. And 't was very provoking that Miss,
before Sir Peter, was always the very pattern of
duteous propriety and kind attention to all her elders.
'T was in vain to excite her to temper and give her
opportunities: they did but reflect on Mrs Deborah
herself and exalt the good humour that could suffer
her so uncomplainingly.

Matters were in this train when Mr Joseph arrived.

Lord, how pleased Sir Peter was, when from the
walk under the elms he espied Mr Joseph ride up the
avenue! 'T was the last thing he desired at the moment, so unsettled and anxious were his views. Love
told him in tones of melting softness that Miss Melissa with her cajoling ways was necessary to his
happiness, while Reason, croaking like a raven at his
dexter ear, pointed out the dangers of an old bachelor
thus giving a loose to his wishes. And here was Mr
Joseph, reason and good sense embodied, arriving as
a reinforcement to the forces he desired to worst.

He cursed Mrs Deborah's officiousness most heartily as he set off to meet the new-comer — Melissa
following behind with downcast eyes.

Even before the first greetings were uttered, 't is
scarce too much to say Mr Joseph had mastered the
situation, even to Mrs Deborah's motive, and under
his profuse smiles he was naturally much disturbed
and annoyed. Like Charles, he was not without his
debts, though carefully concealed. The prospect
of Sir Peter's setting up immediate and nearer

interests was one to be contemplated with dismay.

But the temptation! He was far too good a judge of beauty not to allow that here was a diamond — unpolished, it is true, but still a woman that, powdered, hooped, patched, and perfumed, would turn the heads of half the beaux in London. As for Sir Peter — mercy on him and any that might have expectations from him! To be the slave of her expenses and caprices would be the best fate to be hoped. And the worst, unmentionable!

Mr Joseph resolved immediately on a close alliance with Mrs Deborah as the first step. As to Miss, she viewed him with wonder and pleasure. An agreeable person of a man with an excellent address, soberly but handsomely dressed, she had never seen his like; for the young squires of the county were more roaring blades than anything else and somewhat lacking in the delicacy that commends itself to the female mind. It is possible this might lead to a warmer interest, but that Mr Joseph, far from wishing to arouse his guardian's jealousy and therefore his anger, treated her with the gravest politeness mingled with a coolness which invited no closer acquaintance. All his agreeabilities were reserved for Mrs Deborah.

They sat together one pleasant afternoon, when Sir Peter and Miss Melissa were strolling in the elm walk, and Mr Joseph exclaimed on the beauties of the pastoral scene: the cows cropping the rich pasture where the shadows were lengthening, the pigeons cooing in the cotes, and the notes of blackbird and thrush making sweet melody from every bush.

"Madam," says he, "the man whose heart is not touched by these rural delights must be a stranger to every finer emotion of sensibility: I could not augur well of him. No wonder Sir Peter finds himself at home in such surroundings and with such agreeable society. Ah, Madam, how often have I wished to see my venerated guardian in possession of such a peaceful home of his own and in the company of a wife who could appreciate his worth."

"Indeed, Mr Surface, the wish does you infinite honour," replied the lady, knitting industriously. "But sure much depends on his choice. Mere beauty is no guarantee of happiness."

"Sure, Madam, you can't suppose me capable of such folly. Beauty — what is beauty? The best to be in a few years the prey of the worm! No, what I desiderate for my more than friend is some woman of matured experience, of elegant manners and appearance, no foolish hoyden nor gadabout" — Mrs Deborah cast a glance toward the elm walk — "but one who will oversee his domestics and comforts and provide him with a truly congenial companionship."

Mrs Deborah bridled and smiled. Mr Joseph's words were pointed with a glance that was difficult to misunderstand. He took her hand respectfully.

"Madam, when I received your agreeable commands to wait on you and Squire Parsons I flattered myself with the hope that these visions were to be realised. For where, I ask you, could all the needful qualities be found so united as at Dunton Everard?"

His bow was so conciliating that it induced a most

unusual confidence in Mrs Deborah's bosom. Mr Joseph was so unselfishly disinterested, so truly affectionate in his views, that only the worst of hearts could distrust him.

"Why, Mr Surface, I won't affect to mistake your meaning," said the lady, gently withdrawing her hand, "and I believe Dunton Everard has not falsified your expectations. So far as I am a judge, a warm interest is sprung up between Sir Peter and my niece."

"Madam, you alarm, you terrify me!" cries Mr Joseph. "What? A mere chit of nineteen and my worthy Sir Peter who will never see his half-century more? O, Madam, far, far different were my hopes and expectations! You have planted a dart in my bosom — "

"And so apparently has my niece in Sir Peter's," responded Mrs Deborah tartly. "No, Mr Surface, it has been said there's no fool like an old one, and if I have represented to your guardian that she is even unusually giddy and thoughtless of her age, it was with the wish to spare him the inevitable results of so misplaced a passion."

"And you have done this, Madam, and without avail? Your generosity was wasted? Mercy on me, what a scene opens! But sure the young lady herself can't foresee the dangers of so ill-assorted a union. Your kindly counsel — "

Mrs Deborah shook her head violently. "A headstrong hussy!" was all she said.

" 'T is a lamentable circumstance," replies Mr

Joseph, "that with true happiness at hand, poor human nature follows the will-o-the-wisp that must lead into the sloughs of despair. The man who — "

"The man who should have the courage to represent to Sir Peter that he is sowing trouble that he will harvest very shortly would certainly deserve well of him," said Mrs Deborah snappishly. She gathered up her knitting and left the room before Mr Joseph could say another word.

As for him, he sat in deep meditation. The last thing he intended was to offend Sir Peter, and as to Miss Melissa, had she not stood in the way of his projects, he could have admired her very sincerely. But the very thought of such a marriage was intolerable. It was easy to foresee the interest a beautiful young wife must gain in Sir Peter's heart and purse, and were there to be offspring — S'death! 't was not to be endured. Mr Surface's debts forbade the possibility. But what to do he knew not at present, and could only grope his way, step by step, ready for retreat or advance on the instant.

He now went forth to the elm walk and was gratified that, on seeing his approach, Miss fled like a lapwing, leaving Sir Peter seated, gazing on the cows and the sunset.

"Aha, Joseph, 't is you?" he said. "Come and sit with me and enjoy this peaceful prospect. I declare, so much do I prefer it to the false glitter and noise of London life that I half resolve to rebuild my family seat and settle down to like enjoyments in Sussex. What think you?

"Why, Sir Peter, you know my heart is no stranger to the innocent pleasures of life, and indeed my own sentiments are unsuited to the heartless gaieties of London. But a man who settles down to a rural existence must needs have congenial companionship to soften the change. When every habit is radically changed — "

"Ah, Joseph, Joseph, you speak with all your wonted good sense. Yes, yes, the companionship's the thing. But what if I have discovered the sweetest little tenderest companion that ever a man could desire to be blest with — a little suing, wooing, blue-eyed, yielding, winning, docile, obedient — But I run on! In short, perfection! What then would be your counsel?"

"Lord save us, Sir Peter! I presume not to censure, yet must say that at your age a connection of that kind will give a loose to many tongues that — "

"Connection, Sir! I intend no connection! How dare you suppose — But no, I am unjustly angry. Marriage, Joseph, marriage is what I intend."

"Marriage, Sir, with a little blue-eyed, tender, yielding, docile angel — But sure that gives the notion of a school-girl? You can't intend — Lord bless me!"

"And why, Joseph, should I not aspire to happiness as well as another? The eye at fifty is as sensible of beauty as at twenty, and I have no more pleasure in beholding a disagreeable object than have you. And when with beauty is combined every submissive virtue and a veneration and respect for superior age, which ensures my authority, why, I ask you, am I to throw away so singular a blessing? You, Joseph, who profess such noble sentiments, should comprehend mine."

Mr Joseph, who was already prepared for this announcement, now suffered the anxiety to disappear from his brow, and confronted his guardian with the smile of candour.

"Indeed, Sir Peter, you don't appeal in vain to my sentiments. The man of feeling can readily put himself in another's place, and I who have experienced your benevolent protection can't grudge it to another. Certainly there are dangers and disappointments attendant on a disparity, and the attentions of dissolute young men — But such a nature as you describe is secured by its own elevation. Who is the fortunate lady?"

"Miss Melissa Parsons is to make me the happiest of men," says Sir Peter gravely. "And I accept your sympathy cordially, my dear Joseph, and beg you would communicate the matter to your brother. I know your good sense and moral precepts will be an aid to my Lady Teazle, though I don't expect our lot will long be cast in London, for all her tastes are rural, and I would not have the dew brushed off the flower in the withering breath of scandal, gaming, and vice. As to Charles, he becomes such a rake that I shall not court his company for my Lady, for I would not choose she should even guess the amusements that are his delight."

"You are very much in the right, Sir Peter," says

Joseph eagerly. "With all a fond brother's partiality, I still must own that Charles's vices are — but I can't bring myself to expose them. Let a veil be drawn there. I am inexpressibly honored by your confidence, and will take every opportunity with the lady to inculcate those principles which have ever been and shall be my guide through life. But — Gad's my life! Sir Peter, I must rally you on a double conquest. The old lady within, if I am not much mistaken, is also a victim to the tender passion. You must go warily, Sir — warily indeed. There's a warmth in her words and glances that — indeed I thought I saw in her the future Lady Teazle."

"No, no, Joseph. Such an idea was never in contemplation for one moment," said Sir Peter in great alarm. "I give Mrs Deborah credit for far too much good sense to have entertained such a notion. I look to you to make it all as clear as noonday. I have the highest respect for Mrs Deborah, but if it were nothing else than the asperity with which she speaks of her charming niece — "

"Ay, indeed, Sir, these elderly ladies don't outlive either their vanities or their asperities. You have had a lucky escape. Marriage is a peril that — "

"You think so?" says Sir Peter in some agitation. "Why, so do I if a man were not certain of his ground. But come, Joseph, you must acquaint yourself with more than the lady's beauty, and then I shall be assured of your sincere felicitations. The marriage will take place before I return to town."

Left alone, Mr Surface considered the position

with the nicest care, and he resolved at once to desert Mrs Deborah's party, seeing there was nothing to be gained in that direction, and to ingratiate himself with the future Lady Teazle as the dispenser of favours. Her beauty was not of the order that specially commended itself to his taste, and her manners still less, but the lady who held the key to Sir Peter's purse must never be neglected. And she certainly had charms.

Accordingly, that evening he set himself to the task with the smoothest address. He led her to the spinet and drank in the rusty strains of "John Peel" and other such melodies, as though they had been the song of Orpheus. He drew patterns of the last ruffles ordered by the fashionable Lady Sneerwell from Paris, and the curate not arriving as usual to spend the evening, he played Pope Joan to admiration. It excited the indignation of Mrs Deborah, who could but view him as a deserter, while Miss Melissa must own him a most agreeable fellow, and did so to Sir Peter on the first opportunity.

"La, Sir Peter, I did not like Mr Surface at first. He looked on me so coldly that I suspected disapproval of my attachment to you. But he improves on me daily."

"Why, my dear, I have made him our confidant and he views our union with the warmest sympathy. Pray attach yourself to Joseph, my love. His sentiments are most exalted, his morals of the strictest. Charles, I regret to say, is a very different person: kind-hearted to a fault, jovial, but a rake to the marrow. I would have you keep him at a discreet distance. Your own prudence will make this easy for you."

"Indeed, Sir Peter, your word is law to me, and you will guide all my motions. But can't his sensible brother reclaim him?" says Miss Melissa, privately wondering whether Charles might not be the more agreeable of the two.

"When a man or woman is once addicted to pleasure, there's no escaping. And that's why, my dear, it so gratifies me to know that after a taste of London frivolities you are prepared to settle down as a happy couple at Teazleton. Then it shall be my study to surround you with every evidence of affection, and to look forward to a peaceful old age in your congenial society. What pleasure we shall have in the garden, the farm, the dairy, and those matters in which you are so skilled!"

She responded by a gentle murmur, sweet and unintelligible as the ringdove's cooing, which amply satisfied Sir Peter.

But when the matter was announced, who can depict the amazement of Sir Tivy? He drove my Lady over that they might lose no item of the wonders preparing, and 't would be impossible to tell how he slapped Sir Peter on the back and rallied him on his coming happiness.

"Sir Peter, ain't you the slyest dog-fox in all the County of Kent? Little did I think, when I invited the charmer to dinner the day you come, that I was presenting the future Lady Teazle. Egad, I forgive

her all now — and the more because I'm quite satisfied with my Lady. But Lord, Sir Peter — to take a
buxom girl like that to London! Have you considered
of it? Won't she take the bit between her pretty
teeth and bolt? Won't she — "

"No, she won't!" cries Sir Peter. "And indeed, Sir
Tivy, these prophecies are scarce the part of a friend.
The lady is as docile and obedient as yours, and I
must think it jealousy of my success where you failed
that prompts these — "

"Jealousy, Sir Peter! I'd have you to know that,
so far from jealousy, I compassionate your folly and
rash daring in marrying a young woman whom if
you wanted her company you had much best adopt."

"Adopt, Sir Tivy! Did you consider that when
you went out a-wooing in the same quarter? I'll
not bear these interferences and vexations. I understand 't was with the utmost difficulty the lady could
restrain her laughter at your ridiculous pretensions!"

"Pretensions, Sir Peter? They were as respectable
as yours, and bain't my estate not a whit behind
Teazleton in value? No, no, the lady had more regard
for me than for you, for she refused me and has my
daily blessing for that same, egad! Well, go your way,
and don't look to me for compassion when you regret
your folly too late. Didn't I warn you?"

The altercation grew so warm that at last my
Lady Terrier was compelled to propose a hasty return
to Hardacre Hall, and they parted, scowling upon
one another; and thus ended a friendship of years.

Joseph, meanwhile, penned the letter to his brother

Charles, announcing the intended match, in these terms: —

MY DEAR BROTHER: —
You will doubtless learn with alarm, since it puts an end to any hope of assistance in your debts, but Sir Peter has accepted your advice and is to marry a country hoyden of nineteen before returning to town. The worthy old gentleman is overjoyed at the acceptance of his suit, and though I might expatiate on the almost inevitable consequence, still the man who could ridicule a benefactor in misfortune deserves the reprobation of all feeling hearts. The lady, Miss Melissa Parsons, daughter of Squire Parsons of Dunton Everard, is well enough in looks, fresh complexioned, hair on the red side, blue eyes, manners those of a dairymaid that has the wit to be silent lest she blunder. I know not what underlies this, but may suspect. He does not desire the frequent company of such a libertine as yourself for his lady, but commends her to the graver conversation of,
My dear brother,
Your most obedient and affectionate
JOSEPH SURFACE

This was followed by a reply from Charles Surface addressed to Joseph as follows:

MY DEAR BROTHER: —
Sure I did but jest in recommending a young match to Sir Peter, and can't but laugh to think of the consequence. Still, though it can't be denied he runs a risk, risks are run and survived daily, and not only he but his friends will have a gambler's sport in betting on the event. Lord help us! And the aged discourse to us of wisdom! I have men-

tioned the circumstance to Lady Sneerwell, Mrs Candour
and all the licentiates of the School for Scandal that has its
meetings hereabouts, and already — though I did not
intend it — is a fine tale taken flight as to the reasons for
the match. Let this go no further, and do not advertise
Sir Peter that all his town friends are preparing a warm
reception for his Lady, who will be compelled to join with
them in self-defence. Let me hope she will profit by your
instructions. I will steal a leaf from your book to add that
the man who could let such an occasion escape him
deserves — but you may fill in the rest.

Your affectionate brother and servant,
CHARLES SURFACE

This letter remained private, and the preparations
for the marriage proceeded.

Mr Joseph did his best in the intervals to instruct
the bride in the carriage to be expected of her in
London, and the friends she must meet there. Their
most frequent conferences were in the elm-walk,
where Sir Peter could observe from the window with
what gravity the tutor performed his part, though
not overhearing the lesson.

Let this be a sample of his instructions: —

"Indeed, my dear Madam," says the tutor, "You
need not fear expense. Your notions are too modest.
Sir Peter's is a generous heart, and he will wish to see
his lady not only in the mode but leading it, though
I am sure I need not suggest to such quick apprehension as yours that it would alarm him if he knew now
that this was your view. To be sure, a young wife

must always make the most cautious advances till her foot is sure, and then let her proceed as boldly as she pleases."

"But, Mr Joseph," says she, "I don't even know what I desire as yet. Do but consider that I never was in London in my life, and never saw a lady of fashion nearer than the stand at the races. Lord! how shall I know what to do?"

"Why, Madam, as to that, I believe I have a pretty notion myself of what is expected, and when you have met my Lady Sneerwell and others who are in the height of the mode, you will not be at a loss. Your own advantages of person, combined with Sir Peter's purse, will call every milliner and toy-woman about you directly you arrive. But do nothing without advice. I am wholly at your disposal."

"O Sir, I shall rely on you in everything. You are sure Sir Peter will wish me to be remarked for taste?"

"As surely, Madam, as he will be gratified to see you remarked for beauty."

"But manners, Mr Surface? These are not so easily come by as dress."

"Why no, Madam, and since dissipation is the height of fashion, you must lay aside a little of the bashfulness which is allowable in the wilds. This will become you. Unless I mistake, there is fire under your snow, and a little laughing rogue in either eye that will carry you far. Yet not too far. Observe that I would not have you give that worthy man the least uneasiness. No — the best guardian to a woman's modesty is attention to the faults of others and a freedom in censuring them which gives a high opinion of her own principles. You can't have a better tutoress than my Lady Sneerwell whom I have mentioned to you."

"And yourself, Sir."

"Why, I flatter myself I am no novice in the little agreeabilities expected from a woman of fashion."

"A woman of fashion — " sighs Miss, in a sort of rapture. "O how I long to leave this humdrum hole! What do I not owe to Sir Peter!"

"To your own beauty, which has subjugated him as it will subjugate hundreds of adorers. Do not do yourself such an injustice as to forget this. Yet remember, my charming pupil, that 't is after marriage and not before that a woman recalls to her husband all he owes to her condescension in making him the happiest of men. To do so now would be ungenerous. After marriage 't is a point of dignity."

Miss reflected. "Then you would not have me open all my mind to Sir Peter?"

"By no means, Madam. A half concealment is the sex's resource, and like a gauze scarf flung over an alabaster bosom, is a charm the more. Coquet with Sir Peter as you would with a stranger — that is, if you would secure your own way. But never permit him to explore your mind."

"La, Sir, have you ever been married yourself?" cries Miss Melissa, amazed at all this superior wisdom.

"No, Madam; but have you not heard the proverb that the onlooker sees most of the game? I am but a humble observer of the bliss of others. And there is a further caution I would add. If you would have your husband remain your adorer, pique his jealousy a little, coquet with others — with discretion, you observe, no more, but sufficient to suggest to him that his blessing is coveted by others and that its continuance depends on his good behaviour."

"Indeed, Sir, I will. I hope I do credit to your instruction."

'T is known in Lady Teazle, as a finished product, how very much credit she did to Mr Surface's instructions, and perhaps it may be unnecessary to labour this point. Suffice it to say that daily she received her lesson with a docility that ensured success.

"And if," thought the man of sentiment to himself, "I acquire not thus a controlling interest in Sir Peter's affairs, I have studied to very little purpose in the school of human nature. She may serve my turn much better in eloping with some gay macaroni, than could Mrs Deborah by dying before Sir Peter and leaving him to make a more sensible match."

Thus all parties were satisfied excepting Mrs Deborah, and when the marriage day dawned, clear and smiling as the bride, not a cloud obscured either the general harmony nor yet the sky.

'T was when Sir Peter had handed her into the carriage after the ceremony, the joy-bells ringing from the village church, that he observed with the fondest rapture that this must be the happiest day of his life, and the second when he should hear the bells ringing in the same manner to welcome them to Teazleton.

"For, my beloved Lady Teazle," says he, "you

can never appear so lovely in my eyes as in your linen gown, the prettiest girl in Sussex, tripping to my mother's dairy house in the park. O how I long for that happiness. 'T was in that sweet dress you won my heart."

"What, Sir Peter! To be a dairy-maid! No, thank you! I suppose I have n't had enough of it here! Perhaps you'll expect me to supervise the poultry also!"

"Why, my dearest Lady Teazle, I vow — "

"And I vow 't is cruel! What — am I to have no pleasure, no charming gaieties, no attentions, no — "

"Lord save me! What's this?" cries Sir Peter in deadly alarm. "But, Madam — "

"But, Sir Peter, you promised me my fine house in London, my carriage and horses, my footmen and nosegays, my dresses and entertainments, my parties and cards, my — "

He endeavoured to stem the torrent. "My love, I said as plain as could be that my intention was for Teazleton. I said — "

"Sir Peter, Sir Peter, you said I was to be your joy and delight in London, did n't you now? How can I be your delight if I'm thwarted in everything? Did n't you tell me of your gallantries with all the fine ladies, and the routs you went to, and the ridottos, and the masquerades, and the déjeuners, and the water-parties, and the — "

"Yes, Madam, but I never said you were to take part in them. I said — "

"Sir Peter, did n't you say I was the delight of your

soul, and I was to have my own way in everything, and you could refuse me nothing and — "

"That was when I thought it would be my way, Madam; and you said I was to guide you. And I say, once for all — "

"And I say, once for all, that if a wife is to be scorned and browbeat, she had better be — "

"Had better be what, Madam?"

"No matter! O, why did I marry a man old enough for my Aunt Deborah, that can't so much as keep his sacred promises? Let us go back and be unmarried, Sir Peter! Teazleton! Why I might as well be buried alive here and not be plagued with a husband to cross me. Sure, I might hope a grandfather's kindness from you, if no more!" My Lady's words were interrupted with sobs. She could not at that early stage tiff with the gaiety she was to acquire later.

"And when you've but just promised to love, honour, and obey me! O, Sir Peter, Sir Peter!"

"Lord, Madam, that was *your* promise! But, never mind, my heart's delight! Look up, my angel and forgive me. Don't cry like this and spoil your charming eyes, my love! — Gad's life, how beautiful she is in tears! — What will Mrs Deborah — Joseph — your papa, think? No, no! There! Indeed you shall see London, so you shall, and then we'll discuss the matter further. You'll be reasonable, I know, my life. Come to my arms!"

"And the ridottos? The masquerades? The Pantheon? The — "

"Yes, all, all!" cries Sir Peter, frantic. "So long

as you love me and strive to please me, you shall have your own way. But it must be my way too, for all that!"

"Now, you're my dear Sir Peter!" whispers the bride softly, nestling against his shoulder. "Indeed we'll have but the one, one way between us, and it shall be mine. I knew you could not be a bear to your own Lady Teazle. You shall find me the most dutiful, the most affectionate wife that was ever told of, so long as you humour me. Kiss me, Sir Peter, to seal our agreement."

Sir Peter kissed her. They drew up at the house door.

Later, Mr Joseph stood smiling and bowing with his hand on his heart, as they stept into the coach that was to take them to London.

"Farewell, Joseph! We shall see you soon in town," cries the happy bridegroom, with a face as long as his elbow, as the horses were set in motion. "Farewell, Mrs Deborah!"

"The way of the transgressor is hard!" says Mrs Deborah sourly, turning to re-enter the house.

The world knows the rest.

www.ingramcontent.com/pod-product-compliance
Lightning Source LLC
Chambersburg PA
CBHW022210010726
47493CB00002B/498